THE SUMMER OF THE
ROYAL VISIT

BY THE SAME AUTHOR

The Blackmailer
A Man of Power
The Great Occasion
Statues in the Garden
Orlando King
Orlando at the Brazen Threshold
Agatha
News from the City of the Sun
The Shooting Party
A Glimpse of Sion's Glory

THE SUMMER OF THE
ROYAL VISIT

ISABEL COLEGATE

ALFRED A. KNOPF NEW YORK 1992

THIS IS A BORZOI BOOK
PUBLISHED BY ALFRED A. KNOPF, INC.

Copyright © 1991 by Isabel Colegate

Originally published in Great Britain by Hamish Hamilton,
London.

Library of Congress Cataloging-in-Publication Data
Colegate, Isabel.
The summer of the royal visit/Isabel Colegate.—1st American ed.
p. cm.
"Originally published in the United Kingdom . . . by Hamish
Hamilton, London"—T.p. verso.
ISBN 0-679-40880-0
I. Title.
PR6053.0414S85   1992
823'.914—dc20   91-53118
                                                        CIP

Manufactured in the United States of America

FIRST AMERICAN EDITION

PART ONE

Let us just think for a moment then who I am. No one much. I was born in this City and have lived here most of my life. Educated just the other side of the hill at a school founded in the nineteenth century for the sons of Nonconformist ministers, I did my two years' National Service in the army after the end of the Second World War, and spent most of that time a few miles away on Salisbury Plain. After Bristol University I went back to my old school to teach. Apart from three years teaching English in Florence after my marriage and before the children were born, all my working life was spent in the same place. I retired a few years ago after my wife's death, and live not far from where I was born, alone except for when either of my children, who are both grown up and live in London, come for a visit. I potter about, digging into local history; I read a lot. I walk my dog, I wonder about this or that. I've quite enjoyed my life. I must admit I'm afraid of getting old, becoming helpless and possibly disgusting. I have no views about the meaning of the universe. I walk with my dog on the hill and look down over the City: I think of my grandparents. They seemed to feel things very strongly in those days.

The City is built between hills. The river curls round it, embracing the Abbey, the Town Hall, the streets and squares of the centre. Beyond the centre the City stretches up the south-facing slopes, laid out in lesser squares and streets of fine Palladian houses and imposing crescents. From where I often pause on the hill to the south of the City, beech woods behind me and a grassy slope falling steeply down to the cemetery below me, I can see the Circus like a miniature Roman amphitheatre linked by a street of tall pale houses to the semi-circle of the Great Crescent, which fronts a smooth expanse of grass bounded on the far side by the trees of the Botanical Gardens. The railway station beneath me, just on the far side of the river which lies between the hill on which I stand and the City, expresses with its grandiose castellations those two apparently incongruous Victorian enthusiasms, steam and the Middle Ages, but the greater part of the City was built in its time of prosperity, eighteenth-century idealism expressed as a product of eighteenth-century materialism; those were the years in which the City was a fashionable spa.

Since my retirement I have become a familiar figure in the Reference Library, peering at card indexes and trying to read old copies of the local newspaper on scratched microfilm; most afternoons I walk on the hills and think of the past. If I could go on like this for ever I should be perfectly content; only there is a thin note of fear somewhere in my head, sometimes louder, sometimes quieter, but never wholly silent. When I had Mary to talk to in the evenings this was not so. Not that she necessarily listened when I talked to her; that was not necessary. I don't suppose I listened to her much either. We talked to each other all the same to our mutual satisfaction, and the sound of fear was muffled, heard distantly if at all; this is what I take to be the object of marriage, to keep at bay the fear of the future, the fear of death.

There is a sprawl of building to the south of the river, hardly part of the City proper. The land rises very steeply here. Part of the slope is too steep to build on, and above that declivity the woods and fields have been kept inviolate; only on the westernmost side of the hill, where the road curves down towards the south gate of the City, has building spread. There is a small church near the top of the hill, a twelfth-century foundation, originally attached to a house of shelter for penniless idiots. The latter institution was merged with the somewhat larger Idiot School on the London Road in the 1850s and moved to a purpose-built fortress some miles away (which now houses, incidentally, a training-school for air-traffic controllers), and its former home next to the church on the hill – which is known as Haul Down – became a night refuge for down-and-outs until it was sold in the early part of this century as a private dwelling. The houses which used to crowd round the church in three or four little streets were mostly built in the eighteenth century, to shelter, however meanly, the rabble which had gathered to serve, or hope to serve, or beg from, or rob, the prosperous townsfolk and the even more prosperous visitors. In that robust age visitors were sometimes driven out in their carriages to stare at the poor, perhaps to moralize, perhaps to laugh. Even so, the eighteenth-century understanding of domestic architecture laid out streets of small houses which might have been damp but did have pleasant proportions and an agreeable relation to each other. Not many of them remain. Some of the houses closest to the church were replaced after a fire in the late nineteenth century, and most of the rest were swept away in the 1960s; I suppose they seemed to belong to the bad old days. They were replaced by a straight row of gimcrack boxes marching meaninglessly and regardless of the contours of the land over what used to be allotments.

Of course, those little streets would have been crowded in former times, a hundred years ago for instance, when Stephen Collingwood lived there. They would have been cluttered with refuse, and the pale crumbling stone of the houses would have been blackened by smoke. Most of the houses had too many people living in each room, few of them had sound roofs or adequate drains. Stephen Collingwood was the curate in charge of the church, which was really a chapel, the Chapel of St Catherine, and came under the control of the Rector of the

Abbey. He was not a young man. He had been a lawyer and had taken orders only after the early death of his wife; he was in his early forties when he came to the City. He had asked for work among the poor, but he had never previously come across them, except in a very distant kind of way. He came from a family of minor gentry long established in Worcestershire, and during his marriage had lived in reasonable comfort in London – in Campden Hill, I think it was – and when he came to live in simple lodgings in Haul Down closely surrounded by his parishioners he found himself unable to love them as much as he had intended to; this failure filled him with shame and self-reproach. He left some diaries, which I have read. I feel I have come to know him very well. Like me he walked, often along the same paths. Sometimes I feel I have just passed him, on a spring evening perhaps, striding along with his unnecessarily large greatcoat flapping, his eyes momentarily meeting mine, his smile unsurprisingly intimate, on his way back from Blake Leigh woods to his supper and his evening task of reading aloud to the men in the Haul Down night refuge.

He had read that a fifteenth-century traveller had come upon the chapel by approaching the City from the south 'down a rocky hill, full of fair springs of water'.

'On this rocky hill', the traveller had written, 'is set a fair street outside the City gate, and in this street is a chapel to St Catherine.' It was not exactly a fair street now, dirty and crowded as it was, and as for the springs, perhaps they had dried up, though the stone trough where the coal horses drank was always full of clear water; but his recollection of the passage, together with the impression left on his mind by his walk over the hills on a fine spring evening, made him turn to the Psalms rather than the New Testament for his reading.

The men's night refuge was in the former home for the mentally deficient, and it consisted of a Gothic hall with two rows of beds in it. The beds were close together; only between the two rows was there a wide passage. Each bed had a rough blanket on it, but because that particular night there were only four men sleeping there they had taken extra blankets from the neighbouring beds. Stephen had been told by Mrs Caws, who cleaned the room, that it was his duty to forbid this, but it was too late; one of the men was already snoring. Mrs Caws spoke of lice, and other horrors, but Stephen thought the smell of disinfectant with which she managed to permeate the place would have killed most bugs. The four men had taken beds as far away from each other as possible. The room could hold twenty-four but was seldom full; Haul Down was further to walk than River Street at the bottom of the hill, where there were other dosshouses and cheap lodgings closer to the public houses and brothels of the City's small but active area of iniquity. These men were tramps, as usual, speechless from drink or disinclination, harmless enough. One of them answered his greeting with a sort of groan, one slept, the others pretended to sleep. He walked slowly between them to his stool and began to read.

When he had first taken on this duty he had tried to find improving texts, and even sometimes to invite discussion, in the hope of bringing some of the outcasts to Christianity, but many of those who were not too drunk or too tired or too ill to listen proclaimed themselves Christians already, and indeed often revealed intimate knowledge of the Bible. They blamed lack of work, or poverty, or personal misfortune of a sometimes horrifying nature, for their sorry state. Stephen found it difficult to exhort them to further effort without feeling himself a hypocrite. When occasionally one of the men did seem disposed to talk he usually turned out to be a windbag, who was almost impossible to stop and who aroused the anger of those who preferred to sleep. Stephen soon fell into the way of taking his place quietly and reading for a little while almost as if to himself. He had a good voice, and when he was in church was careful not to use it in a theatrical manner, which he would have thought shameful; but because he liked reading aloud and because on the whole the tramps and derelicts who frequented the refuge hardly listened to him, he allowed himself a freer rein when he was there.

'He sendeth the springs into the valleys, which run among the hills,' he read, as if he could cleanse his small indifferent audience by the sound of his voice, and the thought of those waters. 'They give drink to every beast of the field: the wild asses quench their thirst. By them shall the fowls of the heaven have their habitation, which sing among the branches.'

Sometimes a solitary shelterer, hunched beneath his blanket and confused by drink or physical weakness or mental inadequacy, would watch in silent alarm as the tall figure in the long coat walked quietly past him to the reading-stool, sat down and read, in a voice which matched the powerful but often quite mysterious words, then closed the book and left, pausing only momentarily for a stern 'Good night', leaving the man as often as not relieved by his departure. Sometimes Stephen had even read to an empty room, bringing solace only to himself. On one such evening the door at the opposite end of the room had cautiously opened, and Charlotte Moore had stood there, with a whiteness of fog behind her, quite alone.

From Blake Leigh woods you have a fine view of the City. It is not so famous as the view from Southcliff, which is panoramic, but it takes in more of the surrounding hills, so that you have a clearer appreciation of the lie of the land. Perhaps I like it better because the site of the City below comes as a surprise, on a path through a belt of beech trees, in the course of a walk through the fields which is long enough to exercise my old mongrel. These fields are kept as farming-land and can never be built upon; John Moore, the quarry-owner who owned them, insisted on covenants to that effect. The City is mostly built from the surrounding oolitic limestone, which has been quarried from Roman times.

The Moore family emerged as quarry-owners only in the early nineteenth century, after the heyday of Georgian building, but they knew their business, coming as they did from a long line of stonemasons, and since the stone was famous by that time and in use all over the country, they soon became prosperous. In the 1850s John Moore, the elder of the two brothers who ran the business, built himself a solid, sober-looking house on Blake Leigh, and sent his son Harry to Rugby for an education. From the terraced garden of that house you can look down on the City and see it much as it would have looked to Harry Moore and his wife Charlotte a hundred years ago; the twentieth-century housing estate which has spread over most of one of the hills on the south bank of the river valley as it makes its way towards the sea is not visible from there. I suppose the City would have looked more sombre in those days. Twentieth-century tourism has brought prosperity and twentieth-century understanding of the technology of stone-cleaning has meant that much of the stonework has been returned to its original colour, but a hundred years ago the City was smoke-darkened and in decline, a backwater, still genteel but rather shabby, 'lost in its memories', as a guide book of the time grandiloquently has it. 'Its pavements haunted by the light step of an eighteenth-century beauty hurrying with a rustle of her petticoats to join the gay assembly at cards or a light fandango, or by the stout sandals of a Roman centurion on leave from guard duty on Hadrian's Wall and strolling down to the baths for an evening's relaxation.' I doubt if they ever danced fandangoes in the Assembly Rooms, and I am not absolutely confident about those stout sandals either, but certainly there was a feeling prevalent that something about the City's past made it proper for its inhabitants, staid or unsophisticated or even in some cases wretched as their lives might be, to consider themselves a cut above the rest of the world. This feeling had the perhaps unexpected side-effect of making them very much inclined to quarrel with each other.

They found a variety of causes for disagreement. Apart from personal rivalries and sectional snobberies, of both of which there were plenty, there were such questions as the much-criticized subscription rate for entry to the newly laid out Jubilee Gardens, or the problem of street-lighting, or of refuse collection, or of the regrettable tendency of the children of the poor to fall into the canal and drown, over all of which many people became extraordinarily indignant; the correspondence columns of the local newspaper resound with ferocious epithets backed by high-sounding principles. Of all the controversies the most highly charged and the longest running was the question of the Grand Spa Hotel. The City Council had decided that it should be built. There were those who thought this a mistake, but the Council had been persuaded that now was the time to re-establish the City as a spa of international renown. There was to be an architectural competition to determine the best design. Harry Moore expected to supply the stone for the new building, but such was the comfortable state of his business, and such his own cheerful temperament, that he would not have much minded had the whole scheme come to nothing, which in his experience such schemes often did. Charlotte Moore was interested only inasmuch as she favoured the design supported by her friends Mr and Mrs Tranmer, and was against any proposal put forward by Edwin Hanbury, the City Surveyor, whose wife Marianne Hanbury she thought absurd. Charlotte had an eye for absurdity but did not by and large judge it harshly. The eldest of the five daughters of a country clergyman, she had begun charity visiting in the parish of Haul Down soon after her marriage, finding it natural to continue in the sort of work she had been used to doing since she was a child. When Stephen Collingwood came to the parish he found her intermittent presence a recurrent miracle. Charlotte was aware of her effect on him, and though, being beautiful, she was used to making an impression, she found such vulnerability touching in so serious a character;

she wondered what his wife had been like and was afraid
he must miss her terribly.

'I am on my way to call on Mrs Hanbury. Shall I take her your
regards?' Caspar Freeling waited, his head slightly on one side,
his bright eyes expressing nothing but a desire to please.

Stephen Collingwood hesitated; he could hardly say no, but
the truth was he did not much care for Mrs Hanbury, and
thought that his feeling was probably reciprocated, in which case
the lady might well be surprised to receive such a message.

He said, 'If you like.'

Caspar laughed understandingly, but said only, in an airy kind
of way, 'She likes you, you know,' and smiling an open friendly
smile he raised a hand and walked on. Stephen turned into the
church, feeling vaguely uncomfortable, as he usually did after an
encounter with Caspar Freeling.

Caspar continued to the end of the road, turned the corner and
began to walk with his slightly sideways almost hesitant step
down the steep hill. He was not a tall man but there was a sort
of self-consciousness about his progress which made him noticeable: he patted his pockets, took out his handkerchief, looked at
his watch, in a series of little gestures as if he thought he might
be being watched. He was certainly noticed; two ragged boys
followed him along the high pavement above the narrow road.
When they came near him he said without turning, 'Nothing
doing today. Go home,' and they fell back. The pavement at this
point was two or three feet above the road, from which it was
separated by a cast-iron railing. It was impossible to avoid passing
fairly close to anyone coming in the opposite direction. Caspar
seemed to hesitate at the sight of the woman walking towards
him, then he moved closer to the wall of the men's refuge and as
she approached, which she did slowly as if tired by the climb up
the hill, he turned with his back to the wall and pressed himself
against it, leaving an unnecessary amount of space for the slight

figure which passed him. She wore a long skirt, and a shawl over her head, as was the custom in that part, but the skirt and the shawl were more brightly coloured than was usual, and as she passed him on quiet slippered feet her dark face showed her to be Petchumah, the Indian wife of Wilf the ex-soldier, with whom she ran a lodging-house near the top of the hill. She murmured a greeting as she passed but Caspar did not answer, only closing his eyes for a moment with an evident distaste which she had noticed in him before but which she accepted as she did most things without question. Caspar went on his way, putting her face, and her quiet step, and her gentle nasal voice, firmly out of his mind; he had no wish to examine the cause of this revulsion.

He thought instead about Stephen Collingwood, whom he was prepared to like. At any rate he wanted Stephen to like him. Caspar thought more about what people thought of him than about what he thought of them, and his behaviour was often governed by what he took to be other people's opinion of himself; he liked to fulfil expectations. This willingness to go in the way people wanted him to go (usually as a result of his having first planted in their minds a certain idea of himself) did not mean that in so doing he submitted his will to theirs; the interplay of personality involved was a good deal more subtle than that. It was perhaps this subtlety of Caspar's which Stephen Collingwood, a simpler man, found so puzzling. Whatever it was, Caspar knew that Stephen was wary of him and he thought as he walked on down the hill towards the City that he would like to dispel that wariness. He wished for Stephen's good opinion.

The terrace of small houses on his left came to an end, and was succeeded by a rough grassy slope at the bottom of which, on the floor of the valley, a road, the railway and the river lay between him and the City proper. Two empty coal carts, drawn by thin horses, came slowly up the hill towards him on their way to the drinking-trough opposite the chapel; their drivers walked beside them. Otherwise there was not much traffic, this being a quiet spring afternoon. Such noise as there was came from over the river, where by one of the tall stone warehouses men were loading sacks of grain on to waiting carts. Caspar crossed the bridge, passed the warehouse, and came into a busy street of small shops selling food and hardware. He walked faster here, his step more masterful and his gaze set somewhere above the heads of the surrounding slow-moving crowd. He did not slacken his pace until he came into a small square with a drinking-fountain in the middle of it. A colonnaded street led left towards the calm façade of the bathing establishment. To his right a forecourt fronted the west door of the Abbey. The door was open; a few respectable citizens were making their way towards the late-afternoon service of Choral Evensong. The street ahead of him was wider and less crowded than the one he had just passed through, the shops the most elegant the City could offer. Here he strolled, looking in at the windows, pausing for some time in front of his favourite umbrella shop before looking at his watch and going on his way, with renewed self-consciousness now, up the gentle slope towards that part of the City which spread itself on the south-facing hillside in a series of terraces, crescents and squares until it faded out into the trees, with only a few villas and their gardens interrupting the woods which crowned the hill and which were now dusted with the first light green of spring. Crossing the road and mounting some steps on to a broad high pavement he turned left and then right into a street of houses whose identical four-storied façades stepped their way elegantly up the hill. Only the doorways varied slightly in design and at one of these, which was surmounted by a fine stone pediment, Freeling stopped and rang the bell.

Mrs Hanbury, the wife of the City Surveyor, had been waiting for him, and as soon as the parlourmaid showed him into the first-floor drawing-room she hurried towards him with out-stretched hands and a theatrical cry of delight. ''Tis he!' She tended to indulge the Irish in her when she felt inclined to make some extravagance of speech, or indeed of behaviour, but it came and went, this Irishness, according to her mood or the company in which she found herself. She had lived in England for many years; for most of them she had been married to Edwin Hanbury, the City Surveyor, whom she held, despite her apparent waywardness, in some awe. She had a good deal of dark red hair piled on top of her head and not very successfully held in place by a multitude of decorative haircombs interspersed with quite sizeable steel hairpins. Her white skin had yellowed somewhat with the years, so that the freckles on her nose and cheekbones stood out less noticeably than when she had been a girl, but her large slightly protruding eyes were still a clear blue and her mouth still curved easily into an eager smile.

'Hadn't we just been waiting for you?'

She clasped his hand in both of hers and drew him into the room, not without some difficulty because there was such a clutter of small pieces of furniture, low chairs with high backs, footstools, tables covered with velvet cloths and an assortment of ornaments, standard lamps with heavy fringed shades, sewing-boxes on legs, tables so small they held nothing but one china vase or an enamelled dish. Having guided him safely to the hearthrug before the plain marble fireplace, she introduced him to the two people already standing there.

'Madame Sofia you know. And this is our poet, our very own provincial singer, Peter the Poet.'

Caspar Freeling bent low over Madame Sofia's hand, and acknowledged the young man's greeting with rather less respect. Madame Sofia lowered herself hugely on to a sofa, the back of which was covered by a Paisley shawl. Madame Sofia's stout shoulders were swathed in an almost exactly similar shawl, but there was no question of her merging with her background. Her personality was such that her whole form seemed more than commonly instinct with life; stationary, solid, weighty she might be, but inanimate never. In her rare moments of silence she was given to a tuneless humming; it might well have seemed some kind of audible by-product of the extraordinary intensity of her existence, the very hum of her being. Those enthusiasts who were allowed to accompany her in some of her spiritual exercises spoke of her aura. Whatever it was, this aura, or personality, or physical presence, she made no attempt to shade it; it shone forth generously on anyone who came within its orbit. She patted the sofa beside her and told Caspar to sit down.

'You are tired. The sweet boy will give you some tea. You need to free your spirit. Come. Converse.'

The City Surveyor and his wife had been on a brief tour of foreign spas, funded — well, rather meanly funded: they had had to pay for their own meals — but funded at any rate to some extent by the City Council, in order to learn from foreign success in the exploitation of natural mineral springs. In Baden-Baden they had encountered Madame Sofia, lately arrived from St Petersburg. Mrs Hanbury had insisted on bringing her home, her trophy from the Continent. A Theosophical Society had recently started up in the City; it was favoured by many of those most desirable in Mrs Hanbury's eyes from a social point of view, and the advantages which might accrue to her from having in her house a person so eloquent in the exposition of esoteric doctrine and so obviously possessed of arcane knowledge of the highest order were obvious and delightful.

The sweet boy obediently placed a cup of tea on the occasional table next to Caspar.

'We've passed each other more than once on Haul Down,' he said. He had a soft voice and a marked West Country accent, worn cuffs which looked as if their frayed edges might have been snipped off with scissors, black boots which were cracked with use. He was small and very thin; his light brown hair had been badly cut and was short on top so that it looked as if it might be regrowing after having been completely shaved. The expression on his thin face managed to be both wide-eyed and amused. He looked twelve and was in fact nineteen.

'I go to see my friend the curate up there occasionally,' said Caspar, as if he found the matter uninteresting.

'Mr Collingwood? Oh, I know Mr Collingwood. He's one of the best men I know.'

But Caspar had turned back to Madame Sofia. 'Tell me about St Petersburg. I'd much rather hear about St Petersburg than about anything that happens in this prosaic little place.'

'Yes, Madame Sofia, tell us about St Petersburg.' Marianne Hanbury seated herself girlishly on a footstool, holding out a plate of macaroons. Peter Tilsley (he was known to no one but Mrs Hanbury as Peter the Poet) sat on the edge of a red plush armchair and looked attentively at Madame Sofia.

'I was married in St Petersburg,' she said with a nostalgic smile. 'Such a beautiful city. But the social life so stiff, the political life – but you have no idea, living in England, the home of Liberalism. Such oppressions. You cannot speak, or write, or perform, without running into the stupid censorship of the Tsar. Spies everywhere. I left, taking only my beloved books. I came to India, where I was accused of being a spy myself.'

'Madame Sofia left her husband,' said Mrs Hanbury, proud of her protégée. 'And had no means of subsistence.'

'I started a business with those beautiful Indian textiles. I extended my knowledge of occult matters. Many experiences came to me, many revelations. India is a continent in which religion is in the air one breathes.'

'How I should love to go there,' said Mrs Hanbury enthusiastically.

'There are a number of retired people in this City who have spent their working lives there,' said Caspar Freeling drily. 'They don't look particularly well on it.'

'That Mrs Andrewes,' exclaimed Mrs Hanbury. 'So yellow.'

'There's an Indian lady who lives on Haul Down,' said Peter.

'Have you seen her, Mr Freeling? She walks about there with her coloured shawls and her eyes down, so out of place I always want to talk to her, but I haven't found the occasion yet. You must have seen her.'

'I don't remember.' Caspar spoke coldly, then changing his manner said ingratiatingly to Madame Sofia, 'But do tell us how you came to Baden-Baden, Madame Sofia?'

'Baden-Baden called to me. I was in Bombay and Baden-Baden called.' She closed her eyes for a moment as if remembering the moment when the message came, then opening them again fixed them, prominent and piercing, on Caspar Freeling. 'I am looking for a fine apartment at a reasonable rent. Mrs Hanbury tells me you are in touch with everything in this City.'

'I have begged Madame Sofia to make her home with us,' said Mrs Hanbury, omitting to mention that her husband, the City Surveyor, had been less than enthusiastic on hearing of this proposition.

'Such kindness,' Madame Sofia smiled warmly at her hostess. 'But I have my belongings in Baden-Baden, I need them round me. I think of settling here for a time. I feel a spirituality in the atmosphere, a half-felt remembrance of an older wisdom.'

'I suppose you could say I am here for the same sort of reason,' said Caspar Freeling. 'I am an Oxford man. But I have come here because I am studying pre-Roman religious sects, Druidism in particular. I believe this City to have been an important centre.'

'Ah,' said Madame Sofia, and closed her eyes again. She could have been meditating, or consulting some kind of internal reference, or meaning to convey that Druidism was not her cup of tea. The other three watched her in silence with varying degrees of awe until after two or three minutes she opened her eyes again and said firmly to Caspar Freeling, 'Find me first a jolly set of rooms at a reasonable rent. Then we can discuss these Druids.'

He laughed and said he would see what he could do.

Peter walked back the way that Caspar had come, noticing as Caspar had failed to do the sound of the seagulls over the lower part of the town. He had been born within sight of the sea, and the clamorous birds who frequented the riverside wharves of this inland City never failed to arouse in him that longing for other lands, for adventure, for the future, which he had felt as a child, wandering unwanted and unnoticed about the port in which he lived. His father was a merchant seaman who had never acknowledged him, his mother a country girl in domestic service who had died soon after his birth. He had been brought up in a Home for Waifs and Strays (boys only), a rough place where he had met no particular kindness and where his capacity for wild laughter had been thought likely to develop into madness and his occasional breathless abasement before something that had struck him as beautiful treated as an affectation, intended to tease.

The one shelf of books in the dark front passage of the establishment, put there to impress the governors of the charity which ran it, held besides two copies of the Authorized Version of the Bible, the *Complete Poems* of Tennyson and of Longfellow, *The Last Days of Pompeii* by Bulwer-Lytton, Macaulay's *History of England* and Motley's *The Rise of the Dutch Republic*. The orphans had lessons in reading and writing and simple arithmetic, but the lessons were sketchy and few of the children became proficient in any of the skills; more hours were spent in preparing them for a life either at sea, if they were strong enough, or – which was more probable – as assistants or messenger boys to chandlers or carpenters. Motley's *Dutch Republic* remained an undiscovered country; a leaking pipe in the wall above it had given it an unappealing mouldy look and the first two pages had stuck together; somehow the third had failed to stir even Peter's easily excited imagination, but he had read the other books over and over again, and knew long passages of each by heart. Whenever he could find paper and pencil he wrote down the poems he remembered, and soon began to imitate them on his own account. He began work as the most junior of clerks in a shipping-office, which he found to be drudgery, but in the course of several months he saved enough money to buy a secondhand copy of Palgrave's *Golden Treasury* from a man who took a barrowload of books to the covered market behind the docks and whom he had persuaded to put the book aside for him until he could afford it. He soon became ill with rheumatic fever, and the poems turned into mad music and would not let him sleep, but after the crisis he was sent by the doctor to bathe in the curative waters of the nearby City, which he had never seen. There was a charity hospital which provided beds for twelve indigent patients at a time; they were allowed into one of the small baths in the early hours of the morning and had to go in and out by their own entrance for fear the sight of them might affront more respectable citizens. Improved health and a sense of the absurdity of the proceedings raised Peter's spirits to the extent that he was discharged from the hospital before his prescribed course of treatment had come to an end for 'causing repeated disturbances in the baths', or in other words for splashing. By this time he had made himself known to the City's newspaper. He had written an 'Ode on Learning of the Intended Visit of Queen Victoria' and the newspaper had published it.

Macaulay's *History of England* had taught Peter that he lived in the most fortunate, advanced and free civilization in the world, and that there was every reason to suppose that, under its blessed constitution and its glorious monarch (firmly guided of course by her loyal Parliament), this great Empire would become ever more fortunate, more advanced, more free. Not a great deal in Peter's own experience so far bore out this diagnosis, but Macaulay's literary style was so splendid it would have been almost sacrilegious to differ. The thought of the Queen herself attending the opening of so desirable an institution as a Free Library, and then being driven all through the City so that her admiring subjects might see her, had filled him with patriotic enthusiasm, and his Ode had rung with Tennysonian phrases. He had taken it by hand to the newspaper's office, and had returned the next day to find the editor himself prepared not only to see him, not only to publish his Ode, but to respond to his fervent pleas by taking him on to his staff as a provider of occasional verse (every Wednesday) and a regular contributor to a column of Notes and Queries.

This newspaper, the *City Herald*, was an extraordinarily respectable publication. Its brief reports of national news were deferential of established authority and its more extensive coverage of local affairs was similarly respectful of the Mayor, the Corporation, the Bishop in whose see the Abbey stood, the more substantial of the local shopkeepers and tradespeople, and any distinguished visitors who might be honouring the City with their presence and whose arrivals and departures were duly chronicled on the centre page. This latter custom had begun in the eighteenth century, when the *Herald* had been founded, and when the arrival of an aristocratic personage to take the waters had been such an important event that the bells of the Abbey had sounded for it. A hundred years later the most exalted arrivals were likely to be, for instance, Miss Amy and Miss Edith Brown, maiden aunts of the ex-Governor of Bengal, and the ringing of the bells announced only the imminence of Divine Service.

The Notes and Queries column was expected to have a similarly sober tone. Flights of fancy were discouraged, gossip frowned on; Peter was having to learn to curb his pen. He would have liked to describe Mrs Hanbury's exotic guest, and repeat what she had revealed about her past adventures, but he knew that Mr Crowe, the editor, would call this indulging in personalities. 'We will have no personalities here,' he had said. He was something of an antiquarian, however, and had been pleased with some speculations Peter had made about the Arthurian legends and their (extremely tenuous) connections with the City. Caspar Freeling's mention of Druidism might therefore be a more profitable line to follow, and Peter, having passed through the City and begun the climb up to Haul Down, wondered whether he would be likely to be rebuffed if he were to ask Mr Freeling for some information. He thought Freeling an odd character, though impressive, and had noticed his coolness towards himself in Mrs Hanbury's drawing-room. He was also made uneasy by Freeling's apparent familiarity with that room and with his beautiful hostess. Peter thought Mrs Hanbury's red hair glorious and her warm smile more or less divine; nor had he ever seen anyone so beautifully dressed. Her kindness in writing to him after reading his poem in the *Herald* seemed wonderful, and he hoped very much to write something to justify her interest in his talent. He did not want to speculate as to her relationship with Caspar Freeling, but it had struck him as curiously conspiratorial, and Freeling's disavowal of Haul Down – implying that he only went there now and again to see Mr Collingwood when Peter knew for a fact that he had a room in a lodging-house towards the top of the hill – was even more mystifying, as indeed was the fact that so obviously gentlemanly a person should be lodging in such an inferior part of the town. Perhaps it would be more sensible to ask Mr Collingwood about the Druids.

The thought having occurred to him, Peter quickened his pace and almost ran up the steepest part of the hill. When he had said to Caspar Freeling that he knew Mr Collingwood, he had not meant that he knew him well, and the admiration he had expressed had been based partly on hearsay. He knew Mr Collingwood as a man who did his duty among the poor of his parish with an appealing humility, but he had exchanged only a few words with him. These words had been pleasant and encouraging on Mr Collingwood's part. They had stood in a light rain outside the little church and Peter had talked of his work for the newspaper and Mr Collingwood had understood without having to be told that Peter wanted to be a poet rather than a newspaper reporter: he had asked him to call whenever he liked, perhaps to borrow some books. On the strength of this quick sympathy Peter, never one to hold back from an impetuous decision, had made up his mind that Mr Collingwood was in every way an admirable man. He was out of breath when he reached the door of the house where Collingwood lodged. It was an older house than most of those which surrounded it, a seventeenth-century structure with two gables and narrow windows. As he rang the bell Peter began to cough and leaning against the doorpost tried to stifle the cough with a handkerchief, so that the large bewhiskered soldierly man who opened the door saw only a small figure huddled in the corner of the doorway spluttering into a handkerchief; he took him to be an urchin ringing the doorbell as a trick and told him to be off.

'Mr Collingwood said I might call. My name is Peter Tilsley.'

A spicy smell came out of the house, a smell so unfamiliar to Peter and so spreading and so musky that he wondered whether it might be the smell of an animal, a leopard perhaps or a lion. The soldierly man made him wait, then came down the stairs again to say he might go up. Relieved, Peter took the stairs too fast and arrived at the top coughing. Stephen Collingwood made him sit down and poured out a small glass of Madeira wine for him.

'But you are bleeding.'

'It's nothing. It's from the throat, not from the lungs. The doctor told me.' Peter swallowed the wine. 'I'm sorry. I came up the hill too fast, that's all.'

'Sit quietly then for a little. There's plenty of time.'

'I hope so. I mean, I hope I am not disturbing you.'

The small sitting-room was warmed by a coal fire. Stephen had insisted on lodging in the midst of his parishioners, to the surprise of his superiors, who had expected him to take over his predecessor's set of rooms in the more salubrious part of the City. Having made his point, he had found two pleasant little rooms, brought some pieces of his own furniture, instructed the ex-soldier Wilf with some precision as to his requirements, and made himself comfortable. There was a small brown sofa and a high-backed armchair, a desk in front of the window, innumerable small pictures on the walls and two tall bookcases full of books; more books lay on the desk and in a pile beside the armchair. Tobacco smoke was visible in the air, wreathing gently towards the ceiling; Stephen was an inveterate smoker. Now he knocked out his pipe and extinguished it, thinking the smoke might exacerbate Peter's cough.

Peter sat in a corner of the sofa, breathing deeply. His eyes, red-rimmed from the tears the coughing had induced, looked at Stephen with a kind of hunger, which the latter interpreted correctly as a longing for conversation.

'I have all the time in the world,' he said. 'Tell me what you have been doing.'

'I have been having tea with Mrs Hanbury,' said Peter, with a comical roll of his eyes at the grandeur of it. 'And why I have called on you is because you were kind enough to suggest it, and because as I came up the hill I was wondering about something Mr Freeling had said about the Druids and thinking I could perhaps ask you to explain it, because I know nothing about the Druids.'

'I don't think anyone knows much about them. What is Mr Freeling's concern with them?'

'He thinks this City was a great religious centre in those days. That's why he's come here, to find out about it. He's a scholar from Oxford, it seems.'

'What can he hope to find? There are no records or relics or anything else. He would have to invent it. I suppose it's not the first time a scholar has done that.'

'They were before the Romans, weren't they? That's about all I know.'

'It's supposed to have been the religion of the Ancient Britons.

Caesar's *Commentaries* talk about a powerful priestly caste who held their ceremonies in groves of oak. I expect it was some kind of animism, like most primitive religion. There would have been the spirit of the oak tree and the spirit of the thunder, you know the sort of thing. I can't see what's interesting about it, frankly, when so little can be known. What can I find for you, to tell you about those times?' Stephen went over to one of the bookcases and crouched down in front of it. 'The Arthurian legends are more interesting, I should have thought. You know those, I suppose?'

'Of course. From *The Idylls of the King.*'

'I can lend you those, if you like.'

'I know most of them by heart. I feel as if they were mine. Not as if I had written them but as if they were my possession. I should like to fall under the influence of a less glorious poet. I feel I should turn away from extravagance and concentrate on truth. I am too susceptible to beauty. When I write now I cut out most of it afterwards. I want to pare it down and make it sharp even if it has to be ugly. But I don't want it to be ugly.'

Stephen suggested that he might try Browning. 'I should forget about the Druids,' he added, meaning to imply nothing favourable about Caspar Freeling.

Beyond Victoria Park, beyond the Botanical Gardens, where the northern side of the broad river valley begins to slope gently towards the high escarpment which overlooks the City from the north, a few commodious mid-Victorian villas surrounded by gardens ease the passage from the City to the countryside. The house in which the Tranmers lived was built in the early 1870s and was thus in their time comparatively modern, though not as modern as they might have wished, for the Tranmers believed in the future and would have liked to embrace it in every way. They would have liked to embrace the new Grand Spa Hotel as well, and make it a means both of introducing to the City the kind of building in which they believed and of making the benefits of the mineral springs freely available to all who needed them. They had an architect to propose, who was also their close friend and co-believer in the future, and a proposition for a kind of federation of investors who would underwrite the scheme on a co-operative basis, thus providing, they felt sure, a model for a new kind of enterprise. Charlotte Moore found herself not always able to follow the details of the proposals, and Harry her husband, who was used to more conventional business methods, would sometimes make objections, which would be noisily over-ruled, at which he would laugh and give in, for the Tranmers and the Moores were friends. It was not a friendship which could have been easily foreseen when the two couples first met. The Moores were young and handsome, the Tranmers middle-aged and odd-looking, the Moores had two children, the Tranmers none, the Moores had few intellectual pretensions, the Tranmers many. The Tranmers were disposed to look on the Moores as their disciples, whereas the truth was rather that the Moores found the Tranmers more amusing than most of their other neighbours; but however the friendship had started, there was now much warmth of feeling on both sides.

When Rosalind Tranmer liked someone she gave them advice.

'You're wasting your time with your doleful curate and your bowls of soup. You should be working with me, agitating for proper legislation to sweep away horrible Haul Down and all it stands for.'

'He isn't doleful. He's sometimes very cheerful. And Haul Down isn't exactly horrible. And anyway, people need a bit of comfort in the meantime, until the dawn of socialism, I mean. And anyway . . .' They were in Rosalind's sitting-room, sorting out pamphlets, and Charlotte had a way of letting her thoughts run on when her hands were occupied. 'Anyway they may not need me. I mean it may be just habit, you know, from being a clergyman's daughter. Perhaps I need them.'

Rosalind moved a pile of pamphlets briskly from one side of the table to the other, spilling ash from the cigarette which dangled from the one corner of her mouth.

'Clever girl,' she said, out of the other corner.

She stood up, swept the pamphlets on to her desk, stubbed out her cigarette into the overflowing ashtray and pushed forward another pile of pamphlets. The proofreading had been done hastily and there was an errata slip to be put into each front cover. The title of the pamphlet was *The Road to Collectivism*, the author Herbert Tranmer.

'Has Harry read this, I wonder?' said Charlotte, folding in the errata slips with a now practised hand.

'Why don't you?'

'It looks too boring.'

'It is boring.' Rosalind stood up to reach for another cigarette from her desk, then lighting it began to pace up and down beside the table at which Charlotte quietly worked. 'But it's all part of what has to be done. One can't have only the jolly bits, anarchist meetings and high oratory. It's part of the vision, the only vision in politics now. Apart from the Empire, which isn't a vision, it's a hallucination.'

Charlotte was not much interested in politics, and if there was to be talk of visions she thought she ought to mention the religious kind but knew that Rosalind would disapprove; she changed the subject instead.

'Is Herbert showing Harry the architect's plans? I'd love to see them. I've never liked any of Edwin Hanbury's buildings.'

Rosalind turned with a swirl of her black shawl, swooped on the table and began fitting the slips into the pamphlets at a great rate. 'We'll finish these and go and see. You'll love them.'

Never short of enthusiasm, she often swirled her shawl and swooped in that way; sometimes her deep rather raucous voice rose into a kind of excited squawk, reinforcing the overall impression of an energetic and benevolent crow, whose tatterdemalion wings flapped ecstatically in the keen wind of progress, but whose unceasing activity had about it an occasionally desperate air. She had a big nose and a sharp chin and a poor complexion, thick untidy black hair, bright dark eyes; her smile was unexpectedly warm, exposing a gap between her front teeth which made her seem more vulnerable than her decisive judgements sometimes implied. Charlotte, so much younger and so much in awe of her friend's intellect, had as their friendship progressed been surprised to find herself sometimes feeling almost protective towards Rosalind.

They were bending companionably over the plans, Herbert stolid and Harry more gracefully robust; Rosalind swooped, talking about warm English hearts in the midst of cold classicism, and riverside gardens open to all, and feats of underground engineering to make accessible the beneficent waters of the mineral springs.

'It has to be stone of course,' she explained to Charlotte. 'Though Todhunter likes to work with red brick, but he's going to use mullioned windows and roof gables and echo the Cotswold style just enough.'

'I should think it jolly well does have to be stone,' said Harry with mock ferocity.

Rosalind failed to see to what extent he was joking. 'Oh, but the Council insists on it. You couldn't use anything else here in the City. Anyway we would have insisted, wouldn't we, Herbert? Although of course we know you're so successful already . . .' She looked momentarily confused, seeing them laughing, and then her confusion was redoubled and given a different focus because Janet the maid unexpectedly announced, 'Mr Caspar Freeling.'

Janet looked a little confused too, because although the Tranmers, as they would have put it themselves, kept open house, Mrs Tranmer had no calling hour or afternoons of being At Home, and was completely taken aback by the arrival of someone she knew so little as Caspar Freeling.

He, however, was quite at ease, greeting them each with a firm handshake and a direct gaze into the eyes, rather different from his usual more sideways look, and drawing them quickly into his picture of the new arrival in the City, his mystical Russian friend with her boxes and trunks and crates of furniture and books and exotic relics of one sort or another, all urgently needing housing somewhere in the City and excusing therefore his visit.

'I am asking everyone if they know of anything. She has put me on my mettle by pretending to think I shall be bound to know of something. Of course she's going to be impossibly hard to satisfy. Nothing the agents can show her is up to her standard.'

They wanted of course to know more about her, where she had come from, how long she was staying, whether she knew Rosalind's hero, Prince Kropotkin. He told them all he knew, and a little more, and noticing what it was they had been looking at when he arrived asked in his turn for an explanation of the architect's plans. Herbert Tranmer with his usual courtesy and thoroughness gave it. Caspar Freeling's questions were detailed and accurate and Charlotte, watching the slight almost obsequious form attending so seriously to Herbert's never less than magisterial presence, felt she must be wrong – mean-minded in fact – in feeling that because the plans were supposed to be secret until the closing date for the competition entries, the Tranmers ought not to let them lie about for anyone to see. She listened instead to Herbert, who made anything he explained seem bathed in the light of pure reason. He was a short solid man, bearded and benign, who would have had a fine head but for the bulge of his forehead, which was always rather shiny, an effect perhaps of his white skin. He had written a great deal of political philosophy, and as well as that he was an internationally known expert on butterflies; perhaps it was the mixture of profundity and delicacy in the combination of his interests which made him looked upon by all who knew him as being in some sense set apart, by his learning, his gentleness and his natural moral strength. His wife teased him a little on what she took to be his weak point, that he was in possession of a private income, not large, but enough to keep them both quite comfortably as well as to support their philanthropic projects; this income was based on a family business of merchant venturers in the nearby port, and Rosalind claimed they had been in the slave trade for two centuries. He only smiled when she teased him.

He asked Caspar now if he were a writer on architectural matters. Caspar replied that he was interested, no more. 'My favourite art, you might say.'

'I thought perhaps you might once have trained.'

'I know a little about it. I wrote a book once in Oxford – not about architecture at all, something quite different – but a scornful reviewer said I seemed to know a little about a lot of things and a lot about nothing. It's probably true.'

'How wonderful,' said Rosalind dreamily. 'I mean how wonderful to know a lot about nothing. It's something, I sometimes think, I know a bit about myself.'

Charlotte, who did not like her friend to appear affected in front of someone who hardly knew her, said hastily, 'If you don't then it's the only thing you don't know about, I should think,' and was immediately aware that if Rosalind had sounded affected she herself sounded merely silly. She looked rather desperately at Harry, hoping he had understood. He had, and calmly directed the conversation into more mundane channels.

My friend Arthur Morrison, who is an archaeologist and the most contented man I know, asked me why I spent so much time poring over old copies of the *City Herald*.

'I suspect you of looking for something that isn't there,' he said. 'Or of having improper feelings towards your grandmother.'

I tried to tell him that living as I do in a world in which the condition of humanity between the Tigris and the Euphrates is a good deal more desperate than it was in the time of the ancient Sumerians 5,000 years ago, and when the Assyrian seems to be coming down like the wolf on the fold wherever my anxious glance falls, and when love fails and death is victorious and the wicked flourish as the green bay tree, I am simply looking for someone who went this way before me and left a sign on the wall beside the road. I didn't put it quite like that. Even so he looked at me in deep disapproval.

'And you a historian,' he said.

I told him I was a retired historian, which was different.

I know very well the valley where Stephen Collingwood walked, thinking of the poet Peter Tilsley and of Anne Smallwood of his parish, who had made a scene and caused him embarrassment; I walk there very often myself. Living as I do on the southern heights, in a part of the City which in his time was still a separate village, it is easier for me to reach that particular valley, which is over the hills to the south of the City, than it was for Stephen, who would usually get there by train. The single-track railway which used to run the length of the valley was closed in 1968, but in Stephen's time a ten-minute train ride would take him to the small station at the western end of the valley. There he would leave the train to steam on its way towards the coal country, push open the wicket gate at the back of the platform and climb the steep steps on to the road above. He would cross the small stone bridge over the railway track, where the thick hedgerows seem at all seasons alive with little darting birds whose calls are hardly more than whispers. Stephen, a better naturalist than I am, noticed them too, and was able to name them.

Stephen had recommended direct observation from nature to Peter as a discipline for the poetic imagination, but the only effort in that direction which Peter had shown him so far had been an effusion about clouds which was very far from the scientific precision he had had in mind. He wanted to explain to Peter his feeling that poetry should be both reasonable and more than reasonable at the same time, that the reason should be permeated by the more-than-reason, and the more-than-reason by the reason, in order to give strength, depth, height, resonance to each, but it was a difficult subject, and not one about which it was easy to speak precisely. He remembered conversations with his wife Hannah; they had read together a great deal during their short marriage. He had wanted to educate her, and she had seemed to like it. Such governesses as had passed through the busy household in which she had grown up had left very little impression on her mind; her father was agent to a big landed estate in Herefordshire and she had five sisters and two brothers. She was the prettiest sister, but the gentlest, so meek in fact he had afterwards wondered whether her spirit had been in some unconscious sense schooled to anticipate a short life. She had been three months pregnant and had fallen down unconscious on the dining-room floor. She died three days later; the doctor said there must always have been something wrong with her kidneys. His love for her had been protective, and sentimental; they had not had time to reach much depth of understanding. He thought of her almost every day with a twinge of acute pity. At such times he often said her name aloud, so that Wilf, the ex-soldier with whom he lodged, thought he was suffering from a broken heart, but the pity was for the littleness of her life rather than for his own loss, against which after the first few months he had ceased to rebel.

The valley narrows towards its eastern end, becoming more wooded. Stephen turned into the woods, taking a path which led him beside a small lake, under a tall railway viaduct and over a rushing stream. He began the steep climb across the fields and up the succession of stone stairways which lead between the houses on to the top of the hill. He was walking as he always did to clear his mind; he wanted too to escape an only too familiar self-reproach. He had himself so much resignation in his nature, so much willingness not only to accept the will of God but to see good in it, that he was often astonished by the violent reactions of those who were less reconciled. Why did a woman like Anne Smallwood have to be perpetually in a state of furious lamentation? Even when apparently more or less sober she was a virago. Why? Her husband was often drunk on Friday nights, and then he sometimes beat her; that was unfortunate, but not uncommon among the inhabitants of Haul Down. He was employed as a carter by one of the warehouse companies and was quite a pleasant man when sober. His wife never ceased to rail at him, pursuing him down the street with incoherent shrieked abuse. When Stephen passed their ill-kept cottage the fumes of burnt fat often mingled with the more familiar smell of boiling laundry; she took in washing, though goodness knew who would be rash enough to employ her services in that capacity. She had come up to him that morning as he began to walk down the hill to catch the train, and had clutched his arm and poured out a whole string of complaints about her neighbours; wicked people they were, she said, and what was he doing about it.

'That young man,' she said. 'That Peter. I've seen him going into your place. Thinks he can go anywhere, don't he, speak to anyone, no matter what he's up to the rest of the time. I've seen him. With that Mrs Moore who comes here visiting so nice and ladylike, I know what they get up to, there in the church porch and all. Disgusting, I call it, oh yes, I've seen them.'

He had shaken her off, quite roughly.

'Curb your tongue. Never let me hear you speak like that again.' He had not heard what she had shrieked after him as he strode away down the hill, but when a good deal later his anger had abated he had reproached himself. It was his duty to do more than condemn her malice. He ought to try to change her; that was what he was there for. The trouble was, he could not overcome his repugnance. As usual he found himself a bad Christian.

Reaching eventually the top of the hill, he crossed the main road and took the path through the beech woods towards Blake Leigh, and when he reached the open hillside from which you can see the City spread below you, he paused with the belt of trees behind him and looked, not down at the City but across towards the handsome solid house quite open to view on the hillside with its terraced garden surrounding it. She was there, with the two children, in the spring afternoon. They might have been picking primroses, might now be going in to tea.

He sat down on the grassy slope, his long stick beside him. The grass was damp but there was fitful sunshine between the huge white fast-moving clouds, and the westerly wind was warm on his face and smelt of the spring. A faint blue haze of smoke lay over the City far beneath him; within the mist the shadows of the clouds as they passed changed the colour of the buildings from grey to light brown and back again. Stephen watched the distant figure of Charlotte Moore gently chivying her two small children towards the house. The little girl had stopped to look at something on the gravel path, was crouched in concentration. Charlotte turned to wait, seemed to be expostulating, might have been laughing; the boy had gone on into the house. Charlotte crouched beside her daughter, their heads together. When they stood up the child seemed to be holding something, a flower perhaps, or a worm, or a stone that had taken her fancy. She held it up towards her mother and then the two of them walked slowly into the house, evidently engaged in animated conversation.

Stephen got to his feet and set off down the hill at a great pace; he was smiling. At the bottom of this hill, where a stile leads on to the footpath past the cemetery, the girl from the nearby cottage was rounding up a couple of wandering red hens. She was surprised to see the tall black-haired man with large grey eyes pounding past her at such a pace; seeing by his clothes that he was a gentleman she dropped a curtsy and was rewarded by a greeting of the utmost cheerfulness.

The rooms which Caspar Freeling found for Madame Sofia were only a short walk away from the house of the City Surveyor; Mrs Hanbury looked forward to any number of friendly visits. On one of the first of these she immediately appreciated that Caspar Freeling had achieved another coup; he had brought the Bishop to tea.

The houses here, thirty-two of them with identical façades in a circle broken only at three equal intervals by roads leading away from the centre, were at that time still for the most part lived in by single families of highly respectable citizens. Some of the top floors and a few of the basements were let off as separate flats.

There was one discreet nursing-home, spread over two houses and catering only for such elderly patients as could pay handsomely for the privilege of such a desirable address; and there was one lodging-house, belonging to Mr Arthur Corfield, who owned a great deal of property in the City. It was here, on the first floor, that Madame Sofia had established herself, much impressing the housekeeper and her husband, who lived in the basement. Her possessions had arrived from Baden-Baden, and the well-proportioned drawing-room, which had three tall windows looking out into the Circus, had been transformed into what Marianne Hanbury breathlessly pronounced 'a glimpse of Xanadu, indeed it is'.

Large-leaved palms in pots, with maidenhair ferns clustered at their feet, provided a background for two tall bird-cages of oriental design containing a noisy parrot and a collection of Javanese sparrows. A cuckoo clock on one wall gave rise to a torrent of abuse from the parrot every time it struck the hour. Inlaid tables of Goanese design held a multifarious collection of pipes and hookahs, oriental vases and carved images of gods. A jumble of books and manuscripts covered a larger table, of heavily carved mahogany, on which there was also a jug of barley water, covered by a cloth of beaded muslin. Bamboo chairs and sofas were covered with cushions and carelessly strewn with lengths of Indian material in a variety of designs. There were two tiger skin rugs on the large Turkey carpet, and lurking behind one of the palms was a stuffed ape of unfriendly aspect. In the middle of all this was a huge armchair in the Biedermeier style, with a yellow maplewood frame and brown velvet upholstery, upon which as on a throne Madame Sofia was seated; there was a faint smell of incense in the air.

The Bishop was made uneasy by the smell, which he associated with Ritualism, but put it down to the lady being foreign. He could not believe that anyone living in the Circus could be anything other than highly respectable; besides, Caspar Freeling had hinted at some kind of connection with the Russian royal family.

'You'll have no doubt heard of the impending royal visit?' he asked, leaning forward deferentially with a slight creak almost as if his capacious form might unlike Madame Sofia's be supported by stays (but it was only the bamboo chair). 'You'll have a view of the procession from here. That is . . .' He blew his nose rather suddenly on a large white handkerchief. It had occurred to him that she might be of such exalted rank that she would be among those to be presented to Her Majesty in person at the morning ceremony in the Guildhall.

'So the route of the procession is already known, so far in advance?' said Madame Sofia. 'But I must remember that I am in England, where people do not assassinate their royal families.' She sighed heavily, glancing heavenwards as if in memory of all sorts of dear departed royalty mown down before her eyes.

The Bishop, impressed, nevertheless felt that the English masses should not be let off so lightly. He had serious doubts about them. The spectre of anarchy haunted his dreams. The working classes were not to be relied upon.

He began to impart to Madame Sofia various disquieting pieces of information which he had recently learnt from the newspapers. Madame Sofia's thoughts wandered as they were wont to do at the best of times. She was not much interested in English politics and the Bishop struck her – most unfairly, for who was she to talk? – as too fat.

'Indeed we must all seek humility,' she said distantly.

The Bishop stopped in mid-sentence, confused, but Mrs Hanbury rushed to the rescue; it was a wicked world, she said, the ingratitude, the horrors, and had he read of those dreadful murders? The Bishop, confidence restored, smiled at her benignly; she was after all more or less a disciple of his. She had been to see him some years ago, when she was newly married to the City Surveyor, and had told him she wished to convert from Roman Catholicism to the Church of England; her husband's position in the City was such that it was desirable from every point of view that she should be seen to accompany him to the altar rails when he felt it incumbent on him to receive the sacrament. The Bishop had seen the force of her reasoning. With the co-operation of the Rector of the Abbey – for though the City was within his see the Bishop lived some miles away in the cathedral town which was the centre of the diocese – a dignified little ceremony had been devised, whereby in one of the side-chapels of the Abbey, and in the presence of the two clerics, Mrs Hanbury had forsworn her allegiance to the Pope, renounced a number of doctrines to which she had quite forgotten she had formerly adhered and earnestly prayed for forgiveness for the error of her ways. The fact that they had participated together in this ceremony made both Mrs Hanbury and the Bishop feel afterwards that there was something particular and not necessarily exclusively theological about their relationship. Neither of them had quite the same feeling about the Rector.

Caspar Freeling meanwhile had started to explain to Madame Sofia his theory that the Circus, though built in the eighteenth century, was on the site of a former Druid circle; he was determined to observe how the sun's rays fell at dawn on Midsummer's Day. He even believed that the architect a hundred and fifty years ago in the so-called Age of Reason knew exactly what he was doing. Madame Sofia's loyalty being all to the East, she found the Ancient Britons as uninteresting as the Church of England, but Caspar himself intrigued her. Seeing the Bishop fully engaged in his conversation with Mrs Hanbury, she leant towards Caspar and said rather unexpectedly, 'He is as spiritual as a boiled egg.'

Caspar gave his conspirator's giggle.

She raised a hand. 'Don't think I am ungrateful. You have found me the most elegant rooms in the City and you have made me blessed in the eyes of my neighbours by the visit of this sainted chap. I will ask the permission of my unseen Masters to interest myself in your Druids. And if through your connections with Oxford you know of any scholarly works which need translating, please let me know. There are very few languages with which I am not thoroughly conversant. Naturally in Russian, German, French, English, Polish and Urdu I am top hole.'

Caspar nodded thoughtfully.

'I also need more fresh fruit,' said Madame Sofia.

Caspar, preferring to ignore this last request, concentrated instead on the one before.

'It might be worth your meeting Mr Corfield, who owns this building. It wouldn't be quite on the intellectual level you're thinking of, but he has business interests all over the world and there might be correspondence or contracts or I don't know what over which you could help him with translations. I'll sound him out. Leave it to me.'

Mrs Hanbury had heard the name over her own conversation.

'Corfield, Corfield, everything is Corfield. He thinks he's the great panjandrum himself.'

'Is he out of favour with you?' asked Caspar.

'Indeed he is. He's poking his nose into the business of the Hôtel des Bains, as I call it — no one seems to know what its final name will be. It's so ridiculous to leave the whole thing in doubt and confusion and uncertainty when my husband has the most splendid and practical designs you could imagine. Building could begin tomorrow if they would only leave it to him.'

'They will in the end,' said Caspar. 'As for Mr Corfield, he may not be strong on aesthetics but he has another attribute which many people find attractive.'

'And that is?' asked Mrs Hanbury with a haughty air which she knew became her.

'Opulence,' said Caspar.

Mrs Hanbury clapped her hands and laughed, as if he had produced a rabbit out of a hat.

Peter Tilsley, unlike his mentor Stephen Collingwood, was not much moved by the contemplation of wild Nature. Occasionally a mood of exhaltation might seize him on a country walk, but moods of exhaltation might seize him anywhere, he being subject to them, and his thoughts flowed most freely, and ideas for poems came to him most profusely, when he was wandering through a crowd of strangers. He was becoming known in the places in which he most often wandered in the City, and would exchange greetings with some of the people he saw regularly – warehousemen or baker's boys, whose occupations took them into the streets, washerwomen, housekeepers shopping for their employers, the occasional policeman or school inspector. He was known to these people only as they were known to him, in a kind of territorial sense, but if he happened to meet someone from Haul Down who knew his name or where he lived he felt diminished in his sense of himself as a stranger; this sense was important to the free flow of his imagination. So in the course of time, having walked down the hill and crossed the river and lingered a little by the warehouses and the poorer streets which surrounded them, he took to wandering further from the river and into the centre of the City past the Abbey and the Assembly

Rooms and the Guildhall. Behind the Guildhall he would rejoin the river, wider here and cleaner, spanned by a high stone bridge from which, looking through the windows of one of the little shops which line it, he could see the space on which the new hotel was to be built. It was here that he one day overheard the building being discussed. Three men had come into the little coffee shop, which could hold no more than half a dozen people at a time. The three were so large, and so clearly important, that Peter, sitting unobtrusively in the corner by the window, felt almost crowded out. They asked for coffee and some of the buns for which the City was famous, and stood by the counter talking loudly and scattering crumbs. The two smaller (relatively speaking) of the men had documents with them, rolled under their arms, and talked of dimensions, and drainpipes, and external mouldings; it seemed they were architects, and the big bearded man, capaciously cloaked and smelling of eau-de-Cologne, was their client. It was he who before they left pronounced in the grandest of tones, 'Nothing but the classical is good enough for me.'

Peter immediately began to imagine what pleasure domes they might be planning. He had not thought much about the projected hotel. He had taken in that the site was a splendid one between the Guildhall and the river and overlooked by the bridge, but hotels had never featured much in his scheme of things; it would have been different had someone proposed a library or a place of learning. Now, however, the air of authority of the bearded man, his seeming so important though not exactly handsome, seemed to indicate that something more than merely commercial, something possibly quite splendid, was being envisaged. The reason, Peter thought, might be something to do with the waters. He had swum in those waters, and believed they had cured him (though of what he was less sure); he had felt their beneficent warmth. The others swimming with him – mostly elderly rheumatic patients – had laughed at him when he had said, 'But is it free? This warm, for nothing?' And it had seemed to him miraculous that warm water should spring in such abundance from the depths of the earth year after year. So if the new building was to be seen as some kind of temple for these springs, where people would gather from all over the world to immerse themselves in this divine water or to refresh themselves by swallowing it (it had a disagreeable taste of bad eggs but he had been told that was the sulphur in it), well, then, that was an idea to which the poet in him could respond. The springs of life, the springs of love, the pilgrims, the idea of purification, the wonderful bounty of the Earth, and above all the beautiful building that should house all that, great halls perhaps, built out of chalcedony and blue-grained marble, in which groups of men and women robed in white would wander, conversing on an extraordinarily exhalted level, even singing – but no, perhaps not singing. Peter's little crowing laugh surprised the young lady behind the counter. He loved the vision he had conjured up, he believed in it; and yet he saw that it was funny, so that it was as if the ideal beings he imagined walked their splendid ways accompanied by a leaping, gleeful creator who urged them on with enthusiasm but with no reverence at all. The waitress thought it time to present him with the bill for his cup of coffee. She had red hair but was not very pretty. Her hair put him in mind of Mrs Hanbury, who was not so much pretty as sublime, and then he thought of Mrs Hanbury's husband, the City Surveyor, whom he had never met, and of her frequently expressed wish that it should be he who should be the architect of the new hotel. It must surely be his duty to tell her what he had just overheard. If it was not his duty it was certainly his desire, because it seemed a perfectly adequate excuse to call on her.

As he left the coffee shop the Abbey clock struck twelve, which seemed to him an appropriate enough calling-hour. What he had not bargained for was that, by the time he reached the white front door ten minutes or so later, Edwin Hanbury would have arrived home for the midday meal, as he sometimes did when his affairs did not take him too far afield. Not having met the City Surveyor before, Peter was overwhelmed by his presence. If the men in the coffee shop had been large, Edwin Hanbury was a giant. He stood with his back to the fireplace, hands behind his back, feet slightly apart, a man in full possession of his hearth and home, which included of course the unfamiliarly meek Marianne. His large frame gave the impression of great muscular strength and fitness. His square, ruddy-complexioned face was bordered by side-whiskers which grew from below his ears to underneath his chin; he had a full but well-groomed moustache. His stiff collar, capacious silk tie and subfusc suit all contributed to his authoritative air; his shoes and his watch and chain shone.

Peter wriggled and stuttered until Marianne Hanbury helped him, offering him up for her husband's approval with recommendations which sounded like excuses but which Edwin Hanbury accepted as explanations.

'I know your editor of course, Mr Crowe, an able man indeed. He's always been helpful in putting right the inaccuracies that spread around so easily in a city like this when any change is proposed. The press has a great role to play in this democratic age. There are those who criticize it, but if we can keep it in responsible hands I am not afraid of the future.'

'Many people are,' said Peter. 'Almost everyone perhaps, except those who are in love with it.'

'And which are you?' asked Marianne, smiling her charmingly inane smile.

'Oh, both of course. Afraid of it *and* in love with it.'

Marianne lowered her eyes as if the remark had applied to her, which perhaps it coincidentally did. Edwin Hanbury looked at his watch.

'I wondered,' said Peter, 'whether it was of interest — that's to say, whether you would know who it was I happened to notice talking about the new hotel building just now.' He described the conversation and the appearance of the three men. He was an accurate observer, and at his description of the big bearded man, husband and wife with one accord said, 'Corfield!' and exchanged a glance.

'Corfield is going for classicism,' said Marianne slowly.

There was a slight pause.

'That's as may be,' said her husband eventually, and looked at his watch again.

Peter stood up hastily. 'I mustn't keep you from your dinner.'

Edwin Hanbury shook him firmly by the hand and said, 'Call again, do.'

'Do,' echoed Marianne softly.

Peter hurried out into the street. It distressed him to see the glorious Marianne so subdued. At the same time he was stimulated by the powerful personality of the City Surveyor; here was someone who belonged to the world of action, who understood about money and managing things and how to deal with the press. Even as he walked along the street with the hurried half-skipping gait which betrayed his excitement, Peter could imagine Edwin Hanbury, man of affairs, rocking gently backwards and forwards in his perfectly shining shoes, arms crossed now, expression grave, waiting for the servant girl to bang the gong at the bottom of the stairs to tell him he might descend to his midday beef and dumplings, saying thoughtfully to his docile seated wife, 'You should cultivate that young man, my dear. He might be useful.' But it was not so funny after all. That so much beauty should be subject to that! It made him cough. He had to stop, and lean against some railings, and hold his handkerchief to his mouth until the paroxysm passed.

The Corfield girls were mistresses of the art of making woollen flowers. They had their signature, two or three tiny forget-me-nots in the bottom right-hand corner of the group. When I noticed the recurrence of this modest sign among the displays of such flowers, mounted on velvet-covered stands and covered by glass domes, which used to turn up in the junk shops of the City some years ago, I was sufficiently intrigued to keep it in mind as I pursued my other researches; months later I noticed a paragraph in the *City Herald* of the appropriate date describing the wares on sale at a charity bazaar and mentioning 'Two groups of woollen flowers made by Miss Letitia and Miss Isabel Corfield and signed with their distinguishing mark of two forget-me-nots'. Neither of the sisters married. They died in the early 1950s, having ended their days at a genteel old people's home in a house called Tivoli, just across the road from the impressive gates and laurel-bordered drive of Capo di Monte, their former home. One of their flower arrangements sits on the chest-of-drawers in my bedroom; the colours are still bright and the intricacy of the wire framework on which the sisters so patiently wound the wool makes it more attractive than most such relics, but Mary my wife never liked it; in fact she called it hideous. She would probably have said the same of Capo di Monte, being as she was an uncompromising Palladian, but she would have admired its view over the City.

A rather rumbustious man of letters, a contemporary of Dickens, came to live in the City at one time because he said it reminded him of Florence. Perhaps it was his influence which caused a few large villas in the Italianate style to spring up on the hill to the south-east of the City. Capo di Monte was the largest of these, and the most reminiscent of royal Osborne. Arthur Corfield, who sometimes called himself a simple engineer, liked to complain that the hill was tiring out the horse which pulled him up it, and to imply that it was only to please his wife that they lived in such a place. 'She must have her garden,' he would say. Hetty Corfield was a good gardener according to the taste of the time, as the gardens up there still demonstrate, but in fact he was proud of the house, pleased to have it furnished in the latest and most comfortable style, delighted when visitors complimented Hetty on the garden, highly satisfied to think that his six children (there were four boys as well as the industrious

Letitia and Isabel) were growing up in surroundings so infinitely more favourable than those in which he had spent his own childhood. His fortune, which though great by the standards of the City, where fortunes were at that time not much in evidence at all, was of no more than medium size; it was his evident enjoyment of it which magnified it in the eyes of his neighbours. It was built upon a certain sort of screw, or bolt, which was essential in the making of railway sleepers and which he had noticed in the workshop to which he had gone as a young apprentice. He had persuaded his employer to let him modify the thing in the way he saw it needed to be modified and had then patented it in his own name and eventually bought out his former master and opened a small factory on the flat land between the river and the railway to the west of the City. After that his cleverness had been in not expanding his business too far, and in putting some of his profits into quite small ventures in property, nearly all of which had made more money for him. With the purchase of Capo di Monte and the arrival in due order of his six children he found himself perfectly contented. He was contented with Hetty his wife too, largely on the grounds of her respectful attitude towards himself. Finding her in the garden showing pretty young Mrs Moore her new spring planting, he expatiated on his recent conversation with his architects.

'I told them to go away and think again. No pinnacles, I said, no old-fashioned fancies. I want something to elevate the mind and attract the cultured classes. That's what this City needs if it's to re-establish itself. That's what I can provide.'

'But would you finance it then, rather than the City Council?' asked Charlotte, surprised.

'That's what I'm proposing to them. I'm saying, give the prize to my architects and I'll take the scheme off your hands, I'll be the developer. We'll stick to your specifications and I'll see to the finances.'

'Such a benefaction,' said Hetty Corfield admiringly.

Charlotte, who recognized that the proposition was a business one rather than an offer of charity, was nevertheless impressed. She asked when the competition was to be judged.

'It's supposed to be before the royal visit,' he replied. 'They want to announce it at the same time, show the Queen the winning designs or something of the kind – a model perhaps – but it seems the Oxford professor who's advising the committee and making the final judgement may not be able to manage it in time. He's such a busy man apparently. Anyway we've only another couple of months to get our plans in.'

'Oh, Charlotte,' said Hetty Corfield. 'What will you be wearing for the royal visit?'

Charlotte said vaguely that she supposed she would have something made. She did not like to talk to Hetty Corfield about clothes, or indeed about anything very much except gardens. She liked Hetty, and she believed that Hetty knew it. Certainly her visits to Capo di Monte, which were almost always made in order to learn something about gardening, gave as much pleasure to Hetty as they gave instruction to Charlotte. Charlotte knew that her own garden had never been much loved, either by herself or by her parents-in-law, and she had resolved to take an interest in it. Hetty knew a lot about both the design of gardens and the plants that might be grown in them, because her father had been head gardener at the manor house which overlooked the valley where Stephen Collingwood so often walked; Hetty herself had spent her childhood in the gardener's cottage at its gates. Unlike her husband she had never lost – indeed had hardly modified – her regional way of speech. Thus while Charlotte might reasonably expect to be on visiting terms with the people who lived in the Manor, the Corfields would expect nothing of the kind. This being understood by all concerned, Hetty Corfield was much pleased by Charlotte's interest in her garden.

Pressed by both Corfields to stay a little longer, Charlotte gently disengaged herself. 'I want to be home in time to have tea with the children and I promised to do some district visiting on the way.' She wrinkled her nose prettily to imply that the necessity was a bore, and they let her go, expressing wonder that she proposed to drive herself in her own little pony cart. Would she not let Rogers, who had just driven Arthur Corfield up the hill, take her along to Haul Down and hold the pony for her while she made her visits? But no, Punch was used to it, she said, she always left him by the drinking-trough where the coal horses waited, and there were any number of little boys anxious to earn a penny or two by holding him.

It was a mile or two's drive along the straight road at the top of the hill, past the entrance to her own house, and then down the quiet slope to where the hillside briefly flattened out into a space with a few shops and a post office and then plunged much more steeply down towards the City. Charlotte passed the shops and began the descent but almost immediately drew up in the space near the stone water trough, where a couple of thin horses were tied up and where as usual several small boys appeared and began to compete for her custom. She handed Punch's reins to one of them, but when another insisted that she had promised last time that he should have a turn, she said the two of them could share the job and she would give them a penny each. A third boy, slighter and paler, who had not offered to hold the pony but had stood aside and watched, followed her and said quietly, 'You'll be sorry for that, you know.'

'Will I?'

'You'll have to let two of them do it every time you come. He hardly needs holding anyway, old Punch.'

'You used to hold him sometimes. You're Albert, aren't you?'

He flushed at being remembered; she noticed how fair his skin was.

'You're too old to hold ponies now, I suppose?'

'I've got better things to do,' he said scornfully.

'Better things?'

To her surprise he answered fiercely, 'I get paid more, don't I?'
'I wasn't criticizing.'

He looked sulky but continued to walk beside her. She stopped at one of the little houses.

'I'm going in here, to see Mrs Bennett.'

But the boy was not looking at her. He was looking at Caspar Freeling, who was approaching them, picking his way fastidiously along the road, which was not very clean; there was no pavement here.

'Afternoon, Mr Freeling.' There was something in Albert's tone that surprised Charlotte again. She looked at him and saw that he was smiling at Caspar in a way that struck her as both bold and ingratiating, but when Caspar answered benevolently, 'Hullo, Albert,' and turned to greet her with his usual politeness the boy ran off.

'They tease me round here, these urchins,' said Caspar indulgently.

Charlotte, unconvinced, disengaged herself with a smile and went on into the house.

She was reading *Cranford* to old Mrs Bennett, and they were both enjoying it. Mrs Bennett was in her eighties, as far as anyone knew, and quite blind. She had a daughter of sixty or so, who went out to work every day in a paper mill next to Mr Corfield's works between the river and the railway and who left food and fuel and anything else she thought necessary within her mother's reach; the old woman managed on her own until the daughter came home. Most of the time she sat straight up in her chair with her hands folded on her lap. When Charlotte came to the passage in *Cranford* where Miss Matty had to take a great leap to get into bed because she was not sure there might not be a hairy man underneath it, Mrs Bennett laughed a great deal. Stephen Collingwood, who had looked in to see her as he often did, heard the laughter and hesitated at the door.

Charlotte looked up and made him come in, saying they had

finished their reading and it was time she went home, but he only stood for a few moments with his hand on Mrs Bennett's shoulder, looking down kindly at her blind old face with its protruding and wispily grey-haired chin, saying that he had been passing by and would come again the next day for a talk. By these means he was able to leave at the same time as Charlotte.

As she stepped over some rubble on the road it seemed quite natural for Charlotte to put her hand on Stephen's arm, and keep it there. He told her that he was worried about Peter Tilsley, whose cough seemed to be getting worse.

'I made him go down to the dispensary the other day and all they did was to give him some medicine he doesn't take and tell him he may improve with the warmer weather.'

'Perhaps he will. He told me a doctor had told him he was not consumptive.'

'He told me that too. I think it only shows he's afraid he is.'

Stephen would have liked to tell Charlotte how comforted he felt at being able to share his anxiety, but he was afraid this would be a mistake; she was so astonishingly easy to talk to that it might be that once he started he would tell her everything, and therefore it was better that he should tell her nothing. He wished the little dirty street were longer all the same. As they came towards the end of it, and when they were already quite close to the water trough and the waiting Punch with his two attendants, a swirling muttering figure suddenly stormed past them; he heard the words 'disgrace' and 'hussy' in a familiar harsh whisper. Charlotte's grip on his arm tightened for a moment.

'What was that?'

'Nothing. She's a madwoman.'

'Was it Anne Smallwood? I suppose so. Poor thing. I suppose the hussy's me.'

'She says terrible things of everyone. She's out of her mind.'

'I dare say she's in love with you.'

'Don't terrify me.'

He looked over his shoulder to make sure that the woman had gone on her turbulent way, then slowing his pace even more he said, 'I can't understand these people. I'm no good with them, with any of them. I'm perfectly useless here.'

'But you're useful simply by being here.' Charlotte turned towards him, one hand still tucked into his elbow and the other now laid lightly on his forearm; she looked earnestly into his face. 'They admire you and respect you, they don't expect you to love them.'

'They should expect it, they have every right to expect it.'

But they had reached the end of the little street. Punch had raised his head ready for home, the boys were holding out their hands for money.

'You are so much better at it than I am,' he said, exasperated.

'Oh, but that's because I'm a woman.' She stepped lightly into the pony cart, one hand on his shoulder. 'It's different for men.' She gathered up the reins, smiling now because, looking at him standing there in the road, she thought how much she liked him.

'Why? Why is it so difficult for men?'

'They have to be manly. It must be that.'

He laughed, and protested, but she shook the reins so that Punch broke into a trot. Stephen was left standing in the road, a tall man, smiling, stared at by two ragged boys.

Since he had had his vision of the marble halls and flowing fountains of Arthur Corfield's temple to the goddess of the healing springs, Peter Tilsley had taken a keener interest in the projected hotel. Impressed though he had been by Corfield, he had been even more struck by the tremendous presence of Edwin Hanbury. Being a small man himself, he tended to give undue importance to mere stature. Edwin Hanbury was several inches taller than Arthur Corfield, and he had the broad chest and muscular frame of a rower; most early mornings he was to be seen in a light skiff sculling on the river, wearing a white woollen fitted garment of his own design with short sleeves and three-quarter length legs. Peter had seen him there sometimes before he knew who he was and had thought he must be some famous sportsman in training rather than the City Surveyor taking a turn on the river before breakfast. Who knew what works of genius this great man might be cogitating? He had a most inspiring muse, after all, in Marianne. On the other hand Charlotte Moore had mentioned her friends the Tranmers and had spoken warmly of their plans for some kind of co-operative endeavour to run the hotel for the good of all, and though he had not yet met the Tranmers, Peter was sure that someone as sweet-natured as Charlotte, and at the same time of such a lively intelligence, could not be altogether wrong.

The question of who was to build the hotel seemed of such importance to Peter that he was disappointed to receive a pessimistic response when he mentioned it to his editor, Mr Crowe. Mr Crowe said that he had seen it all before, and that these schemes came and went; even if they decided to do it they would back out, it would end in quarrels and arguments and the Council would say it was all too expensive.

'But if the citizens insist?'

Mr Crowe laughed at the very notion of the citizens insisting. Those few that were interested, he said, would quarrel and argue and say it was all too expensive just like the councillors. At this Peter felt challenged. What was the good of a poet if he could not inspire? He hurried off to the premises of the Institute of Science and Philosophy and settled down to write a contribution to the Notes and Queries column.

The Institute had been founded some years before as a result of the City's having been endowed in the will of one of its longest-serving clergymen with a very large collection of fossils and meteorites, which the good man had put together in a lifetime's devotion to the study of such things. The City councillors, being quite unable to think of anywhere to put the collection, had gratefully accepted the offer made by a group of like-minded citizens to house it in some rather imposing premises which had recently become available, and to make it the focus of an institute whose members might share their scientific interests and attend such lectures and debates as might be organized. This worthy ideal had lost its first impetus. The building, a tall terraced house in one of the parades, overlooking gardens and the river, was not much used, and the occasional lectures on such subjects as 'The Life of the Ant' and 'The Foundation Stones of the Earth's Crust' were poorly attended. Under the articles by which the initial money had been raised the Institute had to be kept open for the larger part of every day except Sundays. A series of low-paid ladies of secretarial background succeeded each other at the desk in the library; the upper parts of the building were let as solicitors' offices. The library was a fine room with pilasters and plasterwork and three tall windows looking out over the river, and though Peter would have preferred that the shelves should have been filled with books rather than rows of dusty stones and faded labels he found it an excellent place to work, infinitely quieter and more comfortable than his lodgings on Haul Down. Merely to sit in so much space and proportion and with such an outlook had inspired him to what he hoped was some of his best work. He still felt himself to be a poet above all else and was beginning to resent the time he had to spend on the Notes and Queries column, but he urged himself on because he needed the money. (Whichever of the bored attendants might be sitting at the desk at the time was occasionally surprised to hear him muttering, 'Dinner, dinner, dinner.') The subject of the new hotel, however, now that he had seen it in what he was confident was the proper light, was easy to write about.

'What do we want of our City? Have we not here the opportunity to make of it something splendid in the eyes of the world? Other cities and towns all over England are growing larger every day. The dictates of manufacturing industry, the demands of an ever-expanding empire, the pressure of an ever-growing population, are making great dark stains on the land, wounds on the glorious face of Nature. Ours is not that kind of city, not only because we are small but because we are favoured. We have our industries, we have our market, we have our daily business, but we are here above all because for thousands of years the earth has yielded up to us an endless flow of the sweet waters of healing. If we allow the hotel scheme to fade away, if we waste the opportunity of having erected on the grand site proposed a building as fine as any of the Roman temples which once stood here, we shall be showing ourselves unworthy of the bounty which Nature yields us. In so small a city as ours, a building in such a position can have an effect far greater than if it were built in Manchester, or Bristol, or London. For our City is small, so small we might almost persuade ourselves we had dreamt it. What shall it be, our dream?'

When he had written these words, Peter raised both hands above his head and croaked in a loud whisper, 'Hurray!' The attendant, who had been dozing, woke with a perceptible jump and looked alarmed, but he had already hurried past her on his way to the newspaper office.

When Mr Crowe inserted the piece he cut the last two sentences; he thought them rather silly.

Caspar Freeling called the room which he rented in one of the houses on Haul Down his 'studio'. It was a large attic, in a big shabby house which had once been a public dispensary. The ground floor was now a hardware shop and the first floor was so much in need of repair that it was hardly safe for anyone to live in; Caspar paid a small rent for it so that it should not be let to anyone else, in order, he explained, to ensure complete quiet for his work. He passed the shabby door to the first-floor rooms every time he went up to his studio but he had only once looked in; he had rooms elsewhere in the City, bachelor chambers overlooking the Abbey forecourt which were a good deal pleasanter than anything on Haul Down. He had made the large dark attic into something like a Turkish coffee house, with soft divans covered with cushions and richly coloured wall hangings; gas lamps in elaborate holders shed a golden light, thick velvet curtains kept out all sight or sound of the street below.

'So mysterious,' said Marianne Hanbury, looking round in admiration and surprise. 'So exotic.'

'I can't think how that woman can have given you the address. I told her she was only to – to give it to no one.'

'I inveigled her. You don't mind? I left the carriage at the top. I told him to wait. Nothing will give you away.'

'It's just that here I can work in peace. I am one of those people who can't work where I live, I have to be away in silence.'

'It's because it was to do with your work that I came. Otherwise I shouldn't have dreamt of it. When I have shown you my findings I'll leave at once.' But she was slipping off her cloak, turning so that he had to take it from her. As he did so she gave a slight shiver. 'It feels so strange here.'

'Yes, it is strange,' he answered coldly.

'Now look.' She picked up a large envelope which she had put down on one of the divans when she came in. 'Here is something to interest you.' She sat down and extracted some sheets of paper from the envelope. 'Look.'

He had to sit beside her in order to see what she held.

'I have torn out these pages from an old copy of *Strand Magazine*. It is all about Druids. Are you not pleased with me?' She turned towards him in supplication.

'If you want something you must ask for it,' he said sternly.

'You know what it is. You have always known.'

'Ask for it.'

'Touch me. Only touch me.'

'Beg me.'

She begged him. He took her quite roughly, holding her down on the soft divan. Secure in the velvet seclusion she shrieked with pleasure.

Her fleshly desires at peace she gently asked him not to look so sad. He rose from the divan and said, 'I don't bring happiness, you know.'

'You do to me, indeed you do.'

'It won't be for long. I have never made anyone happy. Except by the sort of service for which they pay me.'

'You want me to pay you?' she asked, astonished rather than shocked.

'No.' He looked at her. She was leaning on one elbow in the lamplight, half sitting and half lying, her dress disordered and her hair in abundant escape from its restraints; her surprised expression was slightly comical. 'Of course I don't want you to pay me, you dear creature. I'll pay you, one day. Not yet. One day there'll be something, there always is. Something you need me for, something I can do for you, you wait and see. I have a lot of strings to my bow.'

'I know that.' She stood up and began to rearrange her hair in front of a japanned mirror. Smiling at him in the mirror through the reflection of her curved arm she said, 'You're a man of secrets.'

'Talking of that I don't want you to come here again. It's not wise. You're much too noticeable up here. Promise me.'

'I promise. But . . .'

'I'll come to you.'

'Now you couldn't have managed without that article, the one I brought you, now could you?'

'My work would have been held up almost indefinitely without it. I'll come to you for more of the same.'

'Soon?'

'Soon.'

*

Although Charlotte Moore was unwilling to discuss clothes with Hetty Corfield she was quite happy to do so with her friend Rosalind Tranmer, whose husband Herbert was, as Rosalind put it, 'under threat' of being presented to the Queen. The Nonconformist merchant family from which he came had been involved for many years in a variety of charitable works, among which was the indigents' hospital which had enabled Peter Tilsley to take his swimming cure in the mineral waters. It was as a governor of this establishment that Herbert Tranmer had been asked to the reception in the Guildhall before the royal banquet. Rosalind had been asked too but she said there was no fear of her being presented to the Queen.

'The Mayor detests me. He knows I'm an anarchist. I expect I shall be searched to see if I've got a bomb under my skirt.'

'I hope you won't have.'

'I'm much too cowardly.'

They were walking in the Botanical Gardens; Charlotte's two children had run on ahead of them. A mist of blue scillas and grape hyacinths spread under some of the taller trees; the air smelt of almond blossom and mown grass and newly turned earth. Rounding a corner they came upon a bank of pink and white anemones.

'I plant those every year in my garden,' said Charlotte. 'And every year they all come up blue.'

The children were running back towards them, Ella first, looking aggrieved.

'He said "Oy" again.'

Edmund was three and had been his sister's slave, she being two years older. Charlotte had recently arranged for him to go twice a week to play with some slightly older boys, who were his cousins; he was a very pretty boy and she did not want him to become too girlish. Edmund's admiration for these bigger boys had led him to copy some of their less desirable habits. He would sometimes quite unexpectedly and very loudly say 'Oy!', which seemed to him quite excruciatingly funny. Ella thought it shockingly bad manners and wished Charlotte would do something about it.

'Don't say "Oy", Ned darling,' said Charlotte fondly.

Seeing that that would have to do, Ella led him away again, saying they were going to climb a tree. Charlotte knew that climbing trees was forbidden in the Botanical Gardens, but since she knew they were unlikely to climb at all high owing to Ella's extreme caution she hoped they might not be seen. She was happier for the children to play on their own when she was with Rosalind. The Tranmers were childless, and Rosalind, the apostle of liberty in most other fields, had sometimes implied that Charlotte was not strict enough as a mother; Charlotte took this to mean that Rosalind found children a bore.

'Tell me then who else will be there, at this reception?' she asked.

'You would laugh if you could see the list they sent us. All the municipality has to be there. Poor Queen. She comes by train, is met by carriages and the Mayor and the Lord Lieutenant and all that sort of thing, and then at twelve forty-two-and-a-half they arrive at the Guildhall and she meets the City this and the City that — the aldermen, the Inspector of Nuisances, I promise you I'm not joking, the Poor Law people, the Inspector of Weights and Measures, Herbert and me, the Member of Parliament, what a jumble! Then the elect of the elect have lunch with her and she opens the Free Library and drives through the City and climbs back into the train and has a nice doze on the way home. But now quite suddenly —' She took Charlotte's arm and guided her firmly on to another path, whispering as they went, 'We are fascinated, absolutely fascinated by fuchsias.'

'It's too early in the year for fuchsias,' whispered Charlotte. 'Have you seen someone?'

'The mad Madame whatsit. Let's get out of sight. She's such a bore.'

'Caspar Freeling's friend? I've never met her.' Glancing over her shoulder Charlotte saw a heavily wrapped figure moving slowly along the path. 'She looks like Queen Victoria.'

'Bigger and more boring. Mystical, you know. If there's one thing I can't abide, it's a mystic.'

'It's Mr Freeling I don't like. He creeps around with that sly smile and I never know what he's up to.'

'The funny thing is that Herbert says Freeling's all right.' They were now far enough away from Madame Sofia to slow their pace. 'He says he's a scholar and knows all about pre-Roman history.'

'All about it must be very little I should think. There are only a few old stones and bones to go by.'

'Herbert goes to see him sometimes. It does rather surprise me, but Herbert's never wrong about that sort of thing.'

'I can't imagine Herbert being wrong about anything. I wonder if the children will know which way we've gone. I think if we went this way we'd come back to where they were by another path.'

It was a mistake. Rounding an immense thuya they found themselves facing the approaching Madame Sofia. She seemed to roll slowly towards them as if her sizeable feet, hardly visible in their buttoned boots beneath her plum-coloured serge skirt, were set on tramlines; the solid effect was enhanced by the fact that her arms were crossed over her torso, each black gloved hand clasping an end of the large tartan shawl which she wore around her shoulders. It was a mild spring day and she looked hot. The protruding blue eyes in the flushed face seemed to focus with some difficulty on the two women before her, as if her gaze had been fixed on something far more distant.

'Ah!' she exclaimed, recognizing Rosalind. 'Mrs Tranmer! I must tell you that I have heard news of Prince Kropotkin.'

Rosalind introduced her friend, and after a courteous greeting Madame Sofia continued, 'Kropotkin is in England. He has been released from prison in France and is staying here in the land of liberty with some sympathizers in Herne Hill. I don't know their names.'

'I think I might know who it would be. How wonderful. Perhaps we could persuade him to come down here. We could organize a meeting and ask him to address it, but I suppose we'd have to work awfully hard to make this sleepy place pay attention.'

'I am not myself quite convinced by all he says, though my sympathies are with his motives. I am not an anarchist except in the most theoretical sense of the word, because I have seen the true face of anarchy and it is not attractive. My acquaintance with Kropotkin is more on the social side. We had many friends in common in old Moscow.'

Charlotte had seen a faded framed daguerreotype of Kropotkin which hung over Rosalind's desk, and despite his considerable beard and whiskers he had in retrospect a certain facial resemblance to Madame Sofia, the same broad forehead and nose, the same wide-apart eyes and magisterial gaze. Madame Sofia seemed for the moment lost in her memories and Charlotte was relieved when the children appeared. They looked curiously at Madame Sofia, who removing her gloves delved into the pockets of her voluminous skirt and extracted a paper bag from which she took a large magenta aniseed ball and held it out to Ella. 'Aniseed balls,' she said. 'They have been the ruin of me.'

Ella thanked her politely but took the sweet with some caution.

'Eat it, eat it,' said Madame Sofia looking at her benignly. 'One will not hurt you. It is when you are as old and fat as I am that you have to worry.'

'Oy!' said Edmund, and took refuge in Charlotte's skirts.

'Oy to you, my good man,' said Madame Sofia, and held out another aniseed ball. 'But where,' she continued when Edmund had pinkly emerged, whispered his thanks and retreated again, 'where are the others?'

'What others?' asked Ella.

'When you first came running up there were other children with you.'

Ella shook her head.

'But yes,' said Madame Sofia. 'Pale little children, not bright like you. They were there, behind Mrs Tranmer.'

They all turned and looked. There was only the thuya tree. Ella ran behind it and reappeared saying, 'No one there.'

'We must go,' said Rosalind rather abruptly. 'We are expected.'

Madame Sofia, surprised, made polite farewells; as she resumed her tramlike progress she seemed preoccupied.

'Horrible old fraud,' said Rosalind when they were out of earshot. 'How can she have known Kropotkin in Moscow? He's been in exile for goodness knows how long.'

There was a cherry tree in the small garden of the building which had once been the hostel for poor idiots and was now the Haul Down night refuge; it hung over the wall next to the door of the chapel, and shed some of its single white petals on to the pavement. Stephen noticed them as he came out of the chapel and wished the air of spring evening were not tainted as it was by the smell of excrement, equine and human, and the acrid echo of coal smoke; even so it seemed fresher than usual, and he went slowly up the hill towards his lodging, planning a long walk for the following day. Walking and keeping his diary were the things above all which gave him solace; prayer did so sometimes but could not be relied on, because it occasionally left him more dissatisfied with himself than when he started. Sometimes on his walk he felt in communication with God, but he would not call that prayer because he thought that prayer ought to involve more effort from himself. He could not believe it was enough simply to receive, hard though even that could be.

He opened the door on to the familiar smell of curry. Pet-chumah made quite frequent efforts to cook him English food, but the curry smells seemed to have become part of the fabric of the house. Besides, Stephen liked curry, and much preferred it to Petchumah's dreadful thick English gravy. She was pleased by his interest in Indian food and took much trouble to find the ingredients she needed; some of the spices were unobtainable in the City and from time to time she would make the fifteen-mile train journey to the port where Peter Tilsley had spent his childhood and in the spice market behind the docks she would move knowledgeably between the different stalls, testing and tasting until she was satisfied. She was a Tamil girl from the south of India; Wilf had been stationed in Madras and he had watched her walking across the square inside Fort St George carrying the laundry for the officers' mess for months before he had spoken to her. By the time he was invalided out of the army after his second bout of malaria she had become indispensable to him; he could not envisage domestic life without her. To the surprise of most of his fellow-soldiers he had married her in St George's Church, with the blessing of the padré and to the delight of her family, and brought her home with him to England. No one exactly knew whether she was happy there or not; she seemed never to feel quite warm enough. Her cooking on the other hand got better and better.

It was always Wilf who brought Stephen his meals. Petchumah was an unobtrusive background presence whom he encountered only rarely as she slipped in and out to clean his rooms and whom he had to seek out in the kitchen if he had something to say to her; she had been very shy at first and it was only recently that he had been able to extend his conversation with her from her cooking methods to her former life, about which she seemed to speak with nostalgia.

When Wilf with his usual lack of grace (which came not from want of goodwill but from lack of training and from having such large hands) had put on the table a dish of meatballs plentifully spiced with leaves of coriander, a vegetable curry, rice, poppa- dums, brinjal and mango chutney, Stephen, thanking him, said, 'I hope your wife's happy here, Wilf. Has she enough friends?'

'People keep theirselves to theirselves round here. But they're friendly enough to her in passing.'

'I see her in church occasionally, but she slips away without talking to anyone when the service is over.'

'She does feel the cold, that I will say,' said Wilf.

He stood in the middle of the room, his erect and soldierly bearing implying respect without undue deference. Stephen began to eat his meal. Neither felt any awkwardness, each recognizing in the other a certain loneliness, each confident that the other would understand their mutual friendliness as being no impinge- ment upon the boundaries imposed by their being respectively a clergyman and a lodging-house keeper.

'I suppose she must miss her family too,' said Stephen.

'They were always crowded, very crowded indeed. She was used to that. I used to think it would help if she could have a child. But now I think she won't, not here. It's like plants, they don't reproduce in different soil to what they're used to.'

'Could you go back?'

'Not unless we was to work our passage somehow. She has some relations in the higher country, towards the hills. They work in the peach orchards there. I wouldn't mind a more active life to this myself, more physical, as you might say.'

'You're a strong man certainly.'

'I'm a man of action, that's why I liked the army, though plenty hated it. But for the malaria bouts I'd be there still. Never mind, action will turn up again for me some day. Then I'll complain, I daresay. I'll be up again later for the dishes.'

Stephen propped his book up against the little reading-lectern he had been pleased to find in one of the City knick-knack shops, but he did not read, thinking instead of the ex-soldier and the distant peach orchards, and of the soft-footed presence in the house of the woman who could not breed under the cold English skies. When the time came to walk across to the night refuge it was almost dark. He opened the door of the refuge to a powerful smell of alcohol and unwashed flesh and was surprised to see that it must all be coming from the one prone figure who seemed to be the only occupant and of whom there was nothing to be seen except a heap of blankets and a good deal of lank grey hair and beard. He wished the man good evening and was answered by a more or less simultaneous belch and fart, both of unusual volume.

Stephen walked between the rows of otherwise empty beds and sat down on his stool. He prayed silently for patience and understanding, as he often did, sometimes grimly over and over as if he could wear down God's resistance by mere repetition, and sometimes peacefully, as if he felt a hope of grace, but always humbly. Then he read out the Epistle and Gospel for the previous Sunday and followed them with the Collect but could not bring himself to give a blessing. As he left he wished the figure on the bed good night and received the same response as he had had before. It seemed unlikely to be a coincidence; perhaps it was a form of greeting which had taken years to perfect. Or was he being too cynical? Perhaps if you were full of gas, and someone spoke to you so that you stirred where you lay, the gas did escape naturally (and loudly) at both ends. How did he know? And yet he had to fight back the thought that his work was useless and his existence pointless, because despair was the sin against the Holy Ghost.

He almost ran into someone as he came out of the refuge, and in the light of the stars, the moon being behind a cloud, he made out the startled face of a tall man in a high hat, clean-shaven and of ascetic features, who after a muttered apology drew his coat collar up round his face and hurried on down the road. He was not at all the sort of person Stephen might have expected to see on Haul Down at that time of night, or indeed at any time of night or day. His face was faintly familiar, but Stephen was sure he had never seen him there before, nor even, he suspected, anywhere else in the City; it was a memory from somewhere further back that was stirring. London? Oxford? He might have been someone he had known in his undergraduate days, but he had hardly looked like a contemporary. Whoever it was, he must surely have lost his way. Stephen looked round to see whether he needed redirection, but the street was empty.

Of course they had all their own idea of the City; as we have ours. Peter that spring was turning the place in his imagination into the sum of all his hopes, and the reason he was doing that was more to do with what was happening to him than with what was happening to the City. He was ill. He knew that the colour of the blood he was spitting more often now was no longer the colour the doctor had told him was insignificant; it was the bright startling red which meant that it came from his lungs. He was convinced of two things, that nothing must prevent him from writing the poetry he was born to write, and that all he needed to restore his health was the sun. After the summer, after the architectural competition, after the royal visit, he planned to go south; it was every poet's duty to see Italy. He would escape the damp and fog of the English winter and be cured by sun and beauty; all he needed was money. So he flung himself into his work for the *City Herald*. Extra news stories brought him extra money; interesting interviews a fee worth having. He hurried about the City on a number of different trails, and in his increasingly excited state everything he discovered assumed a tinge of the fabulous. He interviewed Herbert Tranmer and saw Progress personified, the wisdom of science and free-thinking philosophy allied to the loftiest of social ideals; Arthur Corfield stood for Industry, for the grinding mill wheels on which a great empire's prosperity depended, and as for Edwin Hanbury, such was the persuasive power of Marianne that Peter was induced to think of him simply as the Great Artist. He secretly found it hard not to see him simply as a Giant, and had occasional wild dreams in which he himself became the Giant Killer and won the beautiful Marianne in some tremendous combat, but this was a different fantasy, not the fantasy of the City. He wrote poems to Marianne, late at night, restless in his little box of a room, but the City could be turned into prose for the *Herald*, and thousands of words that summer expressed his vision of it, the signs and possibilities he envisaged, the past passions he guessed at, the present mysteries he sought to unravel, the network of inter-woven strands of movement, the entrancing multiplicity. It was not solid, his vision, it shimmered a little; it was a city, like its Divine Creator, needing man to bring it into existence. The temptation to exalt man in order to make him worthy of his City was not one which Peter thought it necessary to resist.

Mr Crowe was prepared to accept interviews with distin-guished citizens only on condition that nothing was included which he could possibly describe as a 'personality'; there could be no more than the merest hint of a domestic background of impeccable respectability, no provocative views of any kind were to be allowed to filter through to the published version, and the effect on the reader must be at the same time reassuring and humbling. Peter had wanted to write an article about Haul Down, holding up his friend Stephen Collingwood as an example of Christian devotion, but Mr Crowe had rejected this idea in the strongest terms. The object of the article might be to extol Mr Collingwood's valiant efforts to improve the morale of the poor, but there was a danger that it might be seen as encouraging murmurings against God's dispensations. Mr Crowe would have no murmurings, any more than he would have personalities. Scholarship, however, he was prepared to smile upon; especially if it concerned matters of no contemporary relevance, being thus politically harmless and at the same time likely to induce a proper sense of inferiority in the less educated reader. So Peter went to see Caspar Freeling and asked him about the progress of his researches into the Druids.

Freeling had at first refused to see him, saying modestly that he was sure nothing he could say would interest the *Herald*'s readers, but for some reason not clear to Peter he suddenly changed his mind.

'But I'll talk on this subject only,' he said. 'Nothing about the rest of my affairs.'

Peter explained about Mr Crowe's attitude to personalities.

'There's no need to mention my place on Haul Down either. That's my quiet workplace and I don't want anyone to know of it.'

Peter nodded politely, but thought looking round the room in which they sat that it would have made a more pleasant and a quieter workplace than anything that could be found on Haul Down. It was a panelled first-floor room whose three windows looked over the wide space in front of the west door of the Abbey. From inside the room one saw only the corner of the opposite rooftop and the topmost branches of a huge plane tree in the adjacent small square; every now and then a flight of pigeons disturbed by some passer-by below circled and dispersed; occasionally the rattle of wheels over the cobbles in the nearby streets would obtrude; the Abbey clock chimed the hour and the quarters. Peter would have found it an admirable workplace, better even than the premises of the Institute of Science and Philosophy. He asked Caspar Freeling whether he knew the latter.

'They're always asking me to lecture. I somehow keep on deferring it.' Caspar gave a self-deprecating smile.

'I'm afraid they're not very lively. You would be used to much more stimulating audiences in Oxford.'

'I'm not exactly part of the University. I'd describe myself as more of a wandering scholar. I've travelled a lot, pursuing various researches. I've a pamphlet here I can let you have, on the Druids, if you want the background. It's very drily written I'm afraid – not by me, I hasten to add – but it gives you the facts, such as they are.'

'Since so much is supposition what is it that chiefly interests you?'

'I suppose I am interested in underground streams.'

He had seated himself on a sofa which was placed diagonally across a corner of the room, so that he faced inwards, his back half turned to one of the tall windows. One arm rested on the arm of the sofa, his legs were crossed, his shoes the latest fashion, his attitude casually elegant. Leaning his head back against a cushion he looked across at Peter with a kindly though patronizing smile. Peter, sitting as he usually did on the edge of a chair, was not at ease; this was a mood of Freeling's with which he was not familiar. He knew him better as either cold, even rude as far as his manner towards Peter himself was concerned, or to certain others subtly ingratiating; this friendly condescension was unnerving. Peter thought it best simply to look attentive.

'There are streams of thought,' Freeling continued, 'or more than that of feeling, which emerge from time to time and then disappear, and then break through again with surprising force, having been there all the time, submerged. I think it very likely that Druidism was an early manifestation of this consciousness.'

'And did it reappear?'

'Indeed yes, under different names. Under all sorts of names, in fact, in the Middle Ages. In the twelfth century there were the Cathars, in the seventeenth the Ranters.'

'These were Druids?'

'All part of the same phenomenon.'

'And it was to be seen here, in this City?'

'There's no doubt about it. Findings around the hot-water springs, sacred springs they'd have been naturally, show signs of pre-Roman activity. There are broken remains of what were certainly votive vessels of some kind, and some interesting indications of religious ceremonials, stone altars with signs of repeated burnings, bones and so on. Of course these things only appear when there has to be repair work or foundation laying, there's never been a systematic examination. I'm as certain as I can be that underneath the whole of the centre of the City there lies buried a system of worship of the kind I've mentioned, and that it links up with other signs not far away, the carvings in the chalk downs for instance, even Stonehenge. And then later on we have local settlements of religious brotherhoods in the twelfth century, escaped from France at the time of the persecution of the Cathars. Why should they come to these parts rather than others? I'm certain it was because there was a living tradition quietly carrying on where it had always been.'

'And now?'

'It's time it emerged again, I fancy. We could do with an upsurge of the irrational, don't you think?'

'I don't know, I'm still trying to grasp the rational world myself. I don't think I'm ready for the irrational.'

'It's where you came from.'

'I don't always care to remember where I came from.' Peter's look of dismay was meant to disarm.

Freeling suddenly leant forward, his hands on his knees. 'You want to be a poet, don't you, beyond anything?'

'Certainly.'

'Then so do I want to be a scholar.'

This admission seemed to excite him; it was as if he had never made it before.

'I am a very clever man,' he said intensely.

'Anyone can see that, Mr Freeling.'

'I have a very good brain. Things have not been easy for me, Tilsley. I have had everything against me, everything. I could not gain admittance to the University, for reasons with which I need not bore you. And yet I have a better brain than most men there. By my own reading, my own researches, I have come across a phenomenon which puts all their philosophizing into question. It is a phenomenon hidden in the human soul. It is simply an alternative system, another way of looking at things. I don't say they are wrong. It is simply that they are not exclusively right. What they say may be true, but so is what I say. There is not one right, one wrong.'

'I don't mind that, I suppose. But if there were no right at all and no wrong, the world would be a very grey place, surely?'

'You're thinking of right and wrong in the moral sense. In the sense of your futile Mr Collingwood.'

'Futile? Oh, no, Mr Collingwood is a good man.'

'Good? What is good? And how much opportunity does he have to be bad?'

Freeling threw himself back against the cushions, scorn on his features. 'Collingwood. Collingwood. Do you not suppose if he had the opportunity, if the charming Mrs Moore for instance were at his mercy, do you not suppose he would ravage her?'

Peter burst out laughing, even bouncing a little on the edge of his chair. 'What a shocking scene. But it depends what you mean by opportunity. If one of the huge blocks of stone which Mr Moore's quarrymen move around on their trucks were to fall on top of him, poor man, and if after a decent interval Mrs Moore were to look favourably on Mr Collingwood, he would ravage her with a will, I feel sure. Anything else he would not see as an opportunity.'

Caspar Freeling had closed his eyes. When he opened them again he had returned to his former mode. He crossed his legs and rested one arm on the arm of the sofa, as before, and resumed his cool and condescending tone. 'Mrs Moore does not hugely appeal to me anyway. Pretty but prim. I prefer something more sumptuous.'

'I think she's delightful. But not a great beauty in the classical mould of course, like Mrs Hanbury for instance.'

Freeling seemed amused. 'You admire Mrs Hanbury?'

Peter flushed. 'Immensely.'

'I see.' Caspar Freeling seemed to be thinking, tapping his fingers on the arm of the sofa. Then he stood up. 'Well, we've had enough, I think, don't you? Take the pamphlet. Make what you can of it.'

'I'm very grateful. The article won't be very interesting, but that's because Mr Crowe likes them like that.'

'He's probably right. Nothing inflammatory. Nothing to make anyone think. It's as I say, we're none of us to be relied on. We could all join in a frenzy or a war dance or a human sacrifice.'

'Did they have human sacrifices, then, the Druids?'

'I think it quite probable.'

'Mr Crowe would be very much against any mention of that, I fear.'

Caspar Freeling laughed and put a hand on Peter's shoulder. 'I like you, Tilsley. Come and see me again. I may have some business I could put your way.'

Stephen Collingwood's Christian faith was a simple one, too simple perhaps to be entirely orthodox. It is clear from his diaries that he thought his superiors within the Church might not have been wholly pleased had they known what he believed, or rather perhaps what he did not believe; it is also clear that he had no intention of telling them. He had great confidence in his own self-control, none in his own worthiness. He wrote, 'I can endure suffering myself, but I cannot relieve it in others. I have humility but no human sympathy. This may be what my teachers at theological college were trying to tell me.'

They had said to him that he might be happy in a country parish. They knew that his idea of transcendence had its origins in his childhood wanderings in the hills of the Welsh borders. He was not a young man, having taken orders only in his late thirties. They held out to him the prospect of a village in a pleasant part of the country, with George Herbert as his model. He had said he wanted to work among the industrial poor.

During his training he had spent some time at one of the university settlements in the East End of London, where he found young men and women working in a practical way to provide much-needed housing and perhaps some hope as well, and he felt he could have worked in co-operation with such projects had he only been sent to a parish in Whitechapel or Spitalfields. Instead he found himself far from the stimulus of like-minded fellow workers, perched in the pocket-handkerchief-sized poor quarter of a dilapidated provincial spa, where conditions being so much less terrible than in London and the numbers of people affected so much smaller, poverty came to seem dreary rather than desperate and he had too much time to question his own purposes. Haul Down had a bad reputation in the City and he had done nothing to improve it. Only Charlotte Moore was consistent in her concern, regularly making the fortnightly visits she had begun under the aegis of Stephen's predecessor, bringing cast-off clothes from her friends, and cheese from her brother's farm near Cheddar, and her own unfailing friendliness.

Stephen had found few other friends in the City. The giants and heroes of Peter Tilsley's vision seemed to him boring provincials; both intellectually and socially he was their superior, and rather than confront his own snobbery, of which he was ashamed, he cultivated a reputation as something of a recluse. The friendship of Charlotte and her husband Harry was increasingly precious to him, but though they often asked him to their house he was careful not to go too often; he was aware of being unable to return their hospitality. He foresaw himself getting older where he was, with Wilf and Petchumah and Petchumah's curries, ignored by his superiors in the Church, forgotten by his London friends (whom he made no effort to remind of his existence), filling his diary with nature notes made on his country walks and desultory thoughts on his reading or his failure to improve his religious understanding, and every now and then feeling a leap of wonder, like the wonder once so familiar to him when he seemed to meet God on every path on those re-membered prophetic hills, at the sight of Charlotte picking her way over the cobbles in her shawl with a ragged child or two at her heels. Often he looked forward to the prospect of such a life with equanimity, if not with positive pleasure; but sometimes a kind of wild restlessness overcame him.

'This evening', he wrote, 'the air was so full of expectation that I could not sit still. Evenings in early summer are like that sometimes. I walked up to Southcliff to look at the view. I met the rent collector on his round and asked him not to be too hard on Joan Greenway, who has been beaten again. The father of her children only visits her in order to abuse her and yet the youngest child is only a few months old. She says she is not afraid of him, so it cannot be out of fear that she continues to consort with him. Perhaps he gives her some sort of affection on the rare occasions he is sober. No one else does. On Haul Down they cling to such shreds of respectability as they have and Joan Greenway is not married, no better than she should be, a disgrace to the neighbourhood. He is a miner from ten miles off, married. They despise miners anyway. I have tried to say a little about loving kindness but I understand what a threat that kind of person must seem to someone like Mrs Tucker, who keeps her two rooms and her children so clean, never sends her man off to his work on the railway without a bacon sandwich, sits all day in poor light making brushes, and is unfailingly cheerful even when her usual winter bronchitis is at its worst. Mrs Tucker gives Christian comfort to me, rather than I to her. The Smallwood woman on the other hand haunts me. She is forever rushing past me, mad with rage. I feel I ought to be able to help her, but at theological college they did not teach us how to cast out devils.

'As I walked along the path behind the gardens of the large

houses towards the top of Southcliff all the blackbirds were sending out alarm calls, as they do towards dusk. The sky was a clear aquamarine, except near the horizon, where there was dove-grey cloud. Above this some wisps of darker grey edged with a fiery pink floated imperceptibly higher into the sky as the blue turned paler and became above the band of cloud quite yellow. Against the yellow the trees were a deep greenish brownish black. I stood at the viewpoint looking over the City, from whose chimneys the smoke rose straight into the still air. A continuous rumble of sound came from the variety of horse-drawn traffic on the main road below, a barge on the canal was unloading at one of the wharves, a train steamed away from the station towards London. I felt as if my spirit were frantic to be free. I walked back in the gathering darkness and went into the church. Kneeling there I felt the storm subside, a sort of exhausted calm return. But is it right that I should prefer my church when there is no congregation?'

It was on one such evening that Stephen returned to find Peter Tilsley in a state of collapse on his doorstep.

For some time Marianne Hanbury had been trying to persuade Madame Sofia to conduct a seance in her house. She had imagined a select group of interested and respectful guests gathered in her first-floor drawing-room, the blinds drawn against the afternoon light (the seance would be followed by tea). She had pictured Lady Dalrymple Smythe, widow of a baronet, conversing graciously with the Misses Brown, aunts of the ex-Governor of Bengal, and pretty Mrs Moore captivating with her smile the somewhat rigid Major Spottiswoode, who lived in style in the Crescent and was known to be much interested in the occult. She had reckoned without her friend's temperament.

In the first place Madame Sofia seemed insulted to have been taken as a medium. She was gifted with psychic powers, she explained, but that was quite different. She could on occasion bring through from the astral plane messages or even physical manifestations, though these would usually be apparent only to her. She could also sometimes see standing beside people those absent figures who were of particular importance to them, as if everyone had round them wherever they went a host of visible influences; this capacity she had had since her childhood, but it came and went and could not be called up at will. She was reluctant to use any of these powers.

'You will find that all the avatars have been the same,' she said. 'They have tried to live within the laws of the physical universe. Buddha, Jesus, all of them were quite reluctant to perform miracles. It is also very tiring.'

Marianne had been momentarily silenced. Intense though her admiration for her friend was, she could not help feeling that if Madame Sofia had been of the same order of being as Buddha or Jesus, it would have been somehow more obvious. She was uncertain as how best to continue the conversation. Madame Sofia sighed heavily and closed her eyes.

'However,' she said, suddenly opening them again, 'for a fee I would consider it.'

'Oh, but of course, I only did not like to mention . . .'

'But we will have first a trial session. A few people only, all well known to you. For a lesser fee.'

So there gathered on a sunny afternoon in the Hanbury drawing-room – so sunny in fact that the brown velvet curtains had to be drawn as well as the blinds – a small group consisting of Mrs Corfield and her daughter Letitia (the Corfield ladies were all spiritualists, but Isabel had been overcome by nerves and had had to be left at home), Caspar Freeling, Charlotte Moore and Marianne herself. Madame Sofia, who had not yet arrived, had insisted on including Caspar Freeling; Charlotte Moore had been invited by Marianne, and was there against her better judgement. Up to that very morning she had thought perhaps she ought to send a message to say she could not come. Harry had been against it, saying he thought it unwise to meddle with such things; Rosalind Tranmer, had she known, would have been horrified; but Charlotte's curiosity was too strong for her. She would go just once, she thought, and never again. After all, she had nothing to be afraid of, and supposing she were to get a message from her mother, saying she was happy in Heaven, could anything be wrong with that? But as she sat quietly beside Hetty Corfield she was rather ashamed of herself and wished Caspar Freeling would not look at her.

'How is the poor poet?' he asked her in his cold voice. 'Still lying up with the virtuous Mr Collingwood?'

'Mr Collingwood has taken him in for the moment, yes, to take care of him. He is getting better.'

Madame Sofia's arrival put a stop to conversation. She was enveloped in purple silk, with a black crêpe shawl with long tassels over her shoulders; a smell of mothballs clung about her. Her face was solemn and the expression in her protuberant blue eyes appeared to be disapproving. She shook hands unsmilingly with each guest and took her seat at the round table which had been placed in the middle of the room and covered with the green baize cloth more often used for Marianne's whist parties. Marianne ushered her guests to the table, taking herself the chair immediately opposite to Madame Sofia's. Madame Sofia asked everyone to put their hands on the table, though not touching, explained that it might be necessary to wait for some time in silence, and closed her eyes. Initial embarrassment over, quietness seemed to settle on the group; the noise from the street outside was muffled by the thick curtains. From feeling expectant Charlotte began to feel she might sleep. Madame Sofia began a low chant, something between a hum and a buzz; the words if any were impossible to distinguish. Letitia Corfield stared fixedly at her own hands, her fragile features briefly twisted into a grimace as she fought off an impulse to giggle.

'She should not be frightened,' said Madame Sofia dreamily

opening her eyes and looking over Letitia's shoulder. 'The other girl. She wants to be here but she is frightened.'

Hetty Corfield gasped. Letitia's pale face flushed.

'The small man has his cap on back to front,' said Madame Sofia. 'He is your friend, with dirty hands.'

'But I don't know —' began Hetty, then she grasped her daughter by the arm — 'It's Burnett,' she said breathlessly. 'The gardener,' she explained to the table at large. 'He does wear his cap like that.'

'Quiet, please,' said Madame Sofia, and shut her eyes again. When she opened them she smiled for the first time, directly at Charlotte. 'These children I have seen before, in the park. Your children I mean, not the frightened ones who were also there on that day. But the man with the large grey eyes I do not know. He reaches his hand out towards you, but there is pain there in some way. He loves you and brings you pain.'

Marianne gave an agonized gasp, half a sob. Charlotte turned anxiously to look at her and saw that her excitement was nothing to do with what Madame Sofia had said but was all anticipation. Trembling violently she waited her turn.

'A building,' said Madame Sofia apparently surprised. Marianne gave a small ecstatic groan. 'I see only a building. *Mon dieu*, what a construction.' The look of disapproval had returned. Madame Sofia contemplated the air behind Marianne with what seemed to be profound gloom. 'Portals and porticos, arches, window upon window, an immense thing. And then we have turrets and look-out posts and what seem to be little houses from Simla on the roof. What can this be?'

'Oh, is there a hexagonal room right on the top corner, with a pointed roof? There is? Oh, I know what it is. And is it to be built? Will it be built?'

'This I cannot say.' Madame Sofia closed her eyes again, but before she did so she darted a quick look towards Caspar Freeling. Charlotte saw the look and thought about it afterwards, but could come to no more decisive conclusion than that it had been enigmatic.

When Madame Sofia opened her eyes again she was looking over Freeling's shoulder, in the same way as she had looked over everyone else's shoulder all the way round the table.

'A man in white,' she began slowly, 'with a white beard.' She frowned, and her tone changed, becoming less incantatory and more urgent. 'There are two of them. They have white trousers only, loose. Above that they are naked, brown, they swing swords, no not swords, rifles. They want to hit you. They are sweating, shining. Black hair, moustaches, eyes, wild Indian eyes, they are Indians, these men, soldiers, I think.'

'No.' Caspar spoke loudly, almost as an order.

'They wish you ill. They are enraged. There is blood on one of the guns.'

'No.' Caspar waved his hand from side to side in front of her face. 'You are wrong.'

Madame Sofia sank back in her chair and put a hand over her eyes. Caspar pushed back his chair and stood up. After a moment he went to the curtains and pulled them back. He drew up the blinds and the room was startlingly full of light. The people sitting at the table blinked and looked at each other nervously.

Caspar Freeling came back towards the table and said calmly, 'That was interesting, very interesting. One doesn't want to let these things go on too long. Congratulations, Madame Sofia, you have certainly given us something to think about.'

Peter was finding it difficult to work. He could manage the Notes and Queries, with help from Stephen, and he had polished up a few poems from his notebooks, which he sent to the *Herald* with some reluctance because he felt they were not his best, but he was easily tired, and found it hard to produce those extra pieces, the fees for which he needed so much to swell his travel fund.

Stephen had come back from his evening walk to find Peter

crouched on his doorstep and barely conscious, holding a blood-soaked towel to his mouth. He had called for Wilf and between them they had carried Peter upstairs and laid him on Stephen's bed. Petchumah had silently sponged him with cold water while Wilf went for the doctor. There was no avoiding the truth now; Peter was consumptive and needed complete rest. It had not been a bad haemorrhage, the doctor said, rest and sensible feeding might bring a remission, he should certainly pursue his plans to go south before the winter. The doctor had been an army doctor; his brisk orders were given in a tone familiar to Wilf, though Stephen felt he could have shown more concern for his patient. Stephen moved out of his bedroom into an attic too small to contain much more than a bed, for which Wilf would accept very little in the way of rent. He told Peter he must stay where he was until he was stronger; and tried not very success-fully to curb his own smoking so as not to exacerbate the consumptive's cough.

Charlotte came to visit, putting the odd little household into quite a stir. She was simply dressed, in a grey linen suit with a grey silk high-necked blouse and a dark shawl over her head, her abundant fair hair drawn back into a plaited bun in the nape of her neck, but her clear complexion, her smile, her regu-lar teeth, her small white hands, her little booted feet, had all the effect of making Stephen begin inefficiently to move books about and Wilf to disappear downstairs to reappear carrying a lacquered tray which Stephen had never seen before, on which was a bottle of Madeira wine and some glasses. He was followed by Petchumah, eyes lowered, carrying a spiced cake on a flowered plate. Peter sat up against his pillows prepared to be amused.

'I'm afraid it's not very tidy,' said Stephen, to whom his comfortably shabby room seemed suddenly transformed into a musty den redolent of curry and tobacco smoke and gross masculinity. Charlotte dismissed his apologies and produced from her basket a small round Cheddar cheese, which she gave to Petchumah to be kept for Peter. Petchumah received it with reverence and was escorted from the room by Wilf.

Peter, making light of his illness, turned aside Charlotte's queries by asking whether she had any news of the architectural competition. 'I've written so much about it, I ought to be the first with the news of the result. The last thing I heard was that there was to be a meeting of the full committee this week — that's to say with Professor Dacre in attendance — so it's just possible they might make the final decision there and then so as to announce it in time for the Queen's visit. But how can I be the first to find out? I ought to be hanging about the passages of the Guildhall ready to pounce on them as they leave the meetings.'

'Dacre! That's who it was!'

The pretty face and the pale one turned towards Stephen in surprise at the startled vehemence of his tone.

'I saw him up there the other night as I came out of church in the evening. His face was familiar but I couldn't remember who he was until you said his name. I used to hear him lecture when I was up at Oxford.'

'But what was he doing here?' asked Charlotte. 'Rosalind Tranmer told me he had so many obligations that it was difficult for him to find the time to advise the committee at all, and that they were afraid the result might not be out before the Queen's visit. And yet here he was wandering about in the backstreets.'

'He could have been up to Southcliff, I suppose, to get a general view of the City.'

'Haul Down is hardly the usual way back down the hill,' said Peter. 'Which way was he going?'

Stephen paused, then said slowly, 'Towards Freeling's lodgings.'

They could not make up their minds what this might signify, though they speculated. Peter's suggestions became increasingly wild; remembering his interview with Freeling he posited a revival of Druidical religion with a hold on the seats of learning, but Stephen assured him that the mood of the unorthodox in those places was all towards agnosticism.

'Your imagination runs away with you. It's high time I got you out to walk on the hills. Next week, the doctor said.'

'And then you must walk on Blake Leigh and finish at our house and we shall drive you home again.'

Charlotte stood up to go. Stephen followed her from the room but she would not allow him to see her out, saying she wanted to call on old Mrs Bennett before she went home, and Wilf could very well close the door behind her. She paused at the top of the stairs, glanced at the door to Peter's room, which Stephen had closed, and said quietly, 'You are being very kind.'

He shook his head.

She put a hand on his arm for a moment saying, 'I think so,' then walked down the stairs, pulling on her gloves. At the foot of the stairs she paused, as Wilf appeared in order to open the door for her; with one grey-gloved hand on the banisters she turned to look up at Stephen, smiling, then thanked Wilf and left. Stephen went back into the sitting-room and sat down; he picked up the book he had been reading when she had arrived but did not open it.

Edwin Hanbury was furious when he heard about the seance. Marianne had meant to conceal it from him, but she was so excited about Madame Sofia's visionary building which seemed to fit so well the description of the City Surveyor's design for the new hotel that she could not contain herself.

'It means you are to win the competition, Edwin, it must mean that. I am so proud.'

The City Surveyor lowered himself into his armchair, his expression serious.

'Whose idea was this flummery?'

Plunging immediately into flustered volubility, Marianne

managed more or less to imply that it had been Caspar Freeling's idea. 'Mr Freeling is so interested in so many strange things and Madame Sofia and he have become such friends. And dear Hetty Corfield . . .'

'Did you pay her?'

'Oh, but my goodness me the Corfields are very wealthy people, as you know . . .'

'I mean, did you pay Madame Sofia?'

'No, no, no, just the merest question of possibly an honorarium. To come from my pin money, naturally. But, Edwin, it is what she saw that was so thrilling. The hotel, she described it as you have designed it in detail.'

'I want an exact description of what happened.'

With difficulty, and with increasing incoherence in the face of his increasing disapproval, she gave it him.

He banged his hands down on the arms of his chair. 'Fool, fool, fool. Oh God, that I should have married such a fool.'

She wept into her handkerchief.

'Don't you understand that they are a couple of charlatans? They arranged it all between them before she started. Freeling told her, don't you see? She said nothing that he couldn't have told her.'

'But she knows these things by mysterious means. I have seen her do it before.'

'You let him see my designs, didn't you? And now everyone will know. Mrs Corfield will go back to Corfield and describe my building. Mark my words, his architects will be at work already. And Mrs Moore is the greatest friend of Mrs Tranmer. The Tranmer scheme will be being revised even as we speak.'

'But what could they do, Edwin, so late as this?'

'They can introduce more decorative motifs, they can work out from what she said that I have gone for the new eclecticism, that I have gone for pomp and civic pride, not their milk and water classicism or their homely-cottage-merry-peasant's style.

They will grab my ideas. They will pile on the ornament.' His face was ferocious with grief. 'And it will be your fault. Your fault, Marianne. I shall lose the prize which is mine by right. By right of talent, Marianne, by right of worth. The prize which would have linked my name for ever with this City, the prize which mean-minded little men have been trying to take from me by saying the City Surveyor should not be eligible. It will be your fault. And I have done so much for this City.'

His vast frame began to heave with sobs. She threw herself at his feet.

'But she saw it, she saw it. How could I have known what she was going to see? And if she had been told by Mr Freeling, why was he so angry when she saw murderous savages behind him, tell me that? He went deathly pale, indeed he did.'

He looked down at her, his expression still so full of anguish that she hid her face in her hands with a renewed burst of weeping.

'They will have arranged that, too. Easy enough to pretend he didn't like what she was saying. To put you off the scent, don't you see, to put you all off the scent.'

'But we were none of us on the scent, we were all faithfully believing.' She rose unsteadily to her feet. 'As I do still believe. Or would if you did not – if you did not – forbid it. I will go to my room.'

Holding one hand out before her, as if afraid she might be so blinded by weeping that she would have to feel her way, she reached the door, opened it and without turning round paused as if in hope he might call her back. He was slumped in his substantial chair.

Gazing in front of him, he spoke with bitter melancholy. 'My name was to have been linked for ever with the resurgence of the City. Everyone who came to take the waters – and they would have come, don't you see, they would have come when they could have stayed at such a place – everyone would have known. There was to be a plaque in the main entrance lobby, prominently placed, to record the opening of the hotel and the name of the architect. Everyone would have seen it as they took their first look round, already disposed to be impressed having seen the exterior. It would have been part of their first impression, before they went on to the grand staircase or to the Palm Court to take tea. "Hanbury," they would have said. "What a man, what an architect. '*Si monumentum requiris, circumspice.*'" Foolish dreams, foolish dreams.'

This melancholy mood seeming quieter than his former fury, Marianne turned back from the door to say, 'I cannot promise not to see Madame Sofia again, but I will promise never, never to take part in a seance. And if you would, Edwin —' here her voice took on a deep contralto timbre — 'if you would be so kind, so generous, Edwin, may we never talk about this again?'

He still stared in front of him, massively despairing. After a few moments he said dully, 'I will never speak of it again.'

With a tremulous murmur of thanks she glided from the room, closing the door quietly behind her. Upstairs she lay down on her bed and worn out by emotion went straight to sleep.

They both kept their promises, he because he was slightly ashamed and she out of generosity and perhaps a little guilt, which had more to do with Caspar Freeling than with the seance; they also felt a shared uneasiness, which made them think the occult best left alone for the time being. The announcement was made after the committee meeting attended by Professor Dacre, who had to hurry back to Oxford as soon as the meeting was over: the winner of the architectural competition for the new hotel was Edwin Hanbury, the City Surveyor.

The *City Herald* in its leader calls the decision 'controversial' but says that the ambitious nature of the winning design expresses the aspiration of the City to become once more the preferred watering-place of the cultured élite. There is no comment from Peter Tilsley, who had written so much about aspirations in the preceding few months. The five final designs, including the winning one, were exhibited to the public in the Town Hall for several days after the announcement, and a reporter from the *Herald* was sent round there to gauge the public mood. The public seeming on that particular morning in no great hurry to inform itself about the new building, and that part of it which did turn up at the Town Hall being in general willing to talk to the man from the *Herald* only if it had grievances on quite other matters — such as street lighting, rubbish collection or danger from mad dogs — and being otherwise shocked at the very notion of getting its name in the papers, the reporter retreated quite soon to buy buns at the coffee shop where Peter Tilsley had overheard Mr Corfield talking to his architects. As it was a sunny day he went down to the edge of the river to eat his buns and was contentedly sharing them with two swans and several mallard when Stephen Collingwood arrived at the Town Hall to look at the designs and report on them to Peter. There is thus, perhaps fortunately, no description in the *Herald* of the tall clergyman with large grey eyes who after studying the first four designs with the utmost seriousness arrived at the winner and burst into incredulous laughter.

PART TWO

I read about cities full of violence and crime, and a sense of collapse, and a fear of the future; but our small City remains provincial, echoing only faintly the storms and passions and revolts and despairs of the cities which matter in the history of the world. In my teaching days I saw the generations of its more respectable citizens succeed each other without much fundamental change; I suppose, being mostly concerned with sixth-formers, I could say that the withering away of the idea of Duty, and the subsequent raising of individual expectations as to life being in some completely vague sense for living, only made that irritating but endearing age group more vulnerable and so more touching; but I never made the mistake of becoming too closely involved with any of them. We have vandalism, of course, and drunken fighting when the pubs close. I don't see much of it myself but I've no doubt it was worse in the past, except perhaps for a brief period in the docile fifties when I was young. The threat to our City now is the threat of tourism, which by turning it into a toy deprives it of its dignity. It will soon be nothing but shopping-galleries and traffic restrictions. In fact, I have heard talk of excluding traffic altogether and turning streets which have been busy thoroughfares since they were built into paved areas accessible only on foot, thus excluding the old whose legs are too fragile and the young whose legs are too short and the weak who dislike carrying heavy parcels, and replacing the geometry of road, pavement and dwelling by irrational concrete flowerbeds and optimistically sited litter containers. Through these obstacles will no doubt thread their way the ill-disciplined hordes of foreign schoolchildren and the plodding groups who follow umbrella-waving guides and the drunken evening kickers of beer cans to whom we have decided to hand over our City. But I make no pretence of being unprejudiced, and it may very well be that in some way at the moment not at all clear to me all these measures will turn out to be for the best. It may also be, since the City keeps alive its long tradition of disputatiousness, that such changes as are finally agreed upon will not come about in my lifetime. In the meantime my own tracks, crossing without too much inconvenience the countless other private pathways which form the web of the City's life, take me still to the Reference Library, the two bookshops I frequent, the small French restaurant behind the theatre, the two or three churches whose monuments interest me, occasionally the cinema, occasionally the upstairs room near the Abbey to which the old man who cuts my hair and who once prided himself on being barber to all the local quality has retreated before the influx of more fashionable practitioners of his art. Pursuing my own purposes I am not much bothered by the tourists or by the ever-increasing numbers of itinerant shoppers, but occasionally an old photograph brings home to me the difference between the City now and in the time when Caspar Freeling was lodged in the first-floor rooms of the house whose top floor I now visit when I need my hair cut. The streets were sometimes almost empty. In those quieter times the royal visit was an event of great importance, not only because of the few hours when men in bright uniforms pranced about on gleaming horses and carriages rumbled by with grandees waving and crowds cheering and the Mayor's heart swelling with pride beneath his shining chain of office, but because of the weeks of preparation, and the hours of work all the preparation afforded. There was the painting and scrubbing and tidying up of the streets through which the procession was to pass; the repairing of the ironwork on the balconies, the painting of the railings, the concealing by whatever superficial (and therefore cheap) means were available of the condition of extreme dilapidation of such of the City's basements as might be observable by the royal eye. There was the question of what those who were to play any part, however small, in the ceremonies were to wear, which meant employment for the City's tailors, dressmakers and hatters. There were plants and flowers to be brought forward in quantity, the floral arrangements at the Town Hall and along the route being intended to be lavish and to include for instance many hundreds of salvias and maidenhair fern, banks of potted palms within the Town Hall, begonias, gloxinias, carnations, window-boxes bright with marigolds and lobelias and hanging creepers; the nurserymen of the City were busy for weeks. There were flags to be made, and banners and commemorative knick-knacks. Schoolchildren painted loyal addresses, and the police issued stern warnings about stray dogs. The contribution from Haul Down, where cottage industry was the custom, was mostly in the way of bunting. The City which Peter Tilsley in his wilder moments was wont to compare with Athens was to be decked out for the royal visit with all the gaudy excess of late-Victorian patriotism. Stephen Collingwood, going about his pastoral visiting, noticed the prevalence of reds and oranges and purples spread over his parishioners' kitchen tables, and in particular a rather violent heliotrope on which he comments in his diary. He felt it should be part of the discipline within which he had resolved to live that he should not set himself above anyone else in matters of taste; but he allowed himself an exclamation mark for the heliotrope.

'It often surprises me,' he wrote, 'that these people who are generally supposed to be the lowest of all – that is to say, they are not the rural poor, with whom we are familiar, and who for all their neediness can gather picturesquely enough round their cottage doors to curtsy to the gentry passing by – and they are not the skilled artisans on whom the great machine of industrialism depends, meanly enough tho' it may reward them — they are the truly uneducated, used only for the lowliest services and not needed, at least not needed in this declining City, in such numbers as they present themselves. They are the as yet un-familiar, potentially terrifying, dregs of our vast industrial system. And what do they do? Sew flags for the Queen. Congratulate themselves on being part of the greatest Empire the world has ever known. Despise the foreigner and thank their lucky stars they were not born where he was.'

When Stephen spoke of these things to Peter, who was still living with him though growing stronger every day, the latter was not much in sympathy; their respective views of things were very different.

'You're verging on politics and politics bore me,' said Peter. 'Besides, you're putting so much weight on material things. People accept the conditions of their lives and expect what it's appropriate for them to expect.'

'It is that which wrings my heart.'

'And yet you avoid those of these heart-wringing people who smell too strong. And when you see Anne Smallwood coming you run away as fast as you can.'

'That is exactly the whole of my trouble.'

'One day I will explain to you the mystery of Anne Small-wood. In the meantime I am feeling better and it is your Christian duty to take me for a walk in the country.'

'I am whatever you think I am,' said Caspar Freeling to Marianne Hanbury. 'You may invent me if you like.'

'What I can't understand is what it is really, but really, that you are interested in.'

'I am interested in power. What else is any man interested in?'

They were in Mrs Hanbury's bedroom and she was naked.

Caspar Freeling was still not used to the lack of embarrassment with which she comported herself when in this condition; he was half charmed and half obscurely shocked. The City Surveyor these days was so preoccupied with the planning of his new building that he could be relied upon not to come home in the afternoons, and by prearranging the time of Caspar's arrival Marianne could be sure to open the door to him herself; if Betsey the parlourmaid had her suspicions, Caspar's occasional generosity made sure that she kept them to herself.

'Power over me you certainly have,' said Marianne, disposing herself on the bed like a houri, in which character she had once been painted by a Dublin artist of not much renown (but that was a long time ago). 'Power of personality abundantly. And then of course you deal in magic, that I know. It was your doing that Mr Hanbury won the competition.' She habitually referred to her husband in this way when she spoke of him to Caspar, to the latter's mild amusement. 'I know it was your doing, I don't know how you did it and I don't want to know. You did it for me; that is enough. So that we could be together, Mr Hanbury being so busy. And so that he would be kind to me, having got what he wanted.'

'He has every reason to be kind to you. You do him great credit.'

'Oh, when we are about together, yes. He thinks we make a handsome pair. He is a very vain man. But I have not given him children.'

Caspar was silent, not particularly wishing to go into that.

She sighed. 'I have been too generous, you might say. In my earlier life. It led to difficulties.'

'His buildings are his children,' said Caspar diplomatically.

'Now there's your magic again. How do you know these things? His buildings are his claim to immortality, he's sure of that. I've told you he's vain.'

'They'll give him more pleasure than sons and daughters. And

I've seen his pride in you, I've seen his self-satisfied smile as he follows you into a room.'

'He'd be prouder if I was a cathedral in the Gothic style.'

'Well, then I shouldn't care for you at all. I'm going to kiss you and leave you. I have to see Mr Corfield.'

'Mr Corfield?' She rose from the bed and pulled a blue silk dressing-gown round herself.

'He's thinking of going into politics, now that he's not going to be involved in the development of the new Hotel. He's a raging radical Liberal, all for business efficiency, whatever the cost. He thinks I might make a few introductions.'

'Was he angry that Mr Hanbury won the competition?'

'Not particularly. He has plenty of other fish to fry.'

'And what does Mrs Corfield fry?'

'You know very well that Mrs Corfield thinks of nothing but making her garden grow. She's not even interested in marrying off her daughters. Mrs Tranmer, on the other hand, minded very much about the competition.'

'Mrs Tranmer looks like a scarecrow.'

'She has beautiful eyes.'

'They look in different directions.'

'What rubbish. Also she's a very intelligent woman.'

'Which I am not, I suppose?'

'You are simply impossible. Which I suppose is why I like you.'

She came towards him to embrace him.

'And I like you because you are an enigma,' she said.

'And that is rubbish, too. I am as obvious as the night itself.'

It was true that Rosalind Tranmer was deeply upset at the outcome of the competition for the new hotel. She had looked on it as a certainty, so sure was she of the superiority of the scheme for which she and her husband had worked so hard. She had felt it was going to be a step forward, the first sign of a new progressive spirit in the City which she loved but frequently found exasperating.

'It makes me feel there's no hope for the place,' she said to Harry Moore. 'I'm afraid Herbert has wasted his energies bothering with it at all. I know his writing and his lecturing take him further afield – he's a national figure, of course, if not an international one, now that he's becoming so well known in America – but all the same he's given up a lot of time to schemes for revivifying this little place, just because of its look of having once expressed an ideal of city life that oughtn't to be let go. It's such a waste of effort when no one seems to have any idea of anything. Professor Dacre, for instance. How can he possibly have given his blessing to Edwin Hanbury's fit of megalomania?'

'It's a mystery, certainly,' said Harry.

They were walking on the hill to the north of the City, a Sunday afternoon expedition to the Folly Tower from which a good view of the surrounding countryside was to be seen. Charlotte Moore and Herbert Tranmer were ahead of them, with the Moore children and the hairy and uncontrollable Moore dog.

'Stephen Collingwood went to some of Dacre's lectures when he was at Oxford,' said Harry. 'He was astonished at the decision. He said the design was against everything that Dacre stood for.'

'What could have made such a man change his mind? And then hurry away like that without giving any explanations or answering any questions?'

'If it was anyone less reputable than Dacre one might have thought something was up. Funny things happen in these local affairs, we all know that. But he's a man beyond reproach.'

In front of them Charlotte was leaning on Herbert Tranmer's arm, apparently helpless with laughter.

'So much for Herbert's lecture on George Eliot,' said Rosalind. 'Charlotte's the only person who dares to flirt with him. It does him so much good.'

'Charlotte has her ways,' said Harry, smiling.

Charlotte's ways now required them all to form themselves into a casual group near the tower, with the trees behind them and the grassy sheep-grazed slope before them, and stand quite still while she made quick notes on her sketch pad. The resultant water colour took her much of the rest of the summer to complete, for she was a slow and meticulous worker. It shows Herbert Tranmer in a dark hat leaning on a stick; he is bending towards the figure of Charlotte herself as if explaining the history of the tower. Charlotte has modestly shown herself rather smaller than she really was, but her dress of flowered muslin is lovingly exact. Harry Moore and Rosalind Tranmer are a little way away with Ella standing beside them holding a bunch of wild flowers. Harry stands up well with his fine athletic build, his hat in his hand and his hair bright brown. Rosalind is surprisingly tall and as thin as a stick, her black hair hardly restrained by a bonnet on the back of her head, her eyes as black as her hair and her mouth stretched into a wide grin. She is the liveliest of the figures, as Ella is the prettiest and most detailed, having been always at hand to pose. Edmund and the large hairy dog are running gleefully towards the front left-hand edge of the picture. The tower and the beech trees are most carefully painted. On the back of the picture Charlotte has written the date and underneath that 'Mr and Mrs Herbert Tranmer and Mr and Mrs Harry Moore, Miss Ella Moore and Master Edmund Moore, with their dog Weaver at the Folly Tower'.

When Caspar Freeling had said to Marianne that he was whatever she thought he was he had shown more self-knowledge than he usually did. Self-knowledge was not something he sought; he was less interested in his own motives than in other people's, on which he would have called himself an expert. The one thing he would have said he knew about was what people wanted; he saw himself as someone who often provided it, in return for a variety of favours. It was as if he progressed through life in a series of moves whose direction was dictated by a complicated system of swops, as a result of which he ended up where he wanted to be, which might be not so much in possession of power as simply where the power was. In the course of this game he preferred to see himself reflected in other people's eyes rather than in the mirror; he was prepared to be more or less whatever they wanted him to be, on condition the game progressed; he did not like stillness, any more than he liked silence, or solitude. If there was a sense in which he took his own stillness and silence and solitude with him as he moved about in his private game, that was something of which, being opposed to self-examination, he was unaware.

Marianne Hanbury having endowed him with qualities of mystery, magic and mastery, it was in that character that he proceeded up the hill towards the Circus on leaving her. His customary slightly sideways walk, as if he had a limp although he had not, and his self-conscious fidgety way of patting his pockets and looking about him, made him anyway conspicuous, but Marianne's assurances as to the power he had over her, and which he indeed felt himself to have, gave the slight deprecating smile which he normally wore when walking about in public an extra air of insincerity, as if only a man who was sure of being treated with deference could seem so modest. He had told Marianne that he was going to see Mr Corfield, which was true, but on the way he was going to see Madame Sofia, who had been asked by Mrs Corfield to call, and to describe to her in more detail than had been possible at their last meeting the great Moghul gardens which she had seen in India. Madame Sofia had proposed to Caspar Freeling that they might share the carriage which she was in the habit of hiring when she needed it from the livery stable in the mews behind the Circus. Caspar had not mentioned this proposal to Marianne; he knew that since the seance she had seen less of Madame Sofia than formerly, and he had no wish to go into her reasons.

As he reached the top of the street in which the Hanburys lived and, rather than crossing the road in order to walk over the circle of grass under the trees in the centre of the Circus, turned left so as to follow the pavement round the periphery and so reach the house where Madame Sofia lodged, he came face to face with Major Spottiswoode, who lived in the Crescent beyond the Circus, and was making his brisk military way towards Peter Tilsley's preferred writing-room, the library of the Institute of Science and Philosophy.

'We must get you along there,' he said breezily to Caspar. 'I understand you're an expert on Early Britain. We should be able to rustle up an audience for you. People get lazy, you know, about going to lectures, but we've quite a few keen archaeologists, quite a few. Enough to give you a run for your money, I'd say.'

He gave a snappy laugh, not unlike a terrier's bark, raised his hat and walked on, ignoring Caspar's murmured excuses which, being deaf, he could not hear.

'Insufferable bore,' said Caspar aloud, continuing on his way. He did not care for military men; he had known some in his childhood and felt they had not treated him with the respect he had deserved.

Reaching his destination he was shown up to Madame Sofia's quarters by a comfortable country person who told him quite as a matter of course that Madame would be meditating. Caspar offered to wait.

'No, no, sir, you go on in, my love. Let her down gently, sir, that's all.'

Forewarned, Caspar went quietly into the room and stood by the door without speaking. Struck immediately by the depth of the silence in which he found himself, he put it down to the fact that the parrot was asleep. Instead of shrieking its usual multilingual greetings, it sat with closed eyes and lowered crest, only the firm grip of its large scaly feet on its perch showing it to be alive. The cage of the smaller birds had been covered by a green baize cloth. Caspar coughed politely. Neither the parrot nor Madame Sofia stirred. Madame Sofia was seated in the centre of the room, on her usual armchair. The room was cool, but reflected the brightness of the June afternoon outside. From where he stood Caspar could look through the leaves of the plane trees and past the honeyed regularities of the Circus houses to the street up which he had just walked, at the end of which were the fine houses which made up one side of a square, and the roof of the theatre, and the spire of a church, and beyond those the woods of Southcliff, densely green on the skyline. Only the occasional carriage passed in the street below, footfalls on the pavement sounded unhurried, someone shouted, with something to sell, but soon moved on. The big room, full as it was of Madame Sofia's heterogeneous collection of objects, and her bulky furniture, and her stuffed ape and her eastern shawls and her sleeping parrot, seemed flooded not so much with light as with lightness, as if the air, which smelt of roses, might have been thin, like the air on the high mountains. Caspar coughed again. The parrot muttered something in its sleep. Madame Sofia turned her head towards him but did not speak. Caspar took a step towards her but stopped as she gave no sign of having seen him. She continued to look in his direction.

'Madame Sofia, I rather think our carriage may be ready.'

She peered at him. 'Is someone there?'

'I am here, Madame Sofia, and it is time we went to call on Mr and Mrs Corfield.'

She started back in her chair as he approached.

'I didn't see you.' She seemed flustered. 'You gave me quite a start.'

'You were deep in your meditations.'

'Well, but I am not blind all the same.' She was clearly

annoyed. 'Only too often when I look at people I see more than they want me to see. I assure you it is very rare for me to look at someone and see nothing at all.'

'I was keeping very quiet because I didn't want to disturb your spiritual exercises.'

'Spiritual exercises, my foot. I was doing mental arithmetic, trying to work out exactly how I am being cheated by my German publishers.'

'I thought you had taken your parrot with you into a state of trance.'

'Lazy brute,' she flapped her hands at the bird, which woke with a squawk. 'Well, I am ready. Let us be off.'

The parrot pursued them with what was clearly a flood of invective.

'If you said that in Kabul you'd be shot on the instant,' said Madame Sofia over her shoulder as she led the way towards the stairs.

Seated in the open landau, a rug over her knees, she seemed to recover her equanimity. 'So, Mr Freeling, tell me what is going on. You always know the latest news. What are they thinking about in this charming City?'

'They are not thinking at all. They never do. But they are talking about the royal visit.'

'How he scorns the provinces. That is very English. You can be a country gentleman but not a provincial one. Even in a city which looks so civilized.'

'You can plan what you like for a place. If the people who live in it are silly geese they will be silly geese no matter what you do.'

'I don't agree at all. And besides, there are worse things than geese. If they are geese, which I would question.'

'You question it? After that little episode not so long ago? What could be more goose-like than their behaviour then?'

'I would rather not talk about that. Besides, you can't dismiss a whole population because two or three people are gullible.'

'There's more we could do in that line, you know, if it would amuse you. While you wait for the German publisher to pay up.'

'It does not amuse me. And it did not entirely amuse you, as I remember it. It is not wise to play about with these things.'

'It was not I who was playing about. I know how you got that hint. It was Collingwood. You had been gossiping with Collingwood.'

'If you mean Mr Collingwood the polite and serious clergyman, whom I hardly know, the very idea of gossiping with him seems to me quite inconceivable.'

'He didn't tell you how I hate the woman he lodges with?'

'I know nothing of the woman he lodges with.'

Caspar Freeling's upper lip had begun to tremble. He put his hand over his mouth, though whether this was to conceal a sneer or a smile was not clear.

'Who is this woman?' asked Madame Sofia in genuine mystification.

'Please forget what I said.'

They were both puzzled, and both annoyed. They sat side by side in silence as the open landau, and its two solid brown horses took them over the bridge from which Peter Tilsley had gazed at the site for the new hotel and along the wide road lined with handsome late-Georgian houses which had been one of the later speculations of those old expansive times, and began the long climb over the canal, past the elegant terraces, and the discreet villas surrounded by gardens, to the top of the hill and the imposing gates of Capo di Monte.

'I warn you, these people are unbearably vulgar,' muttered Caspar Freeling as they drove through the gates. He was still in a bad temper.

As it happened, there was little opportunity for Madame Sofia to appreciate the errors of taste within the house, for they were led by a decorous parlourmaid through the front hall and the drawing-room and out of French windows on to the lawn, noticing only on the way a certain pretentious and unlived-in gloom, the family life taking place as it did in what was known as the morning-room. Under the cedar tree on the lawn Mr and Mrs Corfield, and Miss Letitia and Miss Isabel Corfield, were seated on rattan garden chairs awaiting their guests. The ladies were rather over-dressed for the garden, because Mrs Corfield had been given to understand that Madame Sofia was related to foreign royalty. Letitia Corfield, the older of the two girls, was hoping very much to be introduced in due course to a foreign count, possibly Hungarian. Her ambitions did not rise so high as a duke, let alone a prince, but she thought she could settle very happily for a count, and a drawing-room in Vienna, and an occasional ball at which her dancing lessons with Mrs Bowden-Ellis in the Pump Room every Wednesday would enable her to perform most creditably in the waltz. Isabel Corfield, whose fine-drawn face of a frightened hare was not enhanced by her weak blue eyes, always watery in the summer because of hay fever, hoped not to be introduced to anyone, even Madame Sofia, who had sounded from Letitia's dramatic account of the seance much too alarming. Isabel would have liked to be invisible, and by wanting that condition so much she often came near to achieving it.

Relays of servants now brought out tea and disposed it on bamboo tables. There was a vast tray bearing the teapot and the spirit kettle, all of impeccably polished silver. There were sandwiches, scones, biscuits, thinly sliced bread and butter and any number of preserves in silver-topped cut-glass jam pots, and on a separate cake stand, complete with little plates and silver forks and lace napkins and all on rose-patterned dishes with paper doilies, every sort of rich and indigestible cake. Madame Sofia shifted slightly on her chair in pleasurable anticipation. Caspar Freeling's lip curled.

'We are all so excited about the royal visit,' said Mrs Corfield, beginning to pour out the tea.

'I hope the Queen will not be assassinated,' said Madame Sofia, calmly helping herself to strawberry jam.

Isabel Corfield gave a gasp and put her hand over her mouth. Her sister in a fierce whisper told her not to be silly.

'She will have an entire squadron of the local yeomanry to protect her,' said Mr Corfield. 'I don't think we need worry about her safety.'

Mrs Corfield, anxious about Isabel's nerves, began to steer the conversation towards the only subject on which she felt safe, which was the garden. Mr Corfield, having summed up Madame Sofia in an instant as a foreign troublemaker, engaged Caspar Freeling in a quiet conversation about the situation in Parliament, and the two men gradually withdrew from the tea tables and took to pacing up and down on the lawn in front of the house. Madame Sofia talked her way at random through scones and fairy cakes, *mille-feuille* pastry, walnut sponge, chocolate gâteau, pink and yellow Battenberg cake, at the end of which feast and after one last cup of tea she was ready to give her full attention to the garden. Isabel slipped unobtrusively back to the morning-room; woollen flowers were easier to control, she found, than the real thing. Letitia at first trailed round the garden after her mother and Madame Sofia, hoping that the occasional enthusiastic but unfortunately not well-informed comment might cause the latter suddenly to recognize her as being just the thing for dear handsome Rudolph, Fritz or Ferdinand, due for a visit next week; but since neither Madame Sofia nor her own mother paid any attention to her she grew disheartened and wandered back to join her sister. By the time Mr Corfield and Caspar Freeling went to look for Madame Sofia, having finished their discussions on the understanding that one or two leads might reasonably be followed up to mutual advantage, she and Mrs Corfield were discovered in the conservatory, talking of lilies, and agapanthus and zingobars, and in the meantime peaceably potting out gloxinias.

'No gloves, my dearest?' expostulated Mr Corfield. 'My wife is a fanatic,' he explained to Caspar Freeling. 'I tell her she will soon have hands like a gardener's.'

'I am a gardener's daughter, my love,' said Hetty Corfield, placidly.

The weeks immediately preceeding the royal visit were cheerful weeks on Haul Down. Not many men who were able to work had none to do; the women and children sewed flags and rag rugs and repaired cane furniture. The lover of Joan Greenway could be heard shouting at her from time to time and Anne Smallwood still seemed perpetually enraged, but otherwise life was comparatively peaceful. Mrs Scammell, who sometimes took the place of Mrs Caws as caretaker of the men's night refuge, became anxious about her husband, who had been senile for some time but who had only recently taken to setting off at a brisk trot for the blacksmith's forge at the bottom of the hill where he used to work; she would pursue him in her slippers, afraid he would be run into by the coal carts or taken away to the Asylum. Peter Tilsley, sitting in the window of Stephen Collingwood's bedroom with a rug over his knees, would laugh at this recurrent scene.

'I mean nothing unkind,' said Peter on one occasion. 'When people are irrational they are comic. He hasn't had a bad life, old Bill Scammell, and now he's gaga. There's no tragedy. You forget I've lived among people like this all my life. I take them as they are.'

'I hope I do too. I hope I am not sentimental. I would like to be a little useful if possible.'

'Oh, you're useful enough,' said Peter with mock condescension, 'but you think too much.'

'How dare you!' protested Stephen. 'When if we could only stop your wretched little brain from busying itself all day and most of the night we'd have some hope of getting you really strong again.'

'But I'm not thinking, you see. I'm making up poems. That's quite a different thing.'

Peter was not getting better. He complained of pains in his side, and his cough had a hollow sound that Stephen had not heard before. The doctor seemed to think that his kidneys might be affected as well as his lungs but still recommended going south for the winter.

'Many a miracle's been achieved by the sun,' he said in his breezy way. Peter's idea was that he would have built up his strength by September and could then set out on his journey, but Stephen was worried not only about funds, to which he and other friends were ready to contribute, but about the advisability of Peter's going without a companion. For the time being, though, he did his best to see that Peter did everything the doctor told him to. As an alternative to walks, which were of necessity short, he took him one Saturday in Charlotte Moore's pony carriage – having himself first walked to the Moores' to fetch it – for a drive through the beech woods to see the view from Bampton Down over the wide river valley, returning to the Moores' for a picnic lunch.

Peter was quiet on the drive, looking around at the scenery with evident pleasure. Stephen now knew him well enough to understand that his silence was a compliment. The extreme vivacity which made him such an amusing companion was an expression of his active mind but it was sometimes exaggerated; it was not exactly forced, but he once said to Stephen, 'I have to sing for my supper.' That he should feel he could be silent, and give his natural simplicity full play without clothing it in a comicality which, though it did not hide his true nature, dressed it up for company, was a tribute to his friendship for Stephen of which the latter was duly appreciative.

Afterwards, in the field beside the Moores' house, Peter became animated again. They were in the field because Ella had said a picnic was not a proper picnic if it was in the garden; as well as the Moore family, their friends the Tranmers were there. Peter talked fancifully about the Druids, having been doing some copying work for Caspar Freeling from books which quoted early records. Herbert Tranmer gently chided him for seeming to cast aspersions upon Caspar Freeling's bonafides as a scholar, and Peter immediately became more serious and talked of politics and of how Caspar Freeling had suggested that the power of the press in the person of Mr Crowe, the editor of the *City Herald*, should be harnessed on behalf of Mr Corfield and his ambitions. It transpired that Rosalind Tranmer was very much against the radical Liberals because they tried to undermine the socialists by taking over some of their ideas, and Harry Moore had heard that they were atheists and how could you have a moral code without the idea of God, upon which Rosalind Tranmer threw a bread roll at him (delighting the children) and said she had explained all that to him only the other day and would Herbert please explain it again. So Herbert explained about goodness and a person's best self and moral imperatives of one sort or another, with a courteous apology to Stephen, who, being a man of the cloth, could not be expected to think as he did. Stephen was sitting cross-legged on a rug eating a leg of chicken.

'It is just that you seem to leave out evil,' he said. 'Religion is supposed to be a consolation but it's not always that, not by any means. It makes us look at evil, and it seems to me evil should be looked at.'

'I belong to the Pelagian heresy,' said Herbert Tranmer smiling. 'I don't believe in original sin.'

'If anyone expects from me a full account of the Church's doctrine on these matters, they are going to be disappointed,' said Stephen cheerfully.

'I'm so glad,' said Charlotte. 'I want everyone to think about strawberries, not sin.'

Both children moved to sit close to her at the mention of

strawberries, and she put an arm round each. She was wearing a dress of deep rose pink, her hair was the colour of dark honey, intermixed with strands of sunny gold, her eyes were a clear hazel, her teeth as white as Ella's, and her skin had a lustre of health and youth on it as glowing as Edmund's. With her arms round her children (the colours of Ella's silky hair were mingled like her mother's, Edmund's was fairer), she seemed to Stephen a celebration of the flesh at its most glorious; he could not feel it any kind of heresy to eat at her table and rejoice.

It was always a suitable city for a procession. Not a cavalcade of black limousines with bullet-proof glass and armed outriders moving at speed for fear of snipers on the rooftops, but a more leisurely affair of open carriages and polished breastplates and cockades of feathers. The streets are wide enough in most places to accommodate a loyal populace, the route from the railway station to the Guildhall, from the Guildhall to the Circus and the Crescent round the parks and back to the station lends itself to a ceremonial progress, and the buildings along the route have anyway a look, criticized by some, of being a stage set. So when the royal train emerged from the tunnel behind the Caroline Gardens, and steamed along beside the river on the elevated approach to the castellated grandeur of the station where the Mayor and other notables were waiting on the platform, while the local yeomanry pranced and glittered outside by the waiting carriages, everything seemed perfectly appropriate.

The Mayor was short and fat and the Lord Lieutenant of the county was long and thin. The Mayor before he became Mr Mayor had been Alderman Rudge, proprietor of Mills, Carter and Rudge, High Class Grocers and Provision Merchants, and a most active member of the City's Chamber of Commerce. The Lord Lieutenant had been a Member of Parliament before he succeeded to his father's earldom, and he now spoke frequently in the House of Lords on matters pertaining to agriculture and forestry. Representing as he did the monarch in the county he was so infinitely superior to Mr Rudge, who represented only the burgesses in the City, that Mr Rudge would have felt flattered if he had known that the Lord Lieutenant had referred to him on more than one occasion from behind his white moustache (which he wore rather long, though it was always well groomed) as 'a perfectly nice little man'.

'I shall take my tone from you, my Lord,' said the Mayor on the station platform, trying to remember not to rub his hands together, which his wife had told him made him look like a tradesman.

'Well done, Rudge,' said the Lord Lieutenant benignly, blowing out his moustache as he spoke. He shifted from foot to foot with a clink of spurs; his left leg was inclined to ache if he stood about too long; he had broken it once out hunting. He liked getting into his uniform, in which he believed, correctly, that he looked truly magnificent, but it was beginning to feel a little tight. He wondered if he could think of an excuse to give it all up after this royal visit; it would be leaving on a high note. The trouble was, there was no official retiring age for Lords Lieutenant; the last fellow had gone on until well into senility and no one had seemed to mind.

'You're lucky, you fellows,' he said to the Mayor. 'You only have a year of it.'

'Yes indeed, a year will be more than enough for me,' said the Mayor, quite untruthfully.

The train could be heard approaching. The Mayor had always been susceptible to the sound of a train. Perhaps it was just the association with childhood holidays in Weymouth, or with going to meet his wife when they were engaged and she would come over for the day from Salisbury, where she was working as a children's nurse, but the steam and the noise and the banging doors made him feel sick with excitement even without the wonder and terror of meeting the Queen. He had rehearsed his moves so carefully that he went through them without faltering. The red carpet was unrolled as the train drew to a halt. The Lord Lieutenant moved forward. Figures descended slowly from the train. The Lord Lieutenant seemed to be accompanying someone along the red carpet.

'. . . and Mr Rudge, the Mayor.'

He bowed low, his chain of office swinging below him; then he walked slowly forward, following in his appointed place, but he kept his eyes lowered. There would be time enough to look at Her Majesty later, when he was feeling rather calmer.

In the Guildhall the air of anticipation was slightly hysterical, and the smell of flowers overwhelming. A small party of distinguished citizens waited upstairs in the grand reception room with such of the officers of the Council and other officials as were not part of the group at the station. There was an awning over the pavement outside the entrance. Inside, the harmonious proportions of the hall were almost concealed by towering palms and banks of foliage plants in varying shades of green, fronted by armies of scarlet salvias bedded in moss; the windowsills were crammed with marigolds and maidenhair ferns. Upstairs there were more palms, and massive arrangements of delphiniums and lupins and lilies, and on the windowsills there were banks of carnations, and on the raised daïs at one end of the room, lines of geraniums and begonias and gloxinias interspersed with small palms and more maidenhair ferns. As the correspondent from the *City Herald* put it when he was allowed to see the room after the ceremonies were over, 'The air was heavy with the fragrance of innumerable choice blossoms.' As a result, Rosalind Tranmer was sneezing.

'Thank goodness dear Isabel isn't here,' said Mrs Corfield. 'Suffering as she does with hay fever.'

Although Rosalind Tranmer called herself an anarchist – especially in front of people she knew it would annoy – she recognized that her anarchism was of the Arcadian kind, and thus to be borne in mind as an ideal towards which the human race might hope gradually to progress rather than to be looked on as a guide to practical policy. For that she looked to socialism, and if she had not thought the monarchy too irrelevant to bother about she would have been a republican. She had accordingly not bought herself a new dress for the royal visit. On the morning of the day itself there had suddenly occurred to her the retrograde notion that by not wearing a new dress she would be letting down her husband in public. She had asked Herbert Tranmer whether he thought that this was so and he had answered with his usual serenity that he did not, but by then she was in the grip of panic and beyond reassurance. She had gone to her cupboard and brought out a length of bright green silk which Herbert's brother, who took an active part in the family firm's Far Eastern trade, had brought her from Siam several Christmases ago. She had wrapped this round herself over a dress she already had of a similar but unfortunately not identical colour, and fixed it fairly securely with a large number of safety pins. The effect, though dramatic, was rather wild. Charlotte Moore, who was looking as pretty as was appropriate in pale primrose and cream, said to her husband, 'Rosalind has lost her head at the last minute and rather overdone the wrapping. We must go and talk to her soothingly but we mustn't refer to it.'

'To what?' asked Harry.

'To the green silk,' whispered Charlotte, raising her hand in an insincere little wave to Mrs Hanbury, whom she could not forgive for having persuaded her to take part in that embarassing seance. She could not bring herself even to wave to Mr Hanbury, who as winner of the architectural competition as well as in his official capacity as City Surveyor seemed to Charlotte to be so swollen with pride as to be taking up a quite disproportionate amount of space. A model of his proposed building was on display in the new Public Library, which was in another part of the Guildhall and was to be officially opened by the Queen after lunch. Mrs Hanbury was making herself unpopular by sweetly offering around seats for the afternoon at her drawing-room windows, which overlooked the route which the procession was to take after the brief ceremony in the Library. Since she had long ago offered seats to enough of her close friends to fill all the available space at the windows in question – and indeed at her bedroom windows as well, which also overlooked the route (the view from the dining-room windows on the ground floor would be likely to be impeded by the crowds on the pavement) – her present motive was only too easily discernible as being to make it quite clear to everyone that she and the City Surveyor were invited to the lunch to be given by the Mayor for the royal party, which was to be a much more exclusive event than the reception which preceeded it.

'We have so much room, it seems a pity to waste such a good view. I almost wish we could run all the way from the back entrance of the Guildhall and get there ourselves before the procession passes, but Mr Hanbury was horrified that I could even think of leaving before Her Majesty.'

A ripple of lightly sugared irritation followed her beaming progress; there were so many people whose official positions entitled them to the honour of the Mayor's invitation that most of the mere citizens of note who had been asked to the reception were excluded from the lunch. There was thus general satisfaction when Marianne, made over-bold by the effect she was creating, dangled her drawing-room, metaphorically speaking, before the eyes of Lady Dalrymple Smythe, widow of a baronet, who answered in her rich and carrying baritone, 'Adorable of you, dear Mrs Hanbury, but I am under orders to be in the procession myself. Such a bore. One would so much rather watch.'

But there were sounds of arrival below, a flushed face looked round the door and nodded to Mr Emrys Jones, the Town Clerk, who began to chivy people about like a Welsh sheepdog (he had already told them several times where to stand), the string band near the daïs struck up a Mendelssohn air known to be a favourite of the Queen's, the doors were opened and the sound of restrained voices in polite conversation was heard, and there, so seldom seen outside her capital, the small plump soberly clad monarch was among them, in no sense outshone by the resplendent figure of the Lord Lieutenant, who walked slowly beside her with one hand on his sword.

Peter had insisted on a picnic in the Jubilee Park. They sat on rugs on the grassy slope in front of the Botanical Gardens. Peter and Stephen sat on one rug, and Wilf and Petchumah sat a little way behind them and dealt with the food. Until recently, Stephen might have found this situation awkward; much as he liked Wilf, with whom he had often had quite wide-ranging conversations and who probably knew him as well as any man, they were still master and servant. Wilf had a tendency to stand at attention when he was speaking to Stephen and to use words he would be unlikely to use when alone with his wife. To Wilf, Stephen was in the position of an officer, and as such commanded loyalty and in this particular case something close to affection, but there could be no question of over-familiarity. To Petchumah, they were all her masters and she their servant, which did not mean she could never laugh at them; she did so frequently, in her gentle celebratory way. Today she was solemn because of the importance of the occasion and the fact that she was dressed in her most beautiful sari, a silken thing whose cerise and blue and silver were brought to vibrant life by the unaccustomed brightness of an unclouded sun. It had been given to her by her family on her wedding, though in fact Wilf had paid for it as part of what had amounted to a bride price; she had hardly worn it since. She sat very straight on the rug, handing chapatis wrapped in starched napkins to Wilf to put on the plates, and ate with delicacy, inclining her head over the napkin on her knees.

In those days the Jubilee Gardens were for the enjoyment of subscribers only. The attendants were on the look-out for gate-crashers on this particular day, and Stephen had had a few moments' difficulty in persuading them that he and his friends were to be allowed in on the strength of Mrs Tranmer's subscription card; his clerical collar had won the day. Around them were other groups of picnickers, but all of the most respectable kind; the unrespectable were the other side of the fence, on the pavement, ready to face inwards towards the gardens when the procession neared. On the main road beyond them the sellers of meat pies and ginger beer strolled to and fro, shouting their wares and doing a fair amount of business, while an old man holding a cage with three guinea pigs in it seemed to be going through an antique song and dance routine to which no one paid much attention. On the bandstand by the lake – which was really more of a duck pond, though it had a grotto beside it – the band of the local Light Infantry was playing a selection from *The Mikado*.

'Think', said Peter, 'how much less happy we should be if we'd paid for seats in Madame Sofia's drawing-room windows.'

'She was selling them?' asked Stephen.

'Caspar Freeling was her agent.'

'Of course. He would be the agent of the devil, that man. And yet I've the feeling it's more for pleasure than for profit.'

'He told me that what he wanted more than anything was to be respected as a scholar.'

'What's to stop him? He's clever enough.'

'He doesn't like to take the straight road to a thing. He likes just to appear mysteriously, already at his goal. Perhaps he doesn't like to be seen to be trying.'

'Is that it? Pride? He's certainly mysterious to me.' Stephen spoke lazily, only half interested. Peter's irruption into his life had curiously calmed him; he did not worry as he used to. That was why it had seemed to him quite natural to be picnicking in the park with Wilf and Petchumah, and quite easy to let events take their course as to how their differing status made itself felt or not felt. A little time ago he would have been self-conscious, too anxious not to be seen as standing on his dignity; he would have embarrassed everyone by his embarrassment. Peter had simplified his life, if only by providing him with something specific to worry about, which worry he subsumed in an ever-watchful care; so that when Peter announced his intention of going to stand by the northern carriage drive to see the procession approaching and then running across to see it again as it circled round the park and made towards the south gate, Stephen told him he was to do nothing of the kind.

'When we hear them coming we will walk in an orderly manner down the hill and stand near the band. We shall have a perfectly good view of the whole thing from there.'

'I may not cheer, I suppose? Or jump up and down and throw my hat in the air?'

Stephen laughed. 'You may raise your right hand, with your hat held in it, and shout, "Huzzah!" Once.'

'What a man of stone you are. Where's the fun in one cheer?'

After the Mayor's banquet, the royal party was conducted into what was known as Committee Room No. 2, which together with the Mayor's parlour had been completely refurnished so as to provide an appropriate withdrawing room for the sovereign and her immediate attendants. The Town Clerk's outer office had been reserved for the retirement of such other ladies of the royal party as were not required to be in attendance on the royal person at the moment, and the Town Clerk's assistant's room had been made over to the gentlemen. During the brief respite afforded by these arrangements, the Town Clerk supervised a separation of the sheep from the goats among the remaining luncheon guests. It had been decided that there was not room for everyone to witness the opening ceremony in the library, which was to take place after the lunch and before the procession. There was only a narrow passageway leading from the entrance hall of the Guildhall to the smaller but still elegant vestibule which provided a side-entrance and the way into the new library. This library was a fine big room with windows looking over the river, but it had projecting bookshelves and was anyway not as large as the great chandelier-hung reception room or the red-carpeted banqueting chamber. The Town Clerk busied himself among the guests now awaiting the descent of the royal party into the entrance hall. They knew themselves, of course, whether they were to follow the Mayor's procession through to the library or to wait until it had disappeared down the passage and then make their way to the other side-entrance, where their own carriages would be waiting for them, but the Town Clerk felt it his duty to worry at them, lest they had forgotten the instructions which had been sent them weeks ago on several printed sheets. So he busily separated alderman from alderman, councillor from councillor. Those with a special interest in education or culture were to be included in the library party, as of course were the City Surveyor and Mrs Hanbury, whose apotheosis was to be achieved when the royal eye rested upon the model of the new hotel, displayed on a table in the middle of the new library. The City Solicitor was to go with them, but the Director of the Baths was not, the Chairman of the Charity Hospital was, the Medical Officer of Health was not; the Town Clerk wove his way skilfully through the talkative groups, hinting here, hustling there, never snapping, so that when the small figure in the black dress appeared at the top of the staircase, and then began slowly to descend, with the Mayor and Lord Lieutenant on either side, the company quietly conversing below was already in place and the transition to the next movement of the dance was achieved with the utmost smoothness, some moving forward to follow down the passage, some holding back until their turn came to disperse quietly in the opposite direction.

Marianne Hanbury took her husband's arm as they walked along the passage, the walls of which were garlanded with wreaths of stephanotis, embedded in damp moss; thin lines of water had noticeably run down the cream-painted walls but the stephanotis looked fresh and everybody said to everybody else, 'What a wonderful smell,' and one or two added, 'Almost too strong.' Rosalind Tranmer was walking beside her husband, whose capacity as Chairman of the Charity Hospital was responsible for their still being there, whereas the Moores as mere distinguished citizens had gone home before the banquet; she said loudly, 'How I hate the smell of flowers!' This remark was generally ignored as being only to be expected from that extraordinary Mrs Tranmer; her husband looked at her with the utmost kindness, recognizing she must have her protest, hoping perhaps that it would mean she need not make another when confronted by the model of Edwin Hanbury's prize-winning hotel. In the event the moment of confrontation was almost too brief for comment; the Mayor and the Lord Lieutenant both had it in mind that the procession must leave the Guildhall at three o'clock precisely if the programme was to keep to its timetable. The model was indicated. Mr Hanbury was presented, Mrs Hanbury sank to the ground in the deepest of curtsies. The Mayor, moving away, began his speech about the library. Marianne's great moment had come and gone. Such had been its intensity that she cared nothing for its shortness of duration. She was overwhelmed by the honour done to her husband, and by the credit she felt it reflected upon herself; she was fascinated, hypnotized almost, by the Royal Presence; and yet, rising with admirable steadiness from her curtsy, she allowed her gaze to flicker momentarily in the direction of the Lord Lieutenant. His eyes beneath their thick white eyebrows responded appreciatively. The Lady Mayoress noticed and pursed her lips, the Lord Lieutenant's wife noticed and smiled. Marianne would have been pleased by the first reaction, annoyed by the second; she was far too happy to notice either.

Outside the Guildhall the Guard of Honour of the local Light
Infantry was drawn up, awaiting inspection. Mounted policemen
rode slowly up and down seeing that the crowd remained on
the pavements. Round the corner, in front of the police station,
the carriages which were to form the procession were waiting,
all nine of them, while the mounted escort of the Yeomanry
waited beside them with appropriate restlessness, shifting and
jingling in the bright sun and the light breeze. On the far side
of the Guard of Honour the Chief Constable was waiting,
already mounted and ready to head the procession, with the
special escort of mounted police who were to ride with him.
Solid on his solid horse, he ignored the five people behind
him on the pavement who had been waiting there since early
morning. Three poorly dressed women, a tall man with a wispy
red beard and a young man with a white face and a flowing
green necktie, they were gathered round a poster on a stick
which they took turns to hold. On it was written in ornate
green letters 'Fur and Feather Group'. Under that, in smaller
letters and darker ink, but with equally careful calligraphy, 'Why
Torture a Bird to Beautify Your Hat? Why Murder a Noble
Beast to Adorn Your Shoulders?'

At about the time the Queen was due to appear on the steps
of the Guildhall, the wind freshened. It made itself felt throughout
the City in a series of sudden buffets, causing people to grab
their hats and look anxiously at the cloudless sky. The lime
trees in the Jubilee Gardens fluttered the pale undersides of their
leaves in response, the late cherries in the Botanical Gardens
let fall the last of their blossom, the lines of multicoloured
bunting stretched across the streets along which the procession
was to drive swung wildly and pulled at their ropes, and the
larger of the Union Jacks hung out of first-floor windows flapped
like the sails of a North Sea clipper. Major Spottiswoode at

his window in the Great Crescent said, 'Blowing up,' to the few fellows from the County Club he had invited to share his view. 'Have to watch the horses.'

Madame Sofia, seated in her usual chair, behind the line of paying spectators who filled the windows of her drawing-room, said to Caspar Freeling, 'Already I am regretting it. When will they leave?'

The double doors of the Guildhall were thrown open. The band of the Light Infantry played 'God Save the Queen'. Manifested with apparent suddenness at the top of the steps, she could have calmed a far more furious tempest. Or if not calmed it, ridden it out. Her bonnet was firmly secured beneath her chin. What had she to fear from Death, which would only take her to join her beloved Albert? She descended the steps, her faithful Lord Lieutenant to her right, a pace behind. The Colonel of the Light Infantry moved forward to accompany her on her inspection; the band struck up 'The British Grenadiers'. The men of the Guard of Honour stood unflinchingly before her piercing gaze. To inspect the second rank she disappeared completely behind the first; only the fluttering feathers on the tall Colonel's helmet told where she went; the Lord Lieutenant's wife, who had an odd way of looking at things, was reminded of the egrets she had seen on the backs of submerged buffaloes in Ceylon, where her brother had been Governor-General. The inspection over, the Guard of Honour marched smartly off, while the coach containing the Mayor and Mayoress was drawn by its two sensible bay horses round the corner from the police station where the procession had meanwhile assembled, and took its place behind the Chief Constable and his escort. The Queen's carriage, an open landau drawn by four greys, drew up before the Guildhall; she was helped to mount, the Lord Lieutenant took his place opposite her, the other carriages fell in behind them, the escort of mounted Yeomanry surrounded them, the procession began to move.

It moved quite rapidly, with a great clatter of hooves and jingling of harness, supported by successive waves of cheering; the little boys who ran along behind the back of the watching crowds were soon breathless, trying to keep up. Albert from Haul Down was there, who used to hold Charlotte Moore's pony and then told her he had better things to do; he ran with a couple of friends, one of whom was wearing handed-down trousers which were too big and impeded his progress. They began by running parallel to the Chief Constable but on the slope of the main shopping-street they fell back, behind the Yeomanry escort, behind the Mayor's coach, until they were parallel with the Royal carriage itself. Delayed by the need to cross the road before the next slope up to the Circus they found themselves left behind by the carriages of the ladies and gentlemen in waiting and pounding along beside Lady Dalrymple Smythe, who with the City Solicitor and his wife was in the final carriage as the Mayor's guest.

'Charming, charming,' she boomed, raising her hand from time to time to acknowledge the plaudits of the populace.

'Is it not passing brave to be a King, and ride in triumph through Persepolis?' murmured the City Solicitor, a well-read man.

'Don't know the place,' said Lady Dalrymple Smythe, clasping her osprey-feathered hat as the wind met them at the top of the street.

They rattled round the Circus at a fine pace. Madame Sofia's indifference deserted her; she pushed one of her paying guests aside quite rudely, and looked down on the cantering Chief Constable, the beaming Mayor, the clattering escort, the brightly clad cortège and the Queen herself, borne along like a holy icon, black-clad and unsmiling, face to face with her tremendous Lord Lieutenant.

'What a lot of fol-de-rol,' said Madame Sofia, after the procession had passed.

By the time the Mayor's coach had reached the end of the Great Crescent the last carriage was just turning into it, so that the whole procession was visible from the end house where Major Spottiswoode and his cronies from the County Club were lined up at the windows.

'By God, what a sight!' said Spratt of Colley Court, scourge of the local poachers in his role as a Justice of the Peace. 'You're doing us proud, Spottiswoode, with this view.'

But Major Spottiswoode had seen the small black figure. He began to breathe loudly, and shortly afterwards stiffened into a rigid salute. On the pavement below them hats were thrown into the air, flags were waved. Spratt of Colley Court, having no military experience, was unable to salute, but he stood to attention, and found his breathing almost as severely interfered with as Major Spottiswoode's.

As the procession swept into the park people ran across the grass to swell the crowd waiting by the roadside. Peter ran, and Stephen and Wilf and Petchumah followed him, Stephen protesting and Petchumah making little cries of excitement. The procession seemed to burst on them too suddenly; it was all a flash and dash of movement and noise and shouting and scarlet and white and gold; it was moving too fast, passing too quickly.

'We must run back!' Petchumah cried.

But at the curve of the road past the Botanical Gardens the small black figure was seen to lean forward, the Lord Lieutenant to incline his head, to raise one hand; an outrider came forward, then spurred his horse and cantered to the front of the procession; another rode back to carry the message. The Queen had seen the drab crowd pressed against the park railings; she wished the procession to slow down so that the poor could see her. The Chief Constable would have preferred to have taken this part of the route at a gallop, but he reined in his horse obediently and set a slower pace. Behind him the frisky horses of the mounted Yeomanry tossed their heads and had to be pacified, some of the coachmen shouted, 'Whoa!', one of the ladies-in-waiting took a quick sniff of sal volatile in case something awful had happened. The Chief Constable contented himself with giving the crowd on the other side of the railings a fearful glare; they responded with a not particularly respectful cheer. At the slower pace the small black figure amid the panoply looked more solitary, occasionally turning her head to one side or the other, even more occasionally slightly raising her right hand in acknowledgement of the cheers. A group of boy cadets lined part of the route; they received a serious scrutiny, a faint smile. Suddenly a voice cried, 'Let her through! Let her see her Empress!'

It was Peter who, breathless from running across the park and desperate in his determination to extract from the moment everything it held, had seized Petchumah by the hand and was trying to drag her to the front of the crowd.

'It's her Empress,' he was shouting. 'Let her see her Empress.'

'He's got a nigger wants to see the Queen,' said someone.

'Queen to us, Empress to her,' Peter cried.

'Let the little fellow through,' said the same man.

But opinions were divided as to whether to follow his advice or not, and the sound of horses' hooves was growing louder.

'Here. Let me.' Wilf lifted her, carried her high over people's heads, and ploughed his way to the front of the crowd. Peter and Stephen followed in his wake. They were all there as the royal carriage approached, the Indian woman in her brilliant sari, the massive ex-soldier, now formidably saluting beside her, the tall clergyman, wild-eyed with anxiety, and in front of them, hopping about with the curious kind of mopping and mowing movement to which he inclined in moments of intense excitement, the little flushed figure with hair that stood on end who cried, 'It's your Empress, your Empress, Petchumah.'

Petchumah, so pushed forward, put her hands together in her traditional greeting and bowed her head in homage. The black-clad figure turned, leant forward, seemed to speak; the royal hands — both royal hands — were half outstretched. In this small northern city the might and mystery of India, the gardens, temples, palaces, the tiger-haunted forests, the far snow-covered hills, the stone-carved elephants four thousand years old, the sacred rivers, the merciless deserts, the ancient cruel gods, bowed in homage in the person of Petchumah in her cerise and blue and silver sari before the plump elderly widow of German extraction into whose slightly protuberant eyes an extraordinary tenderness had come. Again and again Petchumah made her obeisance. Again and again the palms, the plains, the crowded bazaars, the ancient suffering, the distant wisdom abased themselves, and the outstretched hands seemed to wish to bless, and the royal lips when they moved to say — or at least Peter said that was what they had said — 'Beloved India.'

'She said "Beloved India",' he shouted — had he heard, did he lip-read, did he make it up? '"Beloved India." She said, "Beloved India."'

So that was it really. The Queen was put back on the train, her attendants about her, the soldiery was marched away, back to wherever it had come from, the horses were unharnessed, fed and watered, the uniforms folded and all the caparisons put carefully away. The Lord Lieutenant went home to a quiet evening and an early night; the Mayor, taking no longer to get over it all, wished there had been fireworks.

Stephen Collingwood took Peter Tilsley home, but was unable to stop him talking. Charlotte Moore told Ella and Ned, who had watched the procession with their nurse from Lady Dalrymple Smythe's house in the Great Crescent, a story based loosely on the life of the royal family as she knew it; it gave them a comforting if politically unsound picture of a world held together by the domestic affections, and succeeded at last in sending them to sleep. Marianne Hanbury, returning home with her husband in some triumph, found her drawing-room still occupied by the

friends to whom she had lent the view from her windows,
though the procession had passed some time ago. Having
described to them enthusiastically the Queen's remarkable
graciousness and obvious admiration for Edwin Hanbury's
masterpiece, she excused herself on grounds of exhaustion and
went to lie down. Her husband followed her, without even waiting to see out the guests, who feeling themselves unwanted by
the exalted pair left farewell messages of veiled reproach with
Betsey the parlourmaid. Edwin Hanbury was meanwhile moving
inexorably towards his wife, who lay on her bed feigning sleep.
She felt his weight on the bed beside her.

'I must wake you,' he said, laying his large hand on her breast.
'My health requires it.'

She thought of Caspar Freeling, but Caspar had returned to his
room near the Abbey and was writing a letter to the Lord
Lieutenant, asking permission to visit what he understood to be
the remains of an ancient stone circle on the Lord Lieutenant's
estate, and to explain to him its extraordinary significance. He
had helped Madame Sofia to see off the people who had
watched the procession from her windows; she now sat peacefully
at her desk doing her accounts, while the parrot, who had felt
outshone by the chattering crowd, expressed himself freely in a
mixture of tongues. Major Spottiswoode refilled the glasses of
his old friends with his finest hock and continued his by now not
completely coherent recollections of his army days; a little
further along the Great Crescent, Lady Dalrymple Smythe,
composed as ever, played a game of bezique with her distant
cousin Gwendolen Dalrymple, who served her as companion in
return for her keep.

Of course, if I had been looking down on the City from my
usual place, in front of the belt of beech trees not far from the
house where the Moores lived, I should have been too far away
to see them all going back into their houses, though I should
have seen the royal train steaming out of the station. I suppose I

might have heard some of the later noise; it was a rowdy evening in the poorer streets. There were several arrests for drunkenness and fighting; in one case a woman was attacked by other women outside a pub and blinded in one eye. A child fell into the river; a man, not the father, tried to rescue it, and both were drowned. The report of the day's events in the *City Herald*, though congratulatory in general about the arrangements, co-incides with the Mayor's regrets about fireworks. It was felt that if the populace had had something to look at after dark they might not have got so drunk. But then as the *Herald* points out, the expense to the City of the royal visit had already been enormous.

Peter Tilsley's article for the *Herald* was not printed; he did not finish it. It seems strained, as if he were trying to sustain a mood which had already faded. He writes rather wildly about the City in the days of King Arthur, and the Romans, and the barbarians who sacked it, and how it re-arose, and asks where are our holy relics, our ancient statues, our myths. He concludes that the eighteenth-century architects thought of the Ideal City in terms of the perfectibility of man, and seems about to say that we should do the same. 'But if the royal visit presages our own small Renaissance, ought we to be content with the proposal for the building which is to express our feelings for our healing waters, by which I mean the new hotel; should we not try . . . ' But here he stops, and puts a line through the sentence. No doubt he remembered his revered Marianne, and her misguided belief in her husband's genius. 'Well, we have seen something,' he continues. 'We must snatch at its significance before it eludes us. We live in an age . . .'

Here Stephen came in with a bowl of soup, and gently removing the notebook laid it open on the bedside table, with the pencil beside it.

'Finish it tomorrow,' he said.

PART THREE

My wife and I used to walk in the Malvern Hills sometimes. We favoured the Lake District too, being a typical schoolmaster and his wife. We took the children, and when they got too old to be interested, we took the dog. We knew quite well the farm near Malvern where Stephen Collingwood stayed that summer soon after the royal visit, when he felt he must get away from the City. It is not far from the house where he grew up, which is down in the valley. His elder brother lived there, but Stephen did not call; they had not much in common and the brother thought Stephen should have gone on with his career at the Bar. The house and its small surrounding estate were a sort of lost paradise for Stephen — that is, if you can lose a paradise and not regret it. The hills, though, had kept their hold on him, and he was in the way of going back there every now and then to walk, and perhaps to think, or if not exactly think, then to empty his mind, in the hope that it would refill itself by some natural process of regeneration.

This time he felt very much in need of regeneration. Every day he got up early and walked, taking sandwiches made for him by the farmer's wife and sitting on a hillside somewhere to eat them; he spoke to no one. Returning late, he ate his supper and afterwards fell asleep over his book. His diary of the time is not cheerful reading, and I have to remind myself that he used it to complain to, as people often do use such books, and that he must have had moments of pleasure which he does not mention, walking in that beautiful country in such a famously fine summer. The trouble was that after the day of the visit his friend Peter had seemed to lose his spirit. It must have been that he was exhausted. It was not as if the event could really have meant so much to him that anything after it was anti-climax, because what he had been talking about, and working towards, and planning for was his voyage to the south, which was supposed to take place in September. Perhaps it was that after the diversion of the visit he could no longer avoid facing the possibility that he might not be up to the journey. The doctor came, pronounced him tired, seemed to think the spleen might be affected as well as the kidneys, said he should rest, but still talked cheerfully of the great benefits to be expected from the sun.

'Keep his spirits up, that's the thing,' he said to Stephen as he left. 'The lungs are frightful, no doubt about that, but a lot can be done by keeping the spirits up.'

But it was as if Peter had no spirits left. He turned very quiet, and sat looking out of the window with a rug over his knees. He made no jokes about poor senile Mr Tucker trotting past with Mrs Tucker in her apron running after him, or about Anne Smallwood shouting something furious beneath the window; it was as if he did not see them. Stephen tried putting his notebook in front of him, with the pencil beside it; Peter pushed it aside. Stephen tried reading aloud but though Peter thanked him it was clear he was not listening.

Petchumah tried to tempt him with delicacies; he would only say he was too tired to eat. Stephen persuaded him to go to bed, wishing that Charlotte might come, but not quite liking to send for her. One afternoon the doorbell rang. It was Wednesday, the day Charlotte often came to do her visiting on Haul Down, but it was not Charlotte; it was Caspar Freeling, who had called with some copying work for Peter. Stephen explained that Peter hardly seemed up to working.

'It might cheer him up, poor fellow,' said Caspar Freeling. 'It's easy copying and I'll pay him the same as I did before. May I go up?'

When he went into the bedroom, Peter looked at him blankly.

'Easy copying,' Caspar explained. 'Help with the travelling expenses.' He turned to Stephen. 'I want him to copy some old sources. It's easier for people to read that way, and I don't lose the originals.'

Peter's dry lips moved. 'All lies. Fakes.'

'My poor fellow, you've been brought low indeed.' Caspar laid his pale hand on Peter's forehead. 'I'll come back in a day or two and hope to find you much improved.'

On the way out he said to Stephen, 'I'd get a better doctor if I were you. When the mind begins to wander . . . '

'The doctor prescribed complete rest,' said Stephen rather coldly.

Peter rested, but his quietness was not reassuring. On the fourth day of it he turned his head on the pillow as Stephen came into the room and murmured, 'If I could see her . . . '

'I will send for her, of course she will come,' said Stephen at once.

Peter's eyes had closed again, but Stephen felt that this was the sign he had been waiting for, and with a clear conscience he sent Wilf with a message to Charlotte to say that Peter seemed very ill and was asking for her. She came that afternoon. As he told her what had been happening Stephen found that as usual when he saw her he could unburden himself of all his anxiety.

'You will know what to do,' he said, leading her up the stairs.

When he opened the door and showed her into the room where Peter lay he was so confident of the pleasure he was giving the invalid that he smiled triumphantly. Peter turned towards them with an expression so unexpected that they both paused, just inside the door. He had heard the light footstep, following Stephen's on the stairs. The wish he thought he had expressed to Stephen had been a wish to see Marianne Hanbury, who haunted his imaginings; when he saw Charlotte his acute disappointment was immediately followed by an understanding both of how the mistake had happened and of what it revealed about Stephen's preoccupation with Charlotte. He wished to conceal his disappointment, and to welcome Charlotte, of whom he was very fond, and to show his friend Stephen a proper appreciation of this thoughtfulness; at the same time he felt his heart might break. He sat straight up in bed, trying with one of his comic looks to conceal his emotions, and held out his arms; so intensely was he feeling that when he opened his mouth to speak he was hardly surprised that blood came out instead of words.

Charlotte ran to support him, and laid him back on the pillows. Stephen turned back to the door and shouted for Petchumah and Wilf.

'It doesn't hurt,' Peter gasped through his coughing. 'It is worse for you.'

Charlotte wiped his face, speaking to him gently and continuously as if to calm him by her voice. When Petchumah came she asked her for water and cloths and if possible ice. Stephen shouted for Wilf to fetch the doctor.

'Take Mrs Moore's pony carriage and go as fast as you can. Bring him back with you.'

The note of alarm in Stephen's voice made Peter struggle to sit up again.

'It's not that,' he said 'It's not the end. An ice pack, that's all.'

Stephen was breaking up the block of ice which was kept in the kitchen sink for just such an emergency. Petchumah wrapped it in a towel. When they came back into the room Peter stared at their faces, and then at the blood all down the front of Charlotte's dress.

'No!' he struggled again. Charlotte held him tightly, 'It can't be that. I can't die. I can't, I tell you. I am a poet. The world needs me. I haven't done what I was meant to do. It can't be. I must live. I must.'

'Oh, you must,' said Charlotte. 'You will. Believe me. Be calm. Rest.'

'Peter, my friend, you are in God's hands,' said Stephen loudly.

'God will let me die.'

'No, Peter, no. Now come, look into my eyes.' Charlotte held him back on the pillows with her hands on his shoulders. She spoke with gentle authority. 'Look at the life in my eyes. Take it. Take life from me. Be calm and you will be cured. God will not let you die. Look into my eyes and trust me.'

He looked. There was silence.

'Is it true?' he asked quietly.

'It is true.'

And then he was suddenly convulsed and gushed with blood again and when Charlotte laid him back on the pillows she saw that the thing she had thought unimaginable had happened and that he was dead. Very slowly she moved her arm from behind his head. Stephen leant over her to close his eyes, then with one hand under Charlotte's elbow he helped her to stand up and led her into the next room.

As soon as he had shut the door she said quietly, 'I was wrong.'

'How can you say that?'

'I should have let you prepare him for death. I was quite wrong to say he wouldn't die.'

'It comforted him.'

She turned to him quite violently. 'If I want to make someone happy why do I have to lie to them? What is wrong with the world that that should be so?'

He put both hands on her shoulders; and then she wept. He held her close. It was impossible not to kiss her hair, her forehead, the soft white skin of her temple, and when she raised her head to look at him, her lips. It was a tentative kiss but a shockingly revealing one; nor was it without response from her. But she disengaged herself.

'I will send Petchumah to help you,' he said. 'So that I can take you home.'

'Thank you.'

At the door he said, 'Of course I owe you an apology.'

She looked at him in all seriousness and said, 'The fault was mine. All mine.'

That was how he came to be walking on the Malvern Hills, near the farm which my wife and I used to know quite well.

The fact that the familiar tall figure of the curate was temporarily absent from the small streets of Haul Down, that he was not to be seen in the evening in his long black cassock walking across the road to read to whoever might chance to be spending the night in the men's refuge, or in the daytime striding along trying to hide his embarrassment as Anne Smallwood pursued him with her mysterious imprecations, seemed to emphasize the suddenness of Peter Tilsley's death. People on Haul Down were used to early deaths – most families had lost someone near to them before time – and bereavement was part of the common lot, understood to be tragic, expected to be survived with the help of religion and the support of family and neighbours. It was Stephen Collingwood's retreat which struck people, the fact that he had withdrawn himself from them at just the time when they would have found him most interesting. His fondness for the young man was understood; everyone had liked Peter. Grief for a friend was a proper emotion; but why had he felt it necessary to go away? His absence was felt as a deprivation, in a way which would have astonished him.

'He'd no need to hide himself from us,' said old Mrs Bennett, when Charlotte Moore went in one afternoon to read to her. 'If he'd called in on me the way he used to do we could have had a nice talk about death. I've known a few deaths, I can tell you.'

'He was probably very tired. He had been working so hard.'

'It's not as if death would be new to him, him being a widower, as I understand.'

'He'll be back. You can have a nice talk then.'

'It won't be the same. The heart's more open soon after the event.'

Charlotte had made up her mind not to visit on Haul Down any more, but to take up another district, perhaps in River Street at the bottom of the hill, which was in another parish, but when she heard that Stephen had gone away she thought she would take the opportunity to go round and say goodbye to some of the people she had visited most regularly. She did not want to see Stephen.

Her friend Rosalind Tranmer had accused her of getting too thin.

'How can you say that when you've always looked like a broomstick yourself?'

They had been sitting under the weeping ash in the Tranmers' garden; Charlotte's children were picking blackcurrants.

'I'm meant to look like a broomstick, that's how I am. You're meant to look like a ripe peach.'

'I don't feel in the least like a peach, sweet and juicy. I feel sour and bitter and a thousand years old.'

'Because of the poor little poet.'

'And other things. Nothing is as simple as I thought it was. I am a very silly woman.'

'Ah, the curate.'

Charlotte said nothing, her face turned away and her whole figure, leaning back in the cane garden chair and dappled by the sunlight through the leaves, expressing an unaccustomed lethargy.

'He will have been saddened by the death,' persisted Rosalind. 'He'll be lonely again, as he was before.'

'He has gone away.'

Rosalind said nothing, awaiting further confidences; unusually for Charlotte, they were not forthcoming, and after a pause Rosalind asked how Harry was.

'Very well. Harry is always very well.'

'Look what we have picked.' Ella held out a basket containing a very few blackcurrants. 'Yes, but it's boring picking fruit you can't eat any of. They're so bitter.'

'They make delicious blackcurrant tea when you have a cold.' Charlotte held out her arms and drew the child close to her.

'Well, you have your consolations,' said Rosalind in her dry way. 'And Mr Collingwood we are to suppose has the consolation of religion.'

'Religion is not a consolation,' said Charlotte with her cheek against Ella's head. 'It is something much harder than that.'

'I remember Mr Collingwood saying so, when we were having a picnic in the field near your house. Do you remember that? He and Herbert were arguing.'

'I remember,' said Charlotte, who seemed to herself at that time to remember everything Stephen had ever said.

'Herbert is against religion, as I am. But I don't understand why he spends so much time with Caspar Freeling, talking about ancient cults which no one really knows anything about. Why is he interested?'

'The world seems to be divided about Caspar Freeling. Some people find him fascinating and others see nothing but a sort of lizardy thing. I belong to the second party.'

'I suppose I do too. But why should Herbert, with his brilliant mind, bother to spend time with him?'

'I expect there's something we don't see. Perhaps he's decided not to waste his magic on you and me.'

Charlotte was not much interested in Caspar Freeling; but when, on her last visit to Haul Down, she left Mrs Bennett's cottage, and having looked in briefly on Mrs Tucker began to make her way back down the street towards Punch and the pony carriage, she found that he was walking towards her with as usual two or three of the local children following silently just behind him. Having no alternative, she wished him good afternoon; he bowed as he answered, but did not pause. As she walked on, she noticed a well-dressed woman on the other side of the street, with a voluminous scarf over her hat and fastened under her chin, concealing most of her face. If Charlotte had not happened to know that Mrs Hanbury did not go in for district visiting, she would have thought that it was indeed the City Surveyor's wife, but turning into the church to see whether anyone had remembered to put any flowers there she told herself she must be wrong. Petchumah was in the church, sweeping.

'We are hearing from Mr Collingwood that he is staying there a little longer.'

'You must be missing him.'

'We are missing him, yes, very much.'

When she came out she saw that at the end of the street Caspar Freeling and the woman with the dark scarf seemed to be engaged in an altercation; he was gesticulating as if to tell her to go away. Stephen should come back, Charlotte thought. And then she thought, But not to me.

Isabel Corfield, the more nervous of the two sisters, was dreaming as she often did of her Uncle Arnold, who when he told what he thought was a particularly funny story had a way of slapping his thighs and throwing back his head to laugh much too loudly, showing his gums and his big yellow teeth. When she was about twelve, she had been taken to the zoo in the nearby town and there had been a chimpanzee in a terrible rage. It had shaken the bars of its cage, and run to and fro slapping its thighs with its big hairy hands, and thrown a cabbage at the staring humans; all the time it had shrieked and gabbled, with its lips drawn back to show its gums and its big yellow teeth. It had recurred in her dreams many times since, its face slipping from monkey to man with hideous ease; when Uncle Arnold, who was still really the chimpanzee, metamorphosed while climbing in through the windows of the upstairs ironing-room into the Rector of the Abbey, Isabel forced herself awake, and lay trembling and ashamed in her bed. She knew it was her duty to submit herself to God's will, and if God wanted her to be no higher than a female monkey then she would humble herself, but nothing could cure her horror of male monkeys, especially when, as so often happened in dreams, they climbed through windows. She remembered that she had left her book downstairs, and thinking she would try to read herself back to sleep (a strategy which had usually failed in the past) she put on her dressing-gown and slippers and, finding the lamp in the hall still lit, began to go downstairs. As she did so the door of the morning-room opened and Caspar Freeling came out, followed by her father.

'We will see what we can do,' Caspar Freeling was saying.

'You'll remember what I've said.' Her father sounded grave. 'Nothing beyond the usual.'

Caspar turned; Isabel could see his pale secret face. He took her father's hand in farewell and said earnestly, 'There is nothing usual about you, Mr Corfield.'

There was a note she did not like in her father's voice as he answered; she would not have dared to call it foolish, but she thought is showed an undue susceptibility to flattery.

'It's good of you to say so of course. Most encouraging. But you follow me on the other point?'

Caspar smiled like a conspirator.

'I follow you.'

They went out on to the doorstep and Isabel took the opportunity to hurry back to her room, and to a night of restless speculation. Caspar meanwhile walked down the hill, well enough pleased with his evening's work. It was a warm night, not particularly dark. The City lay below him in a gentle glow of gaslight. The long road down the hill was empty; a black cat emerged from the thick shrubs which overhung the garden wall of Capo di Monte and crossed the moonlit road; it disappeared into the shadows as it leapt on to the wall of the opposite garden, which belonged to the house known as Tivoli. Caspar crossed the road after it, so as to walk on the darker side. It had seemed to him once or twice recently that he might be being followed.

If Corfield wanted to go into politics, Caspar was prepared to help him. Corfield was a man without sophistication, but he was not stupid, and he was rich; something could be done for him. When Caspar had outlined to him a possible plan of campaign, together with an idea of the foreseeable expenses, Corfield had said he did not want anything that smacked of corruption. Caspar had laughed.

'My dear sir, no question of it. No, no, no. Although, of course, if you look at it in the right way, and being careful as to what you mean by what is generally known as corruption, you could say it has its uses. Wheels have to be oiled, paths smoothed. Favours have to be done if they are to be expected in return. You could say a little corruption helps to make the world go round. But we'd call it something else of course.'

'As long as we don't call it bribery.'

'Nothing so crude. No one can say my methods aren't subtle.'

'I'm a blunt man, and I like to get my way. But I want nothing more than what's usual in the way of inducements for people to do what I want them to do.'

'I should think it an honour to guide you as to what's usual.'

The role of the man behind the man whose time had come to move from the provincial stage to the national one held possibilities. It was a move Caspar himself had been waiting for the opportunity to make. He had his web of secret pathways, extending sometimes into surprising sanctuaries as well as along the dark alleys of the less exalted; he needed to extend it, but even now he was ready to use it. There were all sorts of roads to power, and one of them was by way of becoming indispensable to the right people. As he moved quietly but steadily from shadow to shadow down the moonlit hill towards the sleeping City, Caspar's habitual discontent, his feeling of disregarded merit, slept too; he had a task to which to address himself.

It was unusually hot in late July that year. Every morning Stephen looked for clouds, and hoped for rain; but day after day the hills grew paler beneath the sun, and the distance was increasingly obscured by dusty blue haze. At night he leant out of the window of the small farmhouse bedroom to breathe a cooler air, and saw a moonlit countryside of that particular calm beauty which had often in the past seemed to him instinct with the presence of its creator. He thought of Coleridge, who had written of his sense of loss when in dejection; like him he saw the familiar beauty but did not feel it. All day he walked, sweating under the sun; at night when he could not sleep he wrote in his diary.

'I have read Peter's notebooks, and there is nothing in them except sentimental maunderings apparently addressed to the wife of the City Surveyor. All that fire of life and longing to be a poet and hope of the future and dreaming of the City as it might have become, all that's gone. Because he wasn't any good as a poet. One can feel like a poet and live like a poet and then be no poet at all. In the same way I suppose one can feel like a believer and try to live like a believer and then find one is no such thing. In both cases what is lacking must be inspiration. You can prepare the ground, keep the faculties exercised, behave as if ... but if the spirit does not breathe on you it is wasted effort, which is perhaps all the universe is, so much waste matter, existing because of some odd chance only explicable by mathematics. So what you have to do is to pretend, pretend there is a purpose and a meaning and a transcendent godhead, and by pretending make it come true. This must be what faith is. Or say, instead of pretend, imagine; as if God said imagine me and I am there. But what does it mean, imagine? Does it mean create, or does it mean re-create, as when you read a story or hear a piece of music? I am not such as could sing a tune I had not heard before. Too much is asked of me. I can only say, "I can't."

'The grass I walk on is as hard and dry as my spirit. I suppose it will rain and the grass will grow green again. I think I shall not. I have known dry times but never as dry as this. Everything I have done for the last few years has been wrong. To go into the Church with a faith I could not sustain, to choose a parish whose inhabitants I could not care for, to blind myself as to the true nature of my feelings for my neighbour's wife. Whom I covet day and night. Who possesses my thoughts sleeping and waking. If I were allowed to love her–! But I only walk these dry hills.'

He walked from one sheltered old village to the next and over the Worcestershire Beacon and beside the shrunken river Teme. He stood high up on the site of an ancient encampment and saw the corn being harvested in the fields many miles below him. He watched the red kites over the rocks and the kestrels hovering above the bracken-covered slopes. He heard no sound except the singing of the larks and the distant bleating of sheep. One evening, returning late, he heard a young man singing as he walked along the track driving five cows before him.

That night he wrote to the Bishop asking if he might come and see him as soon as possible, and told the farmer's wife that he would be leaving the next day.

I am not quite sure of the sequence of events as the summer progressed, because the business of Mrs Hanbury and her depar-ture for Ireland was hushed up at the time and emerges only in passing from Stephen's diary, he being preoccupied with other matters. It seems that one evening about this time she left the house at dusk, wrapped in a light summer cloak, and instead of walking up the hill towards the Circus (she had told her husband she was going to see her friend Madame Sofia) turned downhill, walked across the square, past the entrance to the hot baths along the colonnaded pavement near the Pump Room, and so to the door of Caspar Freeling's lodgings beside the Abbey. There were no lights on in the house. Receiving no answer to her knock she turned away and walked quickly through the deserted streets where the greengrocers and clockmakers and cobblers and pawnbrokers had all closed and shuttered their shops, crossed the river by the Old Bridge (walking faster than ever here because of the groups of men round the doors of the five public houses in River Street) and took the steep road up to Haul Down. Her steps dragged as she approached the top of the hill, and at the corner of the road, opposite the water trough, she held on to the railings outside the chapel and waited there to catch her breath. It being a warm evening, people were still about, some for no other reason than that it was too hot to sleep in their crowded rooms; Zachary Baber, the father of Joan Greenway's child, accosted Marianne in a familiar manner, but was repulsed by her with such disdain that he shambled off in his drunken way, muttering something about bloody great women, she being con- siderably taller than he was. Wrapping her pale cloak closer round her she continued along the road, turned in at the door of the old dispensary and made her way up the dark stair to the studio. When she knocked, a small panel in the door slid open, so small that she could see no more than one eye looking out at her. It was not Caspar's eye, nor was the voice which said 'Not at home' Caspar's voice. It sounded like a child.

'I want to see Mr Freeling. It's very urgent.'

There was a pause, and then the childish voice said, 'He don't live here,' and the panel was snapped shut. She knocked again, but there was no answer. She heard someone come into the house and begin to walk up the stairs. She concealed herself on the narrow stairway which led up to the attic and waited to see whether it might be Caspar, but it was a middle-aged man of respectable appearance whom she had never seen before. He knocked, the eye appeared, the door was hurriedly opened, and as hurriedly shut behind him. Trembling with rage, Marianne approached the door with the intention of knocking again, but suddenly noticing that the panel had not been closed she applied her eye to it instead. Her view being limited and what she saw at first puzzling, she remained motionless for some moments, then she began to slide down the door towards the floor, the palms of her hands pressed against the dark wood. If she had been about to faint a sound from below brought her to her senses. Afraid of being discovered by another stranger senseless on the doorstep, she turned and ran, breathing heavily now, down the stairs and out into the street, meeting on the way not another stranger in a high hat but a thin scavenging dog who ran away at the sight of her. She swirled in her pale cloak, her face far paler, along the little street and down the hill towards the City. She sobbed as she went, huge uncontrollable sobs of outrage. Over the bridge again she hurried, passing the few brightly lit doorways where loud laughter or singing were to be heard, until she came to the more respectable quarter of the City, where such entertaining as there might be was behind the decorous façades of houses like her own, where Betsey the parlourmaid was waiting in some irritation to admit her.

'The master's gone to bed, 'm. He said to please not wake him as he's had a heavy day. If you'd be so kind, 'm, he said.'

'Of course, Betsey, of course. Go to bed.'

She let fall the pale cloak; when Betsey picked it up she told her to leave it on the hall chair. She went upstairs, but shortly afterwards came down again and went into the dining-room, where she swallowed several tablets which she was holding in her hand, washing them down with gulps of sherry which she drank straight from the decanter. Then she wrapped herself in the pale cloak again and quietly let herself out of the house. She crossed the road and turned down to pass the grander shops; her hurrying form, softly lit by the gaslight, was reflected in the darkened windows of the draper's and the umbrella shop and the hatter's; she passed the entrance to the circulating library and turned towards the river. She crossed in front of the church whose pinnacled tower stands in the angle of two streets, confronting at a distance of a few hundred yards the vaster structure of the Abbey, then slipping into an alley between two buildings on the other side of the road she left the lighted streets behind and with one hand on the damp stone wall made her way to the boat station from which her husband set off most days for his early-morning exercise. She passed his light skiff, inverted on its stand, and pulled forward one of the heavy old river rowing-boats which were for hire during the summer season. Groaning slightly with the effort — for the laudanum she had swallowed was beginning to make her drowsy — she pulled the boat to the foot of the steps and lowered herself into it. Manipulating with some difficulty one of the heavy oars, she pushed the boat out into midstream, and as it began slowly to glide down the darkened river, she loosened her hair and let it fall over her shoulders; then she disposed herself across the rear bench, her cloak draped about her and one white arm stretched negligently along the back of the bench. As the current took the boat silently downstream, her head sank on to her shoulder; she lay as if she had been overcome with sleep on a warm afternoon, some stalwart lover at the oars.

That, of course, was how she hoped to be found, much later, somewhere out towards the sea, when the laudanum had done its work and the coming of the dawn brought the labourers to the fields. As it happened, Zachary Baber, after visiting his mistress and her child, and after his brief disagreeable encounter with Marianne outside the church on Haul Down, had walked down the hill with the intention of taking the road back to his home and his wife in the coalmining town some ten miles away. He often walked this distance late at night, sometimes so late that he had to go straight down the mine without going home first, so he was in no great hurry and decided to have one last drink at the Lamb and Lion in River Street before going on his way. It was some time later that he went out behind the pub to relieve himself beside, or possibly in, the river. When he saw a boat moving slowly below him, entangled in some rubbish and old crates which had drifted across from the warehouses opposite, and when he approached near enough to see that the figure in the boat was the same large lady who had repulsed his advances so decisively a few hours earlier, his reaction was one of superstitious panic. Blaspheming incoherently he blundered back into the crowded pub and called for a tot of rum; he swallowed it, paid and left, but as he went he said to one of the men standing by the door, without looking at him, 'Best go and look out the back. In the river.'

So it was that the City Surveyor, roused by a tremendous knocking at his door, came down in his dressing-gown to find two policemen and a doctor waiting on the doorstep, while behind them on the pavement two strong members of the fire service carried between them on a stretcher the apparently lifeless form of his wife.

Rosalind Tranmer had decided that Madame Sofia was a fraud.

'Her only interest is in money,' she told Charlotte Moore as they sat in the shade of the weeping ash in the Tranmers' garden. 'Or in some sort of mad notion she has of her own social position.'

They had set up a card table between them and were sitting on wooden slatted chairs drawn up to it, putting copies of Herbert's latest pamphlet into large envelopes. The title of the pamphlet was *Sanitary Policy, Principles and Practice*, and even Rosalind's loyalty had not induced her to recommend Charlotte to read it.

'I went to tell her I had arranged for Kropotkin to come and lecture and, do you know, she was distinctly cold? I don't think she knows him at all. She was pretending, because she can't bear that anyone should think there's a Russian aristocrat she hasn't met. When he's thrown all that off years ago and has been living among the Swiss clockmakers and that sort of person, it's too absurd.'

'Swiss clockmakers?'

'They're the most revolutionary people in Europe, you must know that.'

'I don't know anything. Tell me about your hero, then.'

But she only half listened. Usually Rosalind's anarchism seemed to her mad, but amusing, whereas Herbert's socialism was sane but dull, but she was finding it hard to concentrate these days, and her wandering attention was arrested only by something Rosalind said about rivers in Siberia. Exile and imprisonment passed her by, but it seemed this revolutionary prince had in his youth discovered remote and previously unknown rivers flowing into some mysterious far northern sea, and Charlotte's imagination at once took her there, accompanied not by the kindly looking man in the picture over Rosalind's desk, with his wide bald head and huge beard and thin-rimmed spectacles, but by a tall man with intense grey eyes; she thought how, all pain and scandal thousands of miles away, they would float on a raft of logs where the great river took them, always in each other's arms.

'Now why are you smiling? It's not funny, how he has suffered.'

'I am smiling at my own idiocy. I was thinking I should like to go to Siberia.'

'Then go.'

'What about Harry and the children?'

'Oh, of course, you would die for Harry and the children.'

'Sometimes I think I do. Every day.'

'You have also a duty to save your own soul, don't forget. You shouldn't sacrifice yourself.'

'I think perhaps I should.'

'For what purpose?'

'For what I believe in, naturally.'

'Which is?'

'Oh,' said Charlotte, smiling, 'just domestic life.'

'Domestic life? How could you be so bourgeois?'

'I suppose I think it is beautiful.'

'Oh, if you think it's beautiful I can't help you. If you'd said good, or useful, or necessary, I could have argued. But beautiful –! What can I do?'

'You'll have to abandon me to my fate.'

'Well, but I don't want to find you floating down the river like poor Mrs Hanbury.'

'Mrs Hanbury? What happened to Mrs Hanbury?'

Delighted to find that Charlotte had not heard the story already, Rosalind told her all she knew. Her information had come to her through a network of local gossip and gave a slightly garbled version of events, but it was accurate in saying that Marianne's health had recovered, though whether or not her spirits were equally resilient was not known because it seemed she had gone to Ireland.

'I suppose she was tormented by the thought of that atrocious building her husband is perpetrating,' said Rosalind.

'Of course not. She thinks it's a masterpiece. No, I suspect he's cruel to her. I've always thought he was a bully.'

'He's put it about that it's an illness, a sort of brain fever, and that he's sent her back to her family to rest.'

'Poor thing. I thought she wasn't capable of genuine feeling. I must have been wrong.'

'How do we know it was genuine feeling? It led her to do something remarkably silly.'

Charlotte did not answer.

'You think I'm hard-hearted,' said Rosalind, suddenly defensive. 'You think I only care for strangers and not for people I know.'

'What nonsense. I think it's just as important as you do not to be sentimental. Only I feel sorry for her even if it wasn't genuine feeling.'

'There you are then. I don't. I have a heart like a walnut.'

'There might be a lot to be said for walnuts,' said Charlotte quietly.

The Bishop wrote to Stephen and suggested that he might care to come and see him some time in the autumn. His wife had been finding the summer climate enervating and he was proposing to take her down to the Isle of Wight for some sea air; they would be away for several weeks, near Ventnor, a favourite spot. Stephen wrote back saying that as he was anxious to discuss the possibility of resigning from the priesthood he was quite willing to travel down to Ventnor to discuss the matter.

'I seem to be always angry these days,' he wrote in his diary. 'I don't exactly know who with (apart from the Bishop). Perhaps myself. The people of Haul Down have a bad-tempered curate, which may be unfortunate, but it must be said I was not much use to them when I was trying to be benign. The wretched Anne Smallwood appeared from nowhere the moment I returned and followed me up the street accusing me of ignoring her. I turned round and seized her by the arm, in such a ferocious grip that she looked terrified. I dragged her into the porch of the church and told her that if she didn't leave me alone I would send for the police. She looked so aghast that I made an effort to control myself. I told her that her trouble was a biological one and that it was her duty to understand it and to apply her spiritual resources to overcoming it. I told her that her monthly cycle was coming to an end and high time too. What did she want with more children at her age? She should welcome the approach of the next stage of her life and try to become wise and noble and a comfort and example to all round her now that she was freed from the chains of physical necessity. She looked so bewildered that I wondered whether Peter Tilsley had been wrong when he had explained the whole thing to me so confidently. As she continued to gape at me I could think of no way of ending our interview other than to take her into the church and kneel down with her to pray. I prayed aloud that God would send her strength and understanding and help her to welcome each change in her life with joyful submission and healthy curiosity, and then I said the Lord's Prayer and heard her faintly echo some of the words, and I prayed for God's blessing on us both. And then what I can only call a sort of thunderous despair came over me. I had no right to frighten her so, no right to assume the powers of a vicar of God, when my ignorance of that God, of any God, was absolute. Everything that had been my self seemed to dissolve around me into a kind of grey milky nothingness. I knelt there with my head in my hands and heard myself groan. I don't know how long it was before I looked up, but when I did, Anne Smallwood was gone.'

In the evenings he worked his way more thoroughly than he had done before through Peter's notebooks. He could not revise his opinion of the poetry and he was still saddened to think that Peter had had such faith in himself as a poet and had produced such mawkish love songs, but when he re-read some of the essays Peter had written about the City, not all of which had been published in the *Herald*, he began to think that after all they might make a fitting memorial to his friend. He thought that perhaps if he edited them carefully and wrote a brief preface, telling the story of Peter's life and of his affection for the City, he might be able to persuade Mr Crowe, the editor of the *City Herald*, to help him finance a private publication. With this in mind he went carefully through all the papers Peter had left. They were in an apparently inextricable muddle, sheets of loose foolscap covered with half-finished poems, random thoughts, lists of ideas for articles, tucked into or falling out of notebooks containing slightly more ordered drafts of articles or rough copies of some kind of translation work he seemed to have been doing. Among these last Stephen came across some passages which seemed at first inexplicable but which he eventually concluded must be something to do with Caspar Freeling. They were written in a supposedly antique English and seemed to be concerned mainly with religious ritual of some kind.

'Here the priest rayseth the Cup Heavenward and cryeth aloud the Name then shalle the Willinge Sacrifice be layed upon the stone beneath the Oak Bough and eache of the assembled shalle in turn render the Tribute of Touch.'

Pushing the page impatiently aside, Stephen went out into the street with the intention of walking to the shop on the corner to buy some pipe tobacco. He almost immediately encountered Caspar Freeling, who enquired after his health in a manner which Stephen found curiously insinuating.

'I am quite well,' he replied. 'And I have been looking through some notebooks Peter Tilsley left. I remember his comments when you came to call on him when he was so ill. I didn't understand them then but I do now. That's a funny sort of game you're playing. Have you set up a Druid tabernacle in your hideaway up here?'

Caspar looked at him coldly for some moments before he answered. Stephen continued to smile, though hardly amiably.

'Druids didn't have tabernacles as far as I am aware,' said Caspar eventually. 'I should be delighted to show you my studio any time you like to visit it. Perhaps tomorrow, about this time?'

'It's very kind of you, but I'm sure you're busy. Perhaps another time.'

'No, no, tomorrow, I insist. I shall be delighted.' Caspar bowed and went on his way, the victory his. Stephen found himself trembling slightly with anger. He bought his tobacco and went back to his room, where he tried in the heat of the afternoon to think of what was meant by the City of God. Instead he thought of Charlotte. He felt that she returned his love. He could not pretend that she was likely to leave her husband, who had given her no reason for abandoning him, or her children, to whom she owed all the duties of motherhood; but he thought sometimes, particularly late at night, that those obligations need not be affected if just once, before he left, before he went – because why not? – to the other side of the world, he could hold her in his arms and share with her that unity of body and soul to which the grandeur of their love entitled them. So, sitting at his desk, facing a piece of paper on which he had written in his fine flowing hand, 'The Idea of a City', he suddenly said in a loud fierce voice, 'If you want my allegiance back, God, give me a night of love.'

He pushed back his chair and hurried over to the door of the room to see that it was shut. The thought that either Wilf or Petchumah, both of whom were presumably somewhere in the house, might have heard his blasphemy was shocking; he reached for his diary, in order once again to castigate himself.

Caspar, continuing in the direction of the old dispensary, said audibly and with satisfaction, though no one heard him, 'So there is to be a cuckoo in the City Surveyor's nest.' The pleased little smile with which he had parted from Stephen had had its cause not only in the confounding of Stephen's intent to be embarrassing on the subject of the Druids, but in a letter which Caspar had received that morning from Marianne Hanbury. The news it brought was not by any means all good, but there was that in it which afforded Caspar profound gratification. He was bored with Marianne Hanbury. He had other preoccupations. Her conquest had amused him, and her willingness to do anything he asked her had been useful. He did not wish to be unkind to her, but he felt he had fulfilled his obligations. When she had taken to turning up unexpectedly at his lodgings he had had to speak harshly.

The news of her suicide attempt had reached him through Madame Sofia, who had had an engagement to have tea with her on the day after the event and had arrived only to be greeted by the sorrowing husband. Caspar had felt it his duty to call. The City Surveyor had told him with appropriate solemnity that his wife had had a nerve storm and had returned to the bosom of her family and to the attentions of the Dublin physicians.

'They are very strong on melancholia over there,' he said. 'All the Irish suffer from it, you know.'

'I hope she will soon be back with you,' said Caspar politely.

Edwin Hanbury sighed. 'I fear it may be a long business. These afflictions of the brain are difficult to deal with. I shall need all my fortitude to resign myself to her absence.'

The prospect of his martyrdom did not seem particularly to daunt him.

'I shall devote myself to my work,' he said.

It was not until a few days later that Caspar received Marianne's letter. It was a sad and not quite coherent document, in which she said she had searched for him to tell him of her condition, had looked through the sliding panel in his door and seen something she did not understand but which so horrified her that she did not want to live and had resolved to put an end to herself, and her unborn child. 'But He who watches over your child has another destiny in mind for him, and now that I am away from the City and the thoughts which torment me there, I am resolved to devote myself to bringing your likeness safely into the world. You have been unkind to me and I shall repay you by bearing your child, which is to me turning the other cheek. I would come to you wherever you were, I would lose my respectability and become your wife, but you do not want me (but if you do want me please write at once), however, if you do not want me Mr Hanbury will believe it is his child although the dates make this quite impossible, having been mercifully for me so occupied with his work of recent weeks as to have given me some respite from his attentions but he will believe it though the child be your image because he is quite safe from thoughts not agreeable to him, owing to his self-esteem, which cannot be penetrated.'

Indeed it could not, Caspar thought, smiling his pleased smile and turning into the doorway of the old dispensary. The idea that Edwin Hanbury was to have the nurturing of Caspar's child was delightful to Caspar; he thought of the expense, the nursemaids, the clothes, the schools, everything considered suitable for the son of a pillar of the bourgeoisie, and all to be lavished on an interloper, the seed of secrecy and cunning and disdain planted by himself. He would write to Marianne and advise her to stay in Ireland until after the birth. He would write kindly, using the honeyed words she so loved and so distrusted; he would advise her that the best interests of the child would be served by her returning in due course to her husband — her own best interests too, for was he not himself elusive, a man of no property, restless and unappeasable? He knew well enough how to appeal to her, how to bend her to his will. And Edwin Hanbury should pay. Turning the key in the lock of the door with the sliding panel he laughed aloud at the thought.

As soon as he was inside the room he began to dismantle it, unpinning hangings, piling cushions on the floor, removing curtains and screens. He worked quickly, humming monotonously as he transformed the exotic Eastern chamber Marianne remembered into a plain distempered room containing nothing but a table, a few chairs and a large wardrobe. Into this last he bundled the hangings and the cushions, first taking out some books and documents which he scattered over the table. He opened the window, letting in the warm air and the sounds from the street outside. He did not think it likely that there was anyone in the City in whom Marianne would confide, but there would be no harm in being on the safe side. If Stephen Collingwood found nothing but a bare writing-room when he came the following day, what more reliable witness could Caspar call upon should anyone start asking questions? As for when Marianne returned to the City being about to bear, or preferably having already borne, his child, he intended to be gone by then. He had discharged his obligations to her by using his influence with the so distinguished Professor Dacre to make sure that the competition for the hotel was won by the City Surveyor. The pursuit of Corfield's political interests would take them both to London; it was Caspar's intention to move there in the autumn, when Parliament reassembled.

I may have given the impression that I am against change, when I was talking earlier about the threat of tourism; but that would be inaccurate. You can't teach history for thirty years and be against change; equally you can't help noticing that it nearly always brings loss as well as gain. The ratio is hard to determine afterwards and almost impossible at the time. So whether the influx of tourists to this City will despoil it as nothing has done since Ceawlin the destroyer in the tenth century or whether it will bring a new age of prosperity and an unexpected efflorescence of culture, I have no idea, though I suppose it will be something between the two. As I say, I follow my own tracks. One of them sometimes takes me across the space in front of the Abbey and into the little square beyond it, the one which is almost filled by a vast plane tree and in the corner of which in a small house built in the first few years of the eighteenth century lives my old friend Arthur Morrison, who has taken the simple expedient of growing Virginia creeper over most of his ground-floor windows to prevent the tourists from peering in. Such space as the creeper leaves is filled on the inside of the windows by straggling geraniums and jugs filled with dusty dried flowers. There is light enough in his small sitting-room from the window at the back, which looks out on to a walled garden where he grows vegetables with the utmost neatness. The City authorities have suggested to him that the creeper is not in keeping with the image they want to project and should be trimmed; he has so far kept them at bay by feigning madness. It is quite easy for him to do this because he is very old and of unkempt appearance and does not always put in his false teeth; in fact he is an archaeologist of great distinction and his brain is as good as ever.

I sometimes go to see him after I have been to the Reference Library, which is why I pass in front of the Abbey on my way. The assorted summer crowd ebbs and flows and eats ice-cream in the space which Caspar Freeling overlooked from his rooms and which in his time was crowded only at Christmas and Easter or on those Sundays when there was a band and marching cadets or Yeomanry for Church Parade. His elegant self-conscious figure would look out of place now, but in a way it always did; there was something about his walk, his pale face, his sideways glance, which made people look at him curiously, as though they had thought for a moment he might have been someone else. I don't think I should be surprised to see him one day, sidling through the crowd at once self-conscious and aloof; but I can't imagine Charlotte there. Of course I have seen pictures of her, and understood what must have been the great charm of her countenance, but because I have also seen her as Stephen Collingwood saw her I suppose I have had superimposed on her image in my mind's eye a sort of small burning cloud. She did walk there, passing the doors of the Abbey on her way to show her children the hot springs which had been uncovered as part of the plan for Edwin Hanbury's new hotel. New baths had been proposed: vapour baths, douche baths, massage baths, all according to the latest Continental fashions. There was to be a tunnel, a sort of underground passage, to enable the hotel guests to reach the baths without having to emerge in to the outside air. Perhaps it was supposed they would be wearing their dressing-gowns, or sitting in wheelchairs or being carried on stretchers; who knows? The plan was never carried out, partly because as soon as

excavations started such an extraordinary network of archae-
ological remains was uncovered that it was decided it would
be an act of barbarism to destroy them. They were inspected by
a number of experts and then covered up again; the only
alternative was to pull down the buildings on top. It was as if the
buried world down there was just too vast to be exposed. Arthur
Morrison knows as much about it as anyone, and often talks
about it in his sitting-room with the overgrown front windows,
which is much as his parents left it in the 1950s, Arthur being
not so much against change as oblivious to it, or at any rate
unaware of its sequential nature. The Roman City and the pre-
Roman settlement, the eighteenth-century City and our own, all
seem to coexist in his mind, rather than to succeed each other.
He gives the impression that he would be equally at home in any
of them, and perhaps he would. There have probably always
been people like Arthur, single-minded and solitary and curiously
contented. Anyway, he told me about the springs which the
excavations exposed and which Charlotte took her children to
see. Everyone knew the springs were there, and certain of them
were piped into the baths, but this particular spring had been
pouring hundreds of gallons of water at a temperature of about
120° Fahrenheit into the earth around it for goodness only knew
how long, but certainly since long before pre-Roman times for
round its verges were found flints from the Palaeolithic age. It
was its secrecy that had appealed to Charlotte, the thought of its
bounty flowing unrecognized. She had called on Mr Hanbury to
enquire after his wife, had hoped in fact not to see him but to
leave her card and a polite message with Betsey the parlourmaid,
but he had come bounding out of the dining-room at the sound
of her voice, and brushing aside her concern for his wife had
insisted on showing her the plans he had spread all over the
dining-room table. When he offered to show her the diggings,
she said she would like to see them and to bring the children.

So she took her way past the Abbey where I walk when I go

to see my friend Arthur (but I can only imagine that burning cloud), and holding Ella by one hand and Ned by the other allowed Edwin Hanbury to lead them all down into the cellars of the Pump Room and out into the open space where the diggings had exposed some Roman brickwork and a good deal of steaming mud. They had to climb down a ladder which was leaning on some scaffolding; the children enjoyed that, and Ned being disposed as a general principle to be very much in favour of mud was pleased with what they found at the bottom of the ladder. Ella on the other hand was shocked; she did not think it quite proper that a whole City should be built on nothing better than warm mud. Charlotte, irritated by the way in which Edwin Hanbury held her round the waist rather too long while helping her down the ladder, also found herself disappointed. She had expected to see a clear spring, spouting from depths too deep to be anything but pure; she did not share her son's enthusiasm for mud. She listened politely as Edwin Hanbury spoke of hypocausts and heating-systems, theatres and temples, and the equal splendours he was planning to build, but she thought of other streams and other seas. She had wanted to see something beautiful, something that would speak to her imagination. She felt at this time extraordinarily receptive to nature, art, music, poetry; all of those things seemed to impose order on the unruliness of her feelings, not by denying them but by magnifying them, making them something tremendous and inevitable. They also had the effect of freeing her from the confines of her own individuality; they seemed to be the positive side of something which in its negative aspect would be death by drowning.

Madame Sofia, walking under the colonnade opposite the Pump Room, saw Edwin Hanbury escorting Charlotte and her children out into the street. She waited while they said goodbye to him, each shaking his hand, and in Ella's case dropping a little curtsy, and when he had gone back into the building she crossed the road to speak to them.

'I want to ask you the news from Haul Down,' she said to Charlotte when she had greeted the children. 'I am told Caspar Freeling has a place of some sort up there. Does he still use it, do you suppose?'

'As far as I know. I saw him when I was last there.'

'I have had such a strange letter from poor Mrs Hanbury. I think I should perhaps speak to your friend Mr Collingwood.'

'He is not — that is to say, he has been away. But I have heard he has come back.'

'Tell him I shall come and call on him one day.'

'If I see him, I will tell him.'

'You are in suspiciously good looks these days. I suppose you are not expecting again?'

Charlotte burst out laughing.

'You say all the things one isn't meant to say. But no, not as far as I know.'

Madame Sofia was feeling in the pockets of her large blue linen skirts; the children watched hopefully.

'I hope I shall not have to say what one is not meant to say to Mr Freeling. I thought I had some aniseed balls but I seem to have lost them. What have we here? Humbugs only.'

'We like humbugs better than aniseed balls,' said Ned reassuringly.

'Give my regards to your husband,' said Madame Sofia, having distributed the humbugs. 'And to Mr Collingwood, of course.'

She resumed her slow progress beneath the colonnade, pausing only to administer an unexpectedly ferocious blow with her folded parasol on the back of a fat pigeon which was looking for crumbs. Ella and Ned, who were still watching her, laughed, but Charlotte hurried them away.

'Don't laugh,' she said. 'I think it might not be quite safe to laugh at Madame Sofia.'

*

Stephen met Anne Smallwood on his way to call on Caspar Freeling. She was coming down the road towards him carrying a basket of laundry, and as there happened to be a horse and cart in the way he could not cross the road to avoid her as he usually did. He walked faster, frowning as if deep in thought, but she only wished him a good morning as they passed. Surprised, he answered with friendly emphasis but did not slacken his pace; he wondered what had happened to abate her usual fury. Walking faster had the effect of strengthening his resolve to make his visit to Caspar as short as politeness allowed. He walked briskly up the dingy stairs of the old dispensary and knocked on Caspar's door. It was opened immediately to disclose the austere room which Caspar had prepared.

'Let me offer you a glass of Madeira.'

'You are very kind.'

'I wanted you to see where I work. No mysteries, as you see. Do sit down. I often wish we had more time to talk. There are not so many people in the City with whom I imagine either of us has a great deal in common.'

'My days fill up with parish work. With that and reading I don't go out much.'

'Except to the dear Moores, with whom I always seem to see you.'

'Indeed I am devoted to the Moore family.'

'I'm told that Mrs Moore has changed her allegiance, and goes to do her good works in River Street, rather than up here in Haul Down. You won't be seeing so much of her.'

'No.'

'I am asking a few people to tea next week – not here, down in my apartment by the Abbey. I want to try to interest them in some of Mr Corfield's political projects. I shall ask Mrs Moore. Perhaps you would be able to join us? On Wednesday, say.'

'I am afraid I am engaged on Wednesday.'

'Thursday then. Or Tuesday.'

'Thursday would be delightful, if I can arrange to get away.'

'My dear Collingwood, if I may say so, I think you spend too much time trying to be good.'

Stephen finished his glass of Madeira preparatory to taking his leave.

'And I suspect you spend too much time trying to be bad,' he said mildly. 'Perhaps neither is particularly easy.'

'They come to much the same thing in the end, you know. It all runs into the sand.'

Stephen stood up and put down his glass on the table. He had been about to take his leave but Caspar sounded less ironical than usual, and his face in the light which the dirty window allowed into the bare and dreary room was not so much cynical as sad.

'What do you mean?' asked Stephen.

'When you have seen through the fairy tales men have invented to comfort themselves, the thing that is left is courage. Whether what you do is what people call good or what they call bad makes very little difference as long as you are in action, in play, if you follow me.'

'I hardly do.'

'I have not wanted to be nothing. To that extent I suppose you could say I am ready to be anything.'

Stephen sat down again.

'I suppose nobody wants to be nothing,' he said.

Caspar went on talking, quietly but with intensity.

'I was born in India. My father was an army sergeant, my mother came from Vienna. She was the daughter of a trader in precious stones with a business in the north of India. We were besieged. My father was murdered in front of my eyes by those black devils. I was ten years old. You may have noticed I don't care for that savage you keep in your house.'

'She keeps me in her house in fact. But what a horrible thing to happen.'

'We were close to starving. The rumours that we were about to be relieved came and went. We were there for five months, in terrible heat. I remember odd things only, mainly smells. And then we saw the relieving army. That I remember because it was a shock when everyone shouted and I suddenly noticed how cracked and feeble their voices were. Then for days the army didn't seem to move, and there was more confusion. The women and children were supposed to be going to be allowed out and we began to move, with carts and so on, and the men were with us going towards the gates, and suddenly there was an attack and the sepoys were everywhere killing the soldiers. They were mad, or drunk or drugged, screaming. Two of them killed my father with their bayonets, horribly, and then there was more fighting and they were driven off. We got to Calcutta eventually and to a boat home. My memories of it all are confused. I remember the death. It was in a sort of narrow lane with low buildings on one side, all so dirty. I remember odd incidents of the journey but not much.'

'Had you relations to come back to in England?'

'My mother took me to her family in Vienna. She didn't live long. My father had always said I was to be brought up in England and when she was dying she said I was to be sent back there, to his brother. She died from the after-effects of the siege, I suppose. It was all kept away from me. I remember hardly anything of that time in Vienna; perhaps I had in some way cut myself off from what was going on round me. I had always preferred my father to my mother. I think I despised her because her English wasn't good.'

'She must have been a brave woman. She got you out of that terrible place.'

'I was too young to be grateful.'

'And then you came to England?'

'My uncle was a rough sort of man, a bachelor. It was school then and learning to survive. I learnt all right. But there was no money to send me to university. I worked as a clerk in Oxford and educated myself in the evenings. I'm clever. I'm a good mimic, too. I can do all sorts of voices. I'm virtually a ventriloquist. So I became to all appearances a gentleman. A scholar and a gentleman. There now, I have put myself in your hands.'

'I'll respect your confidence, of course.'

'Do you see how I've made myself a philosophy to match my needs? We all do that, don't we?'

'I see that you want a life to which you feel your capacity entitles you. Your capacity and perhaps your misfortunes.'

'I want what I deserve, Collingwood. But I want to be happy, too, and to make other people happy. Why not? It will give me pleasure to bring you and Mrs Moore together in my pretty room that I've made so pleasant. It will make me happy.'

'Then of course I'll come,' said Stephen, standing up. 'And you must come and dine with me some evening where I live. I spend too much time alone.'

Caspar sprang to his feet, smiling.

'I should like that enormously.' He hesitated, and then said seriously, 'But you understand I can't see that woman.'

'Petchumah? Of course I understand. She shall be sent out for the evening. Later on perhaps you'll find out what an extraordinarily sweet nature she has. But don't worry, I shan't rush it.'

Stephen went down the dusty stairs feeling that he had misjudged Caspar. The meeting had not gone at all as he had expected.

Charlotte was playing a Mozart sonata on the piano. It was No. 15 in C major, the only one she could manage. She played expressively and her teacher, Mr Bowden-Ellis (the husband of Mrs Bowden-Ellis who took the dancing classes in the Pump Room), always used to say she had a beautiful touch, but her technique was not very advanced. The sonata sounded pleasing enough to Harry, who had come into the drawing-room to see her but smilingly implied she was not to interrupt her playing.

When she had finished he said, 'Very good,' in rather the same sort of tone he used when Ella showed him one of her drawings.

'I had lunch in the County Club today,' he went on. 'I was down there seeing the lawyers about a contract they seemed to have made a complete muddle of. People were saying that poor Hanbury doesn't seem to expect his wife to recover.'

'What, never?'

'He apparently says he doesn't expect her back from Ireland for at least six months. And even then he doesn't seem to think she will be cured. It's strange. She always seemed to me the last person one would expect to go into a decline like that.'

'Perhaps she has run away with another man.'

'Surely not. Hanbury wouldn't put up with that. He'd be off in pursuit.'

'Is that what a man should do when his wife runs away?'

'Of course.'

'And when he catches her?'

'Beat her, of course.'

'Beat his wife? But I thought it was the man who's stolen her affections he's supposed to beat.'

'Well, she had a mind of her own, I suppose. She must take the consequences of her own actions, not let the poor fellow take the brunt of it.'

'So you'd beat me if I ran away?'

'Of course.'

'But you're not at all the beating sort.'

'I should be in the grip of ungovernable passion. Although I suppose when I come to think of it, as it would be you, if you see what I mean, I should be just as likely to sob and scream and go down on my knees and make a complete idiot of myself. So you would loathe me for a brute or despise me as a cry-baby. Either way it would be most unsatisfactory.'

'I suppose it would,' said Charlotte, beginning to play some desultory chords.

Harry went towards the open French windows, from beyond which could be heard the sound of the children with their nurse in the garden. He stood there for a few moments and then went out. He was perfectly well aware of Charlotte's present mood, although he did not understand it. He was not quite confident enough of himself to ask her any direct question. He did not think of himself as being good with women. He heard men talk about how they were to be handled and kept quiet. He did not like the idea of using cunning in his relations with Charlotte. At the same time he felt that his usual way with women, which was to treat them like men only a little more politely, might lack the subtlety which was due to someone of Charlotte's exceptional qualities. (He did not know, of course, that it was that manner of his which had first drawn her to him.) So for the time being he was only a little more than usually careful of what he said. Her restlessness puzzled him, and the way in which, when he made love to her, she sometimes rejected him and was sometimes extremely passionate disturbed, although it entranced, him. He expected his patience in not questioning her to be rewarded in due course by some kind of clarification. In the meantime he managed with considerable effort not to draw her attention to how well he was behaving.

In the garden the children were playing French cricket with their nurse, a girl from a nearby village who entered as keenly into their game as they did themselves and was at the moment involved in an altercation with Ned, who had been cheating. Harry picked up a pair of garden clippers from the table on the terrace and walked over to his favourite rose bush, which having flowered triumphantly in June was producing a few late-summer blooms, a bonus which only the best of summers procured. He picked the most perfect and called Ned to come and take it to his mother. The boy came reluctantly, hot and indignant, complaining quite falsely that it was Florrie who was cheating.

When he came back from the drawing-room a few minutes later he was smiling happily, the offence forgotten, in a hurry to get back to the game.

'Did you give it to her?' Harry called.

'Yes.'

'What did she say?'

'She said to say thank you.'

When Madame Sofia came out of the front door of the house in the Circus where she lodged, she saw a small white dog with a brown patch over one eye on the grass on the other side of the road. There were five tall plane trees in the middle of the circle of grass, and it was not unusual for dogs to be exercised beneath them. Some people said the plane trees ought not to be there, and no more ought the grass, and the circle which the houses surrounded should be cobbled and the centre of it marked by an obelisk or a statue, preferably equestrian, but somehow or other the plane trees and the grass had got there, and since there were as many people to defend them and with as much sense of righteous outrage as there were to attack them, they stayed.

Madame Sofia paused and stared across at the little dog, for no particular reason other than that she was preoccupied with worries of her own; the dog continued to sniff round the stones which edged the grass. She saw a man behind the dog, exactly in the centre of the slight mound of grass round which the trees were planted; he was standing quite still, looking at her. It was a warm evening, windless, with a feeling of the end of summer in the air. The man, whom she now saw to be of rough aspect, walked towards her, then called his dog and crossed the road slightly to the left of her, going in the direction of the mews behind the Circus. He wore breeches and a brown waistcoat but no shirt; his chest and arms were thickly covered with blue tattoos. Madame Sofia turned to her right and took her slow heavy way along the pavement and down the street towards the Great Crescent; she was not looking well. She passed the chemist where she often called in for her dyspepsia pills, but it was closed, this being her evening walk. In this hot summer the City in its bowl between the hills was sometimes oppressive and Madame Sofia was in the habit of coming out just before dusk when the heat had abated; she would often walk along the street which linked the Circus to the Great Crescent and stand for a little by the railings which separated the Crescent, with its stern sweep of uniform façades, from the smooth green slopes in front of it. She would breathe deeply, looking beyond the grass and the fine large trees to the hills which rose up on the other side of the river, and then she would make her slow way back again, by now a familiar figure in that part of the City. This evening she walked even more slowly and heavily than she usually did; she paused some time before the windows of an antique shop, looking in at an ormolu side-table which had taken her fancy earlier that week and which to her annoyance was now half concealed by a bulbous green glass vase containing several stems of pampas grass. In her present discontented mood it seemed like a personal insult; she was denied even a clear view of the sort of table which her position and her taste fully entitled her to possess.

Financial security had eluded Madame Sofia in a way she found quite mysterious, but she took it to be somehow a consequence of a whole series of misplaced enthusiasms and trusts betrayed. The first of these wretched encounters as she considered them had resulted in her brief and only marriage. She had been light of step then and her ankles had been not the least bit swollen and she had waltzed with a fresh-faced Hussar and let him dance away with everything she had, he being a notoriously unlucky gambler; since when she had had to live on her wits, and on her instructions from her invisible Masters, which were not always easy to interpret. She would have been glad of some guidance now, but felt she was failing to clear the necessary space in her mind. Also the fact was that it had sometimes been necessary for her in the course of this living on her wits slightly to blur the meaning of the messages she received or even to falsify or even invent; which made it harder to tell what messages, if any, there really were. Staring into the window of the antique shop she thought for a moment she saw a face in the gloom behind the pampas grass; then she turned quickly in case it was the reflection of the tattooed man, who might have followed her, but there was no one there. She delved into her pocket and brought out a small round box of Carter's Little Liver Pills. She swallowed one and continued on her way with no perceptible brightening of the expression on her face.

She had hoped so much of Mrs Hanbury, had upped sticks, as she would have put it, entirely at Mrs Hanbury's urging, Mrs Hanbury who was so effusively friendly, so eager to explore the spiritual dimension, so secure in her social position as the wife of a man of substance. But Mrs Hanbury had become increasingly elusive, and Madame Sofia had had to rely more and more upon Caspar Freeling, who puzzling though she found him in certain ways had nevertheless entertained her with his conversation, helped her to find employment as a translator and private language instructor, and apparently made some kind of sense out of the chaos of her account books. And then suddenly Mrs Hanbury had disappeared, leaving all sorts of strange rumours, and had followed her disappearance with a letter so strange and disturbing, and in its possible consequences so personally in-convenient to Madame Sofia, that the latter's first inclination was to dismiss it as untrue and her second inclination was to do nothing about it. It weighed on her mind all the same as she reached the corner of the Great Crescent and crossed the road to stand by the edge of the park, holding with both hands on to the railings so as to take the weight off her feet and looking across the grass, where some boys were playing with a football, and over the trees, beneath which one or two couples were walking, towards the hills and the woods. She felt a sudden longing for the cool clear air of the foothills of the Himalayas, where she had become what she believed to be an adept and where she had heard the voices of those she called her Masters. These perfect beings, whom she understood to have escaped from the wheel of life and death but to have stayed on earth to help humanity in its struggle towards perfection, had seemed to speak in voices clearer than any she had heard since. It was money, she thought, which had muddied the wells of her understanding, money and the unspeakable tiresomeness of so many of the people she had had to accept as associates. Should she not free herself from the trivial demands of these people? What, after all, did she owe to Marianne Hanbury – apart from one small loan to help with the expense of her move into the apartment in the Circus? If Marianne Hanbury had disagreements with people, it was not up to Madame Sofia to sort them out. Her earlier instinct had been right; the letter should be ignored.

Madame Sofia turned back towards the Circus, walking this time on the other side of the street, the side where the terraced houses were rather grander, having walled gardens behind them which backed on to the park, and seemly façades with highly polished brasswork on their doors. She walked faster now, having reached her decision; it was not until she was half-way down the street that she saw the figure approaching her from the other end. It was a quiet time of evening in a quiet street. A few people were arriving by carriage or on foot and being admitted into one or other of the houses, where entertaining of some kind was going on. A carriage or two passed, bound for other destinations and similar occasions, but there was nothing like the traffic and activity of the earlier hours of the day. Madame Sofia had a clear view down the pavement ahead of her, and the figure now approaching her immediately held her attention. It was a woman, no longer young, and no longer slim, dressed in a dark walking-dress with a full skirt. She had wrapped a large Paisley shawl round her shoulders and a loose black scarf, or mantilla, over her head. She moved stiffly, as if she might have suffered from rheumatism or found her weight tiring to carry, but there was a kind of relentlessness about her progress. Madame Sofia's heart began to beat uncomfortably fast. She would have liked to cross the road but the compulsion to continue in the way she was going was too strong. She did continue, but with increasing dread. A man in a frock coat who had just alighted from a carriage crossed her path; he looked at her curiously before going on into the house whose door was already being held open for him by a manservant. There was now no one between Madame Sofia and the woman walking steadily towards her. Madame Sofia continued as steadily but with a face the colour of putty. The two substantial figures approached each other, and did not hesitate. They passed, and continued at the same pace. Madame Sofia had hardly glanced at the face of the other, but she had seen a considerable jowl and eyes that seemed to protrude slightly; she had not met their gaze. By the time she reached the door of the house where she lodged she was trembling so much that she could not fit her latch-key into the lock. She put her finger on the bell and kept it there until the door was anxiously opened by the kindly country woman, her landlady. Madame Sofia stumbled across the threshold.

'Oh, Mrs Berryman, I have seen a tattooed man.'

Mrs Berryman helped her into a chair.

'Now you sit there and collect yourself a minute, my love. You've had a shock. What kind of man was it, then?'

'A man with a waistcoat and a little dog with a brown eye patch.'

'Arms all covered with tattoos, was he? That'll be Jeff Baker, works in the livery stables behind here, odd fellow he is but no harm in him, no harm at all.'

'No, but you see it was first that, first the tattooed man. And then, then it was much worse.' Madame Sofia lowered her voice, and clasping Mrs Berryman's arm continued, 'I met myself, walking on the pavement.'

There was such an expression of horror in her eyes that Mrs Berryman felt no inclination to laugh. Instead she crouched down beside Madame Sofia's chair in the dim entrance hall and said in an anxious whisper, 'What did you do?'

'I walked on past.'

'That was right. That was the right thing to do, my love.'

'I shan't be here much longer, Mrs Berryman.'

'Don't talk so. Let me help you to bed and I'll bring you some camomile tea. I take it myself when I've anything on my mind and I sleep sweet as anything.'

'It means', said Madame Sofia, allowing herself to be led up the stairs, 'that I shall have to do what I was not going to do.'

Although she was no longer trembling, she was still very much shaken. She sat on the edge of her bed with such an air of hopelessness that Mrs Berryman thought it best to undress her. Madame Sofia allowed herself to be unwrapped and unbuttoned and unhooked and unlaced, all of which took some time; then, decently clad in a voluminous calico nightdress, she climbed obediently into bed. Mrs Berryman, quite awed, said as she tucked her up, 'They must have been beautiful, those stays, when they were new. I've never seen such handiwork. Quite historic, as you might say.'

Madame Sofia made an effort to gather her face together into an expression of hauteur.

'They were given to me as a present,' she said distantly. 'By a first cousin of the Tsar of Russia.'

Madame Sofia was prostrated in her bed for two days before she felt able to take the action whose consequences she so dreaded. It was on one of those two days that Charlotte Moore in cool blue linen and undimmed beauty crossed before the west front of the Abbey once again, and having been admitted to the house in which Caspar Freeling lodged, hurried up the stairs to his first-floor drawing-room. She expected to find a polite tea party; she found no one but Stephen Collingwood.

He was standing by the window through which he had watched her cross the pavement below. Against the light she could not quite make out the expression on his face; her own had warmed into the glad smile with which she customarily greeted him.

'I am so pleased to see you,' he said, and came forward to take both her hands with the feeling he so often had on seeing her, that all his anxieties fell away from him. They stood face to face, looking into each other's eyes, holding hands and smiling, until Charlotte said, 'Where's the tea party?'

Turning away to look around the room she continued, 'Let's at least sit down,' and doing so said, 'There now, we are friends.'

'We are friends,' he echoed.

'Freeling, I suspect, is up to some trick,' she said. 'Have you seen him?'

'He was here when I arrived and said he had been unexpectedly called away and might not be back for some time. He looked worried.'

'I don't trust him.'

'We might have misjudged him. He has an odd history.'

He repeated to her all that Caspar had told him in the bare room, so different from their present elegant surroundings. When he had finished Charlotte said, 'To me he still seems too like a lizard, but I am sorry if he is unhappy. I had much rather hear about you and how you have been.'

He told her about Anne Smallwood, for whose mysterious improvement he could still not account, and that he had been walking in the Malvern Hills. He said he had a cousin in New Zealand, which was true, and that this cousin had written asking him to go out and join him there, which was not true.

'So far away.' Charlotte sounded half anxious, half envious.

'Would you like to come with me?' he said simply. 'I think you will say no, but I have to ask you because I love you with all my heart.'

Her courageous gaze did falter at that; she stared at her clasped hands. After a pause she said, 'I should like to come very much. But I also love Harry. And I am completely devoted to my children. I had no idea I could have feelings so mixed and probably so wrong. I shall stay here and try to learn to be wiser.'

'You are wise already.' His voice was very low.

'My dear, dear friend.' She moved impulsively from her chair to sit at his feet, his hands in hers. 'We shall see each other often and all will be well and we shall never, never have a conversation like this again and I will pray for you always.' She laid her cheek against his hands; he kissed her bent head. And in a moment she was on her feet again. 'The lizard might be watching somewhere. I'll go now. When we see each other again we'll be – as we have always been.'

He stood up too, but could not speak. She turned with her hand on the door handle, and looked at him as she had looked from the foot of the stairs in the dim entrance hall of the house on Haul Down, when she had been wearing her grey walking-dress and a dark scarf. It was a look which, wise though she may have become in subsequent years, she was never so wise as to lose.

Stephen watched her cross the pavement to her waiting carriage; he did not hear the door behind him quietly open. When he turned back into the room, smiling as he often smiled when he had been watching Charlotte, he was surprised to see Caspar Freeling.

'Has she gone?' Caspar asked irritably.

'She couldn't wait,' said Stephen. 'She asked me to apologize.'

'It wasn't at all what I intended.'

'Neither of us wanted a party. You know how unsociable I am, and Mrs Moore was kind enough to say she had enjoyed our talk. She hasn't been up to Haul Down for some time and we had plenty to discuss. I must say thank you and be off as well.'

'You are incorrigible. Why do you think I left you alone?'

Stephen was already at the door. 'I shall think the best of you, my dear Freeling. Come and call on me on Haul Down. Some of my books might interest you.'

In that notorious summer the weather did not break until half-way through September. On the particular afternoon of the first week of that month, the afternoon on which Madame Sofia set off from the Circus towards Haul Down in a hired conveyance, the sky was grey but the clouds yielded no rain and the atmosphere was hot and humid; the shrubs in the garden of the square through which she was driven were drooping and the grass was parched. The green of the woods which clothed the hillside opposite was the dull green of late summer, interspersed already with dry brown and occasional yellow. The direct road up the hill was too steep for Madame Sofia's driver, who took the roundabout way instead. Madame Sofia sat very straight and looked out severely at the demure new houses which they passed. Arriving at the approach to the narrow streets of Haul Down she stopped the driver by the water trough opposite the little church and asked him to wait, saying she might be some time. He looked doubtfully down the street she was proposing to enter and asked if she would like him to accompany her. She refused his offer, and set off past the church, holding in her hand a letter, to which she referred for directions.

Oblivious of the curious glances she attracted, she walked slowly down the street, looking at the numbers of the houses she passed. A small boy followed her briefly, aping her lumbering progress and questioning air, but happening to come across no friends to encourage him he lost heart and turned down an alley which led to the blacksmith's forge. Finding herself at last at the entrance of the old dispensary, Madame Sofia first made enquiries of the old man she found behind the boxes and trays of nails and hooks and door knobs and varieties of wire in the dimness of the hardware shop, and then following his instructions found the side-door and made her way upstairs, pausing for breath outside the door to the empty first-floor rooms and then continuing heavily up the narrower stairs to the top floor.

She knocked. The shutter which had so confused Mrs Hanbury opened. Madame Sofia inserted her forefinger and said loudly, 'I am Madame Sofia, come to see Mr Freeling on urgent business.'

'My dear Madame Sofia,' said Caspar, opening the door. 'What can have brought you here?'

He looked surprised but in no way uneasy.

'I am glad to see you.' Madame Sofia walked past him into the room. 'I have had great anxieties. I hope you will put my mind at rest.'

'Of course I shall, but you shouldn't have troubled yourself to come all the way up here. Let's go down again into the City, where I can entertain you more comfortably.'

'I have not come to be entertained.'

The room was in a transitional state. Having dismantled it for Stephen Collingwood's visit, Caspar had not yet returned it to its former condition. He had rehung the strips of coloured felt which lined the walls, and redisposed some of the cushions and mattresses, but he had not yet rehung the curtains, and the oriental screens were still folded in a corner.

'What is this room?' asked Madame Sofia. 'An opium den?'

Caspar laughed. 'What an exotic use for my humble studio.'

'It smells of men.'

'Funnily enough, my friend Collingwood said the same. Or at least he asked if it had been used as a gymnasium. It may have been for all I know. I have made friends with Collingwood at last. Why don't we walk along the road and call on him?'

'You are very anxious to get me out of here.'

'Come now, sit down.' He moved a chair away from the table and closer to the window. 'Tell me why you are in such a strange mood.'

Madame Sofia sat down with her back to the window. Caspar sat behind the table.

'I have heard from Mrs Hanbury,' she said.

'Ah, poor Mrs Hanbury.'

There was a silence. Madame Sofia shifted uneasily in her chair. With the light behind her she was looking into the room, at Caspar sitting at the table with the dark hangings on the wall behind him and the bright cushions scattered on the floor around him.

'All is not well,' she said.

'Mrs Hanbury,' Caspar sighed. 'Such is life.'

'There are too many people in this room,' said Madame Sofia suddenly.

'What are you talking about?'

Madame Sofia was breathing heavily. 'I have seen those Indians before. They were wanting to kill you. But why are there children? Do they want to kill the children? What is this? And men with such faces. Who are these people without clothes? What is this place?'

Caspar jumped to his feet, knocking over his chair. 'Stop that. Remember what I know about you.'

'This crowd — why is that child on the floor? What have you been doing here?'

'Stop it.' Caspar took her roughly by the arm and tried to pull her to her feet. 'If you don't like this room we'll leave it. It was a gymnasium, that's what you're seeing.'

'It is something much worse than a gymnasium now.' Madame Sofia sat solidly in her chair. 'Mrs Hanbury wrote to me to say that she had looked through your door and seen a naked man. She also heard a child. She was afraid you were indulging yourself in some horrible practices. But it was far worse than she thought. You were not indulging yourself. You were indulging others.'

'You know that I can have you turned out of this country to-morrow.'

'Of course. But I will bring you to justice today.'

'You are mad. You have no evidence. No one will believe you. Come with me now to hear what Collingwood has to say. He has visited me here. He knows it is my studio. I have lent him the essay I have been working on. He has been reading it.'

'I do not need evidence. I know.'

'Other people need evidence if they are to believe you.' Caspar's upper lip was trembling uncontrollably. 'They won't believe you. They will say you are a mad old woman who has listened to the hysterical ravings of a rejected mistress. Ungrateful bitch. Didn't I see to it that her husband won the competition for the hideous hotel she was so anxious he should build? Not that she cared about him. She only wanted to be able to queen it in the City among her paltry friends.'

'How did you see to it?'

Caspar made an effort to control his anger. He spoke more calmly.

'Professor Dacre is a friend of mine.'

'A friend? Or a victim?'

'Come now. You are overwrought. We are both overwrought. We shouldn't quarrel. Let us calmly walk along the road and see Collingwood. He will set your mind at rest. He knows I work here, we'll talk about my work. You'll come to your senses, indeed you will.'

'I am willing to see Collingwood.'

Madame Sofia stood up and went to the door.

'You have completely misinterpreted everything,' said Caspar, following her. 'That's what it is, misinterpretation. You will understand that and then I will forgive you.'

Madame Sofia said nothing, beginning her slow descent of the narrow stairs.

Stephen Collingwood was trying to write a sermon. The Bishop had responded unfavourably to his offer to go down to Ventnor, saying that a matter of such importance as the possibility of leaving the ministry would need much thought and prayer and that to delay their meeting until mid-September could only be beneficial. Stephen had decided that the outcome of his interview when it eventually came about was a foregone conclusion and had written to his cousin in New Zealand proposing a visit. The brief exhilaration – exhaltation even – which had resulted from his encounter with Charlotte had not lasted. She had her family to go home to; fond though he had become of Petchumah and Wilf they hardly constituted a similar tie. He was not happy, but he was able to forgive himself. So in his diary he wrote of practical matters, parish affairs and preparations for his journey. He read everything he could find about New Zealand, he visited blind Mrs Bennett, indigent Joan Greenway and the now bed-ridden Mr Scammell, and he offered them no more than small talk and his mere presence. Mrs Caws succumbed, as she had been threatening to do for some time, to her rheumatics, and Stephen accepted Anne Smallwood's surprising offer to replace her as cleaner to the men's night refuge. He turned a blind eye to Anne's rather ghoulish interest in the men's physical and mental welfare, telling himself that it was a better way for her to cause him embarrassment than her former methods and that he could hardly expect her to stop being embarrassing altogether. He walked on the hills as usual but no longer haunted the grove of beeches from which he might hope to catch a glimpse of Charlotte in her distant garden; he tried to improve the accuracy of his nature notes. In his sermons he expounded as simply as he could what he took to be the Christian ethic. 'What did I expect of myself?' he wrote in his diary. 'Saintliness? Even perhaps some kind of renown? What arrogance! I shall become a labourer, a shepherd of real sheep instead of human ones. I shall do better there.'

When Madame Sofia and Caspar Freeling called on him he was putting together his sermon for the following Sunday. After the long dry summer there was the possibility of a water shortage on Haul Down. In the past Stephen might have been tempted into all sorts of metaphors; in his new realistic mood he proposed to advise his parishioners to take their turn at the standpipe with consideration for their neighbours and to remind themselves that it could not be long before it rained. Not much inspired by this theme, he was relieved to hear a knock on the door and to be told shortly afterwards by Wilf that Madame Sofia and Mr Freeling had come to call.

'How delightful to see you both,' he said at once, going to meet them. As they came into the room he added, concerned by their appearance, 'Has something happened?'

'Oh, we've had a stupid argument, that's all,' said Caspar airily. He put his hand over his mouth for a moment and went on, 'We need only to talk a little, regain our sense of proportion. Madame Sofia thinks all sorts of strange things about me.'

'I am sorry to hear that.' Stephen pushed forward his largest armchair. Madame Sofia sat down heavily and in silence.

'Oh, she'll soon cheer up,' said Caspar in the same tone. 'Now tell me, how did you get on with my essay?'

Stephen turned the chair on which he had been sitting away from the desk and sat down. 'You make me feel like a schoolmaster. I'm no judge.'

'I'd like your opinion all the same.'

'I'm not in touch with the sort of work with which it ought to be compared,' said Stephen weakly.

'You're too modest.'

'Let me say then that I'm impressed by your learning.'

Caspar Freeling looked at Madame Sofia with an expression so fiercely triumphant that Stephen, bewildered, could think of no alternative to honesty. 'Very impressed. And I see all the apparatus of scholarship. But I cannot quite accede to – that is to say, I cannot altogether find – the content.'

'Exactly!' said Madame Sofia loudly. 'This is because he is a void. He can pretend to anything, he can assume any voice. But there is nothing there. He is a void, a fraud.'

Caspar almost shrieked with rage. 'Listen to her. She calls me a fraud. How many gullible idiots has she cheated by pretending to hear voices from the dead? For money. And she calls me a fraud.'

Stephen raised his hands in the air.

'Stop! I have no idea at all what either of you is talking about.'

Madame Sofia leant forward in her chair and fixed her dolorous eyes on Stephen's.

'Mr Collingwood, there is evil here.'

Stephen found himself unable to look away from the extraordinary solemnity of those pale slightly protruding eyes.

'What do you mean?'

'This man has been providing the means for weak men of low desires to satisfy those desires, he has used the hold he has thus gained over them for improper ends, and he has corrupted, or used, or for all I know destroyed, children.'

Stephen, his gaze still held by hers, was convinced of her sincerity, and surprised by her authority; but he could not yet quite grasp what it was that she was telling him, and he clung to the idea that she might be deluded. He forced himself to look at Caspar, and was not reassured. Caspar had assumed an expression of pitying superiority, but the anger which he had made an effort to control still made him tremble, and he was sickeningly pale.

'The woman is out of her mind,' he said in a thin voice, falsely calm. 'I can only assume that she is trying to discredit me because she regrets having told me certain things about her private financial affairs which she knows would be of interest to the authorities in Baden-Baden.'

Stephen looked questioningly at Madame Sofia.

'This is true,' she said. 'He can ruin me.'

'Men of the utmost distinction come to my studio here to discuss antiquarian matters,' continued Caspar more firmly. 'Nothing could be more innocent. Ask Tranmer, for example. Everyone knows Tranmer will vouch for me. Go and ask him. Go now, and finish the matter.'

Madame Sofia was silent for some moments. Then she said slowly, 'Poor woman. Ah, poor woman.'

Caspar said quickly, 'All this was started by Mrs Hanbury. She's a poor woman indeed, mad with jealousy.'

Madame Sofia shook her head slowly. Then she said to Stephen, 'I have a man waiting at the end of the street with a fly. Do you want him to drive us to Mr Tranmer?'

As Stephen hesitated, Caspar said, 'Yes, yes, go, the two of you. Tranmer will tell you you're making a ridiculous mistake. You'll come back and apologize. I'll be along there in my studio. I've work to do.'

A faint violet haze over the City now foreshadowed darkness. The shops and markets were closed, the evening train drawing in to the station brought workers returning home from nearby towns, the rumble of traffic from the streets was reduced, and the sound of the seagulls round about the warehouses by the river seemed louder as a result. Rattling over the bridge, Madame Sofia and Stephen sat side by side in silence behind the impassive back of their driver; they heard the clamorous birds and felt the awful seriousness of their errand. Madame Sofia's silence was morose, and at the same time portentous; she felt herself to be the agent of retribution, but she took no pleasure in the role, even the pleasure often felt by those who do their duty. Madame

Sofia was not interested in duty. As they turned towards the Botanical Gardens, skirting the centre of the City, she sighed deeply. Stephen said nothing. Shocked, confused, and now that he was alone with Madame Sofia embarrassed, he was determined to suspend judgement until he could talk to Herbert Tranmer, whom he liked and respected.

'Perhaps', he said hesitantly, 'I ought to speak to Tranmer alone?'

'He would bamboozle you. I shall leave at the right moment.'

So they were both shown in to the comfortable study which looked out on to the garden and the apple trees which Charlotte Moore's children had been climbing only that morning. The house smelt of the apple and mulberry jam which Rosalind Tranmer had been making. She was out at a meeting, the maid told them, but was expected back soon.

Herbert Tranmer rose from his desk to greet them with his customary warmth, tempered as it often was by a lingering air of preoccupation, as if he had been considering matters of high import but was content to put them momentarily aside in the interests of friendship.

'Of course, you will tell us we're quite wrong,' said Stephen, impressed as always by Tranmer's presence. 'I hope you'll forgive us.'

'Mr Collingwood will never come to the point,' said Madame Sofia. 'I have been to see Mr Freeling in his so-called studio on Haul Down. I have accused him of running an immoral establishment and making prostitutes of children. I have absolute proof. He persists in denying it all and has sent us to you to support his denial. Or not, as the case may be.'

Herbert Tranmer sat very still, his face magisterially grave.

'What is this absolute proof?'

'I have seen it.'

'You have seen . . .?'

'I have seen what happens in that room.'

There was silence for several minutes. The grandfather clock in the corner of the room ticked, Madame Sofia's breathing caused her corset to creak, Stephen Collingwood looked at Herbert Tranmer.

Madame Sofia rose to her feet. 'Now it is time for me to go,' she said to Stephen Collingwood. 'I must start my packing.'

Since Tranmer made no move, Stephen followed Madame Sofia to the door as if to show her out, but she put one hand firmly on his chest and said, 'Go back. You have him now.'

Tranmer was sitting motionless in his chair. There was no colour in his face and his protuberant white forehead was shining with sweat.

'Oh, my dear Tranmer, how can this be?' said Stephen.

Tranmer's voice was unrecognizable; it had become thick and nasal, as if some injury had afflicted his larynx.

'I knew something would happen. Ever since the competition, I knew. He used all this to get what he wanted. It might be anything, sometimes something quite trivial, nothing much at all, just to feel his power. I knew he'd go too far.'

'The competition?'

'Dacre was one of them. Freeling made him give the prize to Hanbury to please Mrs Hanbury, who's his mistress. I've been in Hell. I wanted to get out of it. Why are we made like this?'

'But how did you know about it? Why did you go there?'

'He could tell. He got me there on some pretext. It was supposed to be about the Druids. He did it with a show of ritual. We had instructions. We had to wear masks.' Tranmer's large frame began to heave and tears poured down his cheeks. 'I only looked. At first I only looked.'

'I shall go to the police as soon as possible in the morning. I must. Otherwise he could simply move on.'

'He moved here from Oxford. He thought someone was suspicious. He meant to stop. He told me that. He thought it was too dangerous. He wasn't interested in it himself. They followed

him, Dacre and one or two others, begged him to go on. It was
the meetings, the ritual, the dressing up, it made it all seem
unreal, that's to say possible, the impossible was possible. He
called himself the enabler.'

'But you, of all people?'

The sobs increased. 'I didn't hurt them. I was always kind.
Some people hurt them.'

'Kind?'

Tranmer gave a loud groan and dropped out of his chair on to
his knees at Stephen's feet.

'Despise me. Oh, but forgive me. You must forgive me. You
are a clergyman. It is your duty. I will come to your church.'

'No. Go to a church where you can sit out of sight. When you
dare to join in the general confession, knowing what you know
about the devices and desires of your own heart, join. That is, if
you truly repent. I am not a good enough clergyman to allow
you the luxury of pouring out your soul-sickness at my feet. I
haven't the patience.'

He turned away and leaving the house began his last walk
through the City.

It seems he felt as though Peter Tilsley were with him. When he
reached his room on Haul Down and, unable to sleep, sat down
at his desk, he wrote in his diary, 'It was as if Peter danced and
hopped around me, with his wild hopes and his unexpected
earthiness, pleading with me not to despair. I think I ignored him
at first, poor little wraith, but then as we climbed the steep hill to
Haul Down it seemed he was pulling me up it. I was always
surprised by his wiriness. I left the miserable Tranmer without
pity and tramped along to the Circus as if I were on a route
march through the desert. Past the gardens where the crowd
once gathered to see the Queen – now emptied by evening,
waiting for rain – past the cold perfection of the Great Crescent,
whose abstract harmony disdains the discordant world, along the

street of seemly façades (seeing my dour reflection in the window of an antique shop), round the corner towards the house where Madame Sofia lodges. And then I hesitated. What could I do but tell her she was right? She knew that already. I saw the lights in her windows between the drawn curtains and imagined her moving slowly to and fro consigning the strange properties among which she lives to trunks and boxes, putting the parrot and the sparrows in their travelling cages, labelling the stuffed ape. I found a piece of paper and a pencil in my pocket. I wrote, "I go to the police early tomorrow morning. I will come on to see you and to offer you what help I can." I crossed the shadowy gaslit circle of houses. Its elegance seemed a fragile imposition; a stage set for a comedy of manners in which no one had learnt their part and half the cast were drunk. Peter I suppose would say, yes, but you still have to set the stage, imagine the play, and then I would say, remember who your actors are. Anyway, Peter died; what kind of scene was that?

'So I marched down the hill towards the centre of the City thinking of Peter, not of Tranmer, nor of Freeling, because Peter had always given me something to think about, and I wanted then to think, not merely to feel. By the time I had walked down the street in which the Hanburys live – there were no lights on in their house, she being, I suppose, still in Ireland and he not at home – crossed the quiet square into which it leads and come to that part of the City where people move around even at night, I found that my mind was clearer. I could think of Freeling and Tranmer with a coolness which surprised me. I can see no alternative to going to the police about Freeling; he has to be stopped. He moved to the City from Oxford because he was afraid of being found out. Then he continued his activities. Something drastic has to be done to stop him. If he has to go to prison, so be it. He is a deceiver and a self-deceiver; he will emerge from prison under another name and become another man; whether he will ever be a better man, I can't tell. As for

Tranmer, I shan't mention him. I believe he is as likely to repent without punishment as if he is ruined by scandal. If later on he wants to resume relations with me of course I shall not refuse, if only for the sake of his wife; but I shall hope to have dealings with him by correspondence only, for I mean to be very far away. All my hopes now are pinned on this.

'In the part of the City which I had so far crossed the streets had been quiet, such carriages as passed sedate, such scenes as I had glimpsed through the windows peaceful, calm first-floor drawing-rooms, dignified dining-rooms where servants were snuffing out the candles, all the pretensions, all the pretences, in place. When I came to the older part of the City there was noise and movement. Some kind of trading seemed still to be going on, small shops were lit up and selling tobacco and grog. The public houses were open and noisy. Some barefooted children asked me for money and a mongrel dog barked after them when they ran off with the pennies I gave them.

'Perhaps the dog started the trouble; however it was, there seemed suddenly to be other dogs fighting under my feet, three great brutes doing their best to kill each other. And then everyone seemed to be shouting and screaming and two men were hard at it with their fists, presumably each championing his own dog. One woman was shrieking at a drunken fellow leaning against a wall who seemed to have caused the trouble by having a bitch in season. Others, both men and women, were laughing horribly and shouting indiscriminate encouragement at fighting men and fighting dogs. A big man with some authority among them – perhaps the publican – came out with a bucket of water and threw it over the dogs, drenching them; no one seemed much concerned about the men, who continued to struggle and curse. This was not the City I knew. This was Pandæmonium, the City of Satan. A woman put her hand on my arm as I hurried towards the bridge. She grinned horribly. "Want to talk?" she said. Two others standing in the shadow of one of the warehouses shouted at me but the sound of the train steaming over the bridge on the other side of the river drowned their voices. Raucous singing came from a barge tied up beside the quay. Taking the steps which lead up the hill I began to climb until I could look back and see the dim night-time City behind me, the towers of the Abbey clearly discernible in the middle, the ghostly crescents and squares receding up the hill behind. I thought of Peter urging me on and I wanted to say stop, think, what is the use of a vision which bears no relation to reality, and he seemed to be dancing on ahead with his wild laugh, his queer hoarse voice, saying "It does. It is. Reality's only a step behind. Come on."

'So I came on and sit here and tell myself to obey the psalmist and forbear to occupy myself with great matters which are too high for me. Think of that country the other side of the world, think of great spaces of grassland and untouched forest, clear rivers, fruitful seas, mountains untouched by man.

'I saw a merlin the other day, a little hawk I used to see at home on the Malverns. I had never seen one in these parts, and know them to be very rare. It was a female, on her way south perhaps, a bird of passage. I had stopped on a walk above the quarries and was sitting still on a rock when I noticed her below me on the steep hill, perched on a fence. I had plenty of time to watch her, being behind and above, and I could see the detail of her soft grey-brown plumage, the wide dark bands on her long tail, and then, as she turned to look about her, her bright yellow eye and the delicacy of the fawn and cream feathering of her throat. She turned her head right round to look at me before she flew straight and fast back into the wood. I felt the intensity of her existence and her glorious independence of me. So now I remind myself that there are places in this world which are not the City, and species in this world which are not Man.'

When he had finished writing in his diary, Stephen felt calmer, and able to compose himself for sleep.

*

The light in Caspar's studio burned late. He sat in an armchair in the middle of the room, waiting. The rest of the furniture was piled together behind him, the hangings and cushions on top of it. From time to time he took his watch out of his waistcoat pocket and looked at it. About midnight there was a scratch on the door; Caspar ignored it. It came again, and he opened the door. He looked coldly at the white-faced child who stood there, and said, 'You're not wanted.'

It was Albert, who used to hold Charlotte Moore's horse until he told her he had better things to do. He leant against the door frame nonchalantly.

'I'm hungry.'

'Go home.'

'She's out at work, and left me nothing to eat.'

Caspar looked at his watch again.

'You can have some bread and cheese, I suppose.'

The boy came into the room, with an odd half-swaggering, half-cringing walk which was like a caricature of Caspar's own.

'Wait,' said Caspar. He went over to the pile of furniture and bending down beside it took up a large earthenware jug. 'Take this to the Bear, the boy there'll still be around, he sleeps under the bar. Tell him to fill it up with beer, say I sent you. Here you are.' He pulled some coins out of his pocket. 'On your way back you can tell the others, Tom and his sister and her friend, tell them if they come with you they'll get bread and cheese and beer. You can sleep here if you want.'

The boy took the jug and disappeared down the stairs. Caspar returned to his armchair and waited for some time. When Albert eventually came back he was silently followed by three other children about his age, that is to say, between eight and twelve.

'Go and wash,' said Caspar, irritably.

Hustling together they went into a corner of the room where there was a jug of water, a flowered china bowl and some soap, and made attempts to clean their hands and faces. Caspar meanwhile produced two loaves of bread and a large piece of cheese and set them on the floor beside the jug of beer. He pulled some of the cushions from the pile he had made and threw them down beside the food. The children fell on the food and ate, tearing the bread with their hands; as their hunger abated they began also to pass round the jug of beer, lifting it to their mouths one by one.

'Has any of you told anyone about this place?' said Caspar casually.

They shook their heads.

'You told us not to,' said one of the girls, a black-haired ten-year-old who might have had gypsy blood.

'And it hasn't been so bad has it, coming here?' said Caspar.

They shook their heads again. The girl who had spoken before, who seemed less sleepy than the others, patted her tangled black curls as if she were in front of a mirror and said with a false smile and a strangely genteel accent, 'It's been very nice, thanks.'

Caspar, disconcerted, wondered for a moment if she might be mocking him, but then from her glazed eyes deduced she was either very stupid or feeling the effects of the beer. The other children looked away. Albert kept his pale remoteness but the older girl looked frightened and the boy Tom made a brief desperate grimace. Disorientated though they were, determined also in their varying degrees to cling on to their meagre payments and bury their secrets, they knew that 'very nice' was not an adequate description of what usually happened in that room, and they felt obscurely that they might be punished for that inaccuracy.

Caspar got to his feet and pulled out more cushions.

'Go on, sleep, make yourselves comfortable. Food and rest, what more d'you wan̊t?'

With relief they accepted the cushions and bedded themselves down. They were tired and a little drunk; in a very short time all four of them slept, deeply as children do.

'Yes, but you are meaningless,' Caspar said dispassionately, seeing from his armchair that they were all asleep. 'Meaningless, meaningless, meaningless, the whole lot of you.'

He had written a letter to the Home Office containing all he knew about Madame Sofia, her financial speculations in Baden-Baden and the charge laid against her there of obtaining money on false pretences. He had posted it on his way down to his rooms near the Abbey, where he had gone as soon as Stephen Collingwood and Madame Sofia had left in the hired carriage to go and see Herbert Tranmer.

Caspar's anger against his denouncer had faded with her disappearance; he had become practical. She must be informed upon, and would therefore have to leave the City and most probably the country. Then he must clear his own passage. Once back in his City rooms he had packed his belongings and left with two leather bags. He had told his landlady that he would send for his heavy trunks later. He had paid his rent, made his excuses (urgent business, unexpected changes to his plans, nothing to concern herself about), had left, deposited his two bags at the station, climbed the hill to Haul Down once more, and set about the thorough dismantling of the studio. Then he had sat on the chair and waited. His mind was quite clear and his thoughts unemotional. He thought it possible that Tranmer might stand fast. If so he expected Collingwood to come and apologize, and he was ready to forgive, prepared for a long talk about the vagaries of women, with instances of Madame Sofia's previous delusions and remembered remarks of a Viennese uncle of his mother's who had worked for a physician specializing in hysteria. As the hours passed this conversation seemed less and less likely to take place. Caspar began to think he had better be ready to cut his losses. Perhaps because he had so often had to think quickly in order to save himself from humiliation of one kind or another, he was very quick to adjust his view of things. His past life, or his own vision of his past life, consisted of a series of superimposed and more or less merging histories, each created to meet the needs of the moment, each convincing because he himself believed in it. To the extent that he knew that some of these stories – or some parts of them – were not history so much as fiction, to that extent there was a continuous undercurrent of anxiety in his life, expressing itself sometimes in a sharp irritability, but that knowledge was buried very deep. There was a sense in which he was a brilliant impersonator, so brilliant that he even fooled himself.

As he sat there in his bare room, the furniture piled behind him and the children asleep on the cushions in one corner, and the one oil lamp burning lower and lower, he seemed to watch Stephen Collingwood fade from a potential friend and fellow scholar to a narrow-minded provincial clergyman whom he had never liked; the City became a boring interlude in a life of adventure and promise, Madame Sofia a madwoman who had lost her head over his well-meant attempt to entertain a few friends too sophisticated for this dull abode of respectability. London was the proper field for his exploits. He would lose himself in its darker corners for as long as necessary, and emerge when the time was right. All he had to deal with for the moment were a few immediate practicalities.

By first light – the faint preliminary pallor that comes before sunrise – the oil lamp had burned very low. Caspar looked at his watch once more and saw that it was time to walk down the hill, collect his bags and catch the early mail train to Paddington. None of the tired children stirred as he stood up, took the lamp and left the room. Holding the lamp before him to light his way, he went quietly down the stairs, paused in the dingy entrance hall to look around him for a moment, then put the lamp on the floor, tipping it slightly so that it leant, guttering, against the wooden banister. He shut the door of the house behind him, hesitated momentarily, then quickly turned the key in the lock and hurried along the narrow street. Keeping close to the wall he turned down the alleyway which led eventually to a narrow flight of steps which took him down the hill towards the river and the railway. As he crossed the bridge over the river he put his hand on the rail and let the key fall into the calm water.

When some of the little streets of eighteenth-century cottages on Haul Down were pulled down in the 1960s they were replaced by ill-designed boxes running counter to the contours of the hill, but on the other side of the church, and beyond the few old buildings immediately behind it, there is a better example of similar redevelopment, a terrace built in late-Victorian times. The houses have gables with wooden pinnacles on top and strips of stained glass in floral designs beside their front doors; they might be in a quiet back street in some Isle of Wight seaside resort. They were built to raise the tone of the area, perhaps to attract a respectable lower-middle-class element which would modify Haul Down's reputation for squalor. It was an attempt to make a virtue out of necessity after the fire; an attempt which I suppose you could say succeeded.

The fire destroyed the old dispensary and gutted several of the houses on that side of the street. After the long dry summer all the woodwork, much of which was rotten anyway, was food for the flames as they spread along the street. None of the structures was sound; walls crumbled and roof beams crashed to the ground surprisingly quickly. The fire brigade took a long time to come because of the steepness of the hill the horses had to climb; by the time they arrived the great cloud of black smoke could be seen from every part of the City, shot through every now and then by gaudy tongues of flame.

Madame Sofia did not see it; she was in the train half-way to the nearby port. Reasoning that a day or two's stay at a quiet hotel near the harbour would hardly attract attention, she planned to arrive early, running no risk of underestimating Caspar Freeling's success in activating the authorities against her, and at the same time giving the impression of having just arrived in

England rather than of planning to leave it, thus arousing no suspicions on the part of the hotel staff. She intended to send for her heavier luggage, consign it to the care of the shipping line and book her passage on the first boat to America. She carried with her letters of the most encouraging kind from a community of seekers after truth in Vermont. No one could say she had lost her spirit of adventure.

She may have waited on the station for the westbound train and looked across the line in the pale early-morning light, before the flames on Haul Down would have been visible from where she stood, and seen Caspar Freeling pacing irritably up and down on the opposite platform, waiting for the London train. I can imagine the scene quite clearly, the quiet platforms, the few early travellers, wrapped up against the autumn chill, the one waiting porter with his trolley, the sudden recognition before the steaming engines came thundering between them, but I think it is a delusion; the London train left half an hour before the earliest one Madame Sofia could have caught. They must have made their separate flights without their paths recrossing, she bound for the New World, he for a very old one.

The sound of fire woke Stephen before the shouts. He slept with his window open, and thought at first a great wind must have started and come rushing through the trees and down the street; the sound was so unfamiliar and at the same time so frightening that he had run to the window before he was fully awake. Even when he looked down the street and saw the billowing smoke he was still thinking of air rather than fire and shouted to the man below, 'What is it? What's happened?'

'Fire,' shouted the running man, raising his hand, in which clanked a bucket.

Stephen pulled on some clothes and shouting for Wilf ran down the stairs and out into the street.

'Where is it?'

'The old dispensary!'

It was Ernie Tucker the railway worker who answered. He too was carrying a bucket. It seemed only a matter of moments before a chain of men and women had formed itself and was passing buckets of water from hand to hand between the stand-pipe and the fire. Apart from one or two shouted directions, they mostly worked in silence. A few women carrying or leading children hurried past in the other direction.

'Go into the church,' Stephen called. 'It's open, go in.'

'I'll get blankets.' Anne Smallwood ran to the door of the night refuge.

Another chain had been formed, passing buckets from the water trough. And then a terrible shriek came down the street, a woman's cry of terrifying despair.

Stephen ran forward. A dishevelled woman – could it have been the one who had tried to stop him as he crossed the bridge? – screamed, 'Albert! He's in there! He's with that Freeling!'

Stephen shouted into the smoke. 'Freeling, are you there? Where are you? Answer!'

The smoke seemed to swirl away from him and he could see the closed window of the studio, the flames leaping in the building below. He looked round for something to throw at the window and seeing nothing seized an empty bucket from the man behind him and hurled it. He heard the crash of breaking glass but the smoke came down again as if it had been thrown at him; then it thinned for an instant and he saw a white face, small and terrified, with long hair on either side of it.

'It's a girl. There's more than one of them in there.'

He pulled off his coat, and put it over his arm, ready to hold it in front of his face. He was stopped by a shouted command.

'No, sir. Wait here.' It was Wilf who had roughly pushed him aside, Wilf gigantic amidst the swirling bitter smoke. 'It is my right.'

Of course it was. It was Wilf's right, because he was a hero.

Stephen seized a full bucket and scrambling after him threw the water towards the foot of the staircase, then tossed the bucket back to the figure he could see waiting with hands outstretched behind him.

'Coming up.' It was Tucker again with a full bucket. Stephen seized and threw, gave back an empty bucket, received a full one, until through the smoke he saw the great Wilf with a child across his shoulders and running forward took the child and passed her back into the waiting arms behind him and took another bucket and threw it, and watched for Wilf until he came with the flames behind him now and another child, apparently unconscious, whom Stephen held briefly in his arms and handed on to Tucker while Wilf turned back into the flames. Stephen took another bucket and ran forward with it, trying to keep the flames from spreading up the stairs; he smelt his own hair burning; threw the water, ran back for another bucket, ran forward. With a loud crack the door jamb gave and the front wall of the house collapsed. The beam caught Stephen on the back of the neck and he smelt the stone as it thundered round him. Even as he fell he knew that the hands which were held out to receive the children and which all along the street were keeping steady the chain of buckets, full and empty, would dig for him. These people would bend to listen for him, their voices would encourage him, the strength in their arms and shoulders would heave him out. That was what he would do for them, if he could. The half-thought came to him in the darkness that he should sing, to show them where he was, but then he thought he would sing in a minute, because he wanted to concentrate. He wanted to be able to say to himself, who would have thought (like George Herbert), who would have thought my shrivelled heart could have recovered greenness, but he could hardly even ask himself, why now. Not because his mind was not clear, rather that it was too clear. That which had been true long ago on the hills was true again. Insofar as there was room for thought, he did not want to think. His consciousness was too full of what was beyond thought. Pushing all the same a thin probe of reason into that consciousness he found only affirmation. It was so. If it was music, it was a tune he knew. Crouched in the heavy darkness, his head on his knees, he was wrapped in sublime astonishment, feeling himself held in the hand of God.

PART FOUR

I like the idea that no one knows how migrating birds navigate; I've read somewhere that scientists think it quite probable that different species use different methods, some relying on the trade winds, some responding to the earth's magnetism, some guided by the sun or the stars. There's seldom a single explanation for anything, and you can make most things shift or tilt or change their focus according to which explanation you favour. I believe myself, though many don't, that one may arrive at a truth that's as near absolute as will do for a human brain; only one needs to know such a vast amount of detail to get there. I remember trying to say something of the sort to one of my A-level class who was being very decided in his views about the causes of the English Civil War (all Charles I's fault, he thought). He looked at me kindly and said, 'I know, Sir, but I don't want to muddle the examiners.' He got a scholarship. What's more he ended up in Mrs Thatcher's Think Tank; perhaps he identified her with Oliver Cromwell. Anyway, the motives for Rosalind Tranmer's dedication to the improvement of primary education, for which she later became famous, may have been many, and it would be wrong to make too much of the fact that her decision to concentrate on practical social reform rather than on revolutionary politics dates from the autumn of the year of the royal visit, soon after the evening on which her husband was confronted in his study by Madame Sofia and Stephen Collingwood. Thirty years later, when Charlotte Moore wrote to congratulate her on having been awarded the CBE, she wrote in answer, 'Do you remember all those years ago when that strange old Madame Sofia said she could see poor pale children behind me in the Botanical Gardens, and I was so angry with her because I thought someone must have told her that I minded not having children of my own? I think of it sometimes and wonder if they might have been some of the ones I've been able to do something to help – but perhaps I'm getting sentimental in my old age, and anyway didn't we agree she was a fraud?'

If she had known exactly what had taken place at that confrontation in her husband's study – or perhaps one should say if she had allowed herself to know exactly – she might not have reminded Charlotte of the episode in the Botanical Gardens, because there was another possible interpretation of the children's manifestation, which was that they had more to do with Herbert than with Rosalind. However it was, the balance between the two of them seemed to change from then on. Rosalind became increasingly active in public life and Herbert after a period of obscure ill-health devoted his energies only to writing. The pamphlets became books; from critiques of Fabian policies he proceeded to a history of the world. Rosalind was elected to the local school board, where she was soon agitating for medical inspections, then she found allies in London and went to work in children's clinics in the East End. She was endlessly busy, writing, speaking, organizing. She persuaded Herbert's family trust to endow infant schools in Stepney; they still exist. There was a time when Herbert's white face and large protruding forehead were to be seen in a poorly lit side-pew in the Abbey during Matins, but how long his church-going lasted is not clear; the Tranmers shortly moved to London, and lived in Bloomsbury. Rosalind spent much time at meetings in Stepney and Herbert often worked in the library of the British Museum.

What Rosalind knew about Herbert, and what Herbert knew about himself, remains obscure. What is clear is that Herbert must have felt himself remarkably lucky when he realized the implications of the news which travelled round the City on the morning after the fire and which was so widely mourned, that the eager hands which dug for Stephen Collingwood, as he had known they would, had found him dead. Caspar Freeling had got away with it, if only by the skin of his teeth.

It may have been rarer in those days for a woman to keep her beauty beyond her first youth. Or it may have been something about the particular incandescence of Charlotte's looks which made them so remarked upon. No reference that I have found in such diaries and letters as I have been able to dig up omits to mention the effect on people of her appearance, her smile, her manner. She would have been a familiar sight to the people of Haul Down, but she and her husband must have made a sad contrast with their surroundings as they walked down the half-destroyed street, Charlotte holding tightly on to Harry's arm, through the tired survivors of the fire. They came as soon as they heard of the disaster, and did what they could to help organize recovery. It was Harry who having been told by Wilf of Stephen's brother in Worcestershire wrote to tell him the full story of Stephen's death and to offer any help he could over funeral arrangements (this was before they were taken out of everyone else's hands by the Bishop). Charlotte went upstairs with the weeping Petchumah and knelt for a little beside her dead friend, trying to draw comfort from his serene face and aware only of the absence of anything that was him. The modest Wilf said nothing of his own heroism in saving the children; when the story emerged from the accounts of those who had witnessed it he shrugged it aside, only blaming himself for having failed to reach Stephen in time to save him too, though the fact seems to have been that Stephen died from internal injury rather than suffocation.

The brother and his wife came over from Worcestershire.

They stayed in a hotel but accepted lunch from the Moores. Harry pressed them to stay, saying they would have more privacy than in a hotel, but Charlotte knew they would refuse; she had seen at once that in Mrs Collingwood's cold eyes a provincial quarry-owner's family could not be considered the social equals of the landed gentry.

Harriet Collingwood was a plump person with useful practical qualities but no imagination.

'It amazes me', she said to Charlotte, 'that my brother-in-law could have lived so long in a pleasant city such as this and never got to know anyone of his own sort.'

Charlotte said a little sadly that she had not thought of it like that.

'I wrote to him when we first heard he was coming here,' continued Mrs Collingwood undaunted. 'I told him about the Templetons, who came to live in one of those nice houses in the Great Crescent when General Templeton retired from the army. She was a Meade, one of the Warwickshire Meades, I used to see a lot of her as a girl. I don't believe Stephen ever followed it up. Such a strange thing to do, don't you think, to cut yourself off from your own kind?'

'Your brother-in-law was much liked in his parish.'

'Oh, parish work, yes, that's one thing. I'm sure he was always conscientious. My husband used to worry sometimes that he was too much that way. You know what I mean, like those dreadful Dissenters. But I always said he was never anything but a Broad Church man. He would never have been an Evangelical, I'm sure of that.'

'He was just a Christian, as far as I know.'

'Oh, my dear, as if it was ever as simple as that.'

Charles Collingwood had enough of his brother in him — though he was a more conventional version — and Harriet Collingwood enough unthinking arrogance to make any time spent with them distressing to Charlotte on a number of different counts. Finding her sitting quietly in an armchair in her bedroom one day after the Collingwoods had called to say they would be driving straight back towards Worcestershire as soon as the funeral was over, Harry was struck by the unfamiliar sight of Charlotte idle, rather than sewing or reading.

'You mustn't let that silly woman's patronizing ways lower your spirits,' he said. 'She's too stupid to notice what she's saying.'

'I know.'

'As for her husband, though he's a nice enough fellow he's not half the man his brother was.'

'No.'

'He valued his brother though. I've talked to him. He understands what a friend we have lost.'

'Stephen didn't like the wife.'

'That doesn't surprise me.'

'He said he hadn't much in common with his brother either. But they had been boys together.'

'Charlotte,' said Harry. 'Shall I fetch the children?'

She had been staring out of the window but now, surprised, turned to look at him.

'Why?'

'I thought you might like to play with them.'

'Oh, Harry, I am afraid I have been – I am sorry if I have been – difficult. I don't mean about being sad for Stephen's death, I mean before.'

Harry thought for a few moments. Charlotte waited, aware that there were things she hoped he would not say, anxious lest she had been unwise in giving him the opportunity to say them.

He said eventually in sober tones, 'I shall probably be difficult myself some time. And you will bear with me out of the goodness of your heart. It will even itself out in the end, you'll see.'

She gave him her warm smile and said she hoped she would do as well as he had done.

Charlotte had, I suppose, her way of explaining things. Or, one might say, her expectations. Or perhaps her faith. Or her myth. Being, as I am, her descendant, it may be that I have been heir to the myth, and have spent too much of my life trying to reconcile it with what I know of reality. Mary, my wife, was never very sympathetic towards my vague musings about and around my grandparents, partly no doubt because I was so imprecise. Mary was a very precise sort of person herself. So when I talked about people's ideas of themselves or about successive concepts of the ideal human being, or about changing styles in moral behaviour, she never quite gave me her full attention, preferring to be doing something else at the same time, like sticking in photographs or sorting socks. She never understood that I was not interested in family history and that I was using all these things as no more than islands in my own fantastic sea. Once she said, 'It seems morbid somehow, always thinking about the past.' I was shocked that she should betray such carelessness of what to me were the springs of joy.

The Bishop must have understood something about myths, or perhaps it was just a matter of what would now be called public relations. He decided to take possession of the martyrdom of Stephen Collingwood. He saw at once that it was too good an opportunity to miss. A curate of the Church of England had died in trying to save the lives of children, and what was more they were children of the slums, the lowest of the low. There were lessons to be drawn, about faith and works, about the impeccable standards of the Church, too often impugned by free-thinkers, Dissenters, Disestablishmentarians and other such troublemakers, about the imperative upon the poor to be ever more grateful to their betters, and about the particularly self-sacrificing ethos instilled into all his clergy by the Bishop of the diocese. The fact that Stephen had recently written the Bishop a letter, in which he said that, owing to the Bishop's unwillingness to see him despite the urgency of his request, he had been driven to take his decision without the benefit of the Bishop's advice and would be leaving the priesthood as soon as possible, could be conveniently forgotten.

'I know that sort of temperament,' the Bishop said to his wife, to whom he had complained about the letter when he received it. 'Moody, you know, up and down. I should soon have talked him out of it. A momentary depression. A moment's faltering in the path of faith. In view of later events it would be quite unfair to him to let his little temporary weakness be known. You didn't mention it to anyone, I suppose?'

She had not mentioned it; she seldom mentioned anything, except her health, and the weather, and the grandchildren. She quite agreed that it would be best forgotten, checking her thoughts well before they came to the conclusion that it might have been just as well it had all ended as it did. The Bishop made it known to Mr Charles Collingwood that he would be pleased to conduct his brother's funeral himself and that he would do so in the Abbey.

It was the beginning of two days of anxious negotiation. Charles Collingwood had his own views about what was appropriate. He would have preferred to have transported the coffin to Worcestershire and interred it in a corner of the quiet graveyard where several of the Collingwood ancestors lay, after a funeral service of customary seemliness attended by his neighbours and tenants, many of whom would have known Stephen as a boy. He recognized the Bishop's right to an interest, but asked him if he would not consider travelling to Worcestershire for the service and allowing himself and his wife the honour of putting him up for a night or two. The proposition did not suit the Bishop's purpose, and in saying so he managed to cause offence

to Mrs Collingwood, who felt that he was belittling the Collingwood family.

'Bishops are all very well in their way,' she said to her
husband. 'But in my view they should stick to their prayers and
not meddle. A funeral is a family affair. Families are judged by
their funerals. If he likes to take the service, well and good, as
long as he does it the way we want it, which it must be said we
can always rely on our own Mr Croker to do, but it is really not
up to him to decide where the ceremony should take place, or
indeed where your poor brother should be interred.'

Her husband, who was often amused by her incisiveness, said
he did not think she could get away with such a high-handed
attitude to any but their local bishop, who was anyway not very
important, being only a suffragan bishop; but as he more or less
agreed with her he did try tactfully to persuade the Bishop to
change his mind. In this he was supported by Harry Moore,
whom he had adopted as his adviser on local affairs. Harry,
advised in his turn by Charlotte, who knew a little though not all
of Stephen's relations with the Bishop, gave it as his view that
Stephen's love of his boyhood home and the hills he had known
so well made the quiet Worcestershire churchyard the most
appropriate resting-place. Here the Bishop in his turn took
offence; aspersions seemed to be being cast on the Abbey
cemetery, which had been laid out in the previous generation on
one of the hillsides overlooking the City and was widely agreed
to be an education in itself in regard to careful planting and
excellent monumental sculpture.

Charles Collingwood retired from the argument feeling that
his brother had been under the Bishop's command and in the last
resort would have to obey orders even after death, but, still
advised by Harry, he insisted on a simpler funeral than the
Bishop had at first envisaged. He was also surprised to be visited
in his rooms at the hotel on the morning before the funeral by
Charlotte, who begged him to allow Wilf and Petchumah to

follow the coffin behind himself and his wife. This request, which at first seemed to him an odd one, he acceded to after Charlotte had explained to him what the two of them had been in his brother's life, how he had interested himself in them and hoped they might have children, how they had joined with him in nursing a poor sick poet, and how they had gone together, the ex-soldier, the Indian woman, the poet and his brother, to watch the procession when the Queen came to visit the City. It gave Charles Collingwood, a man of good heart and ordinary enough ambitions, an idea of his brother's life which he did not wish to expand upon but which he found sobering; he conceded it gave Wilf and Petchumah the right to follow the coffin.

His wife disagreed.

'A black woman? You must be mad.' She had been out shopping when Charlotte called. Although she was in deepest mourning, it had seemed silly to miss the opportunity to buy a few nice pairs of gloves and perhaps some shoes; the shops in the City were so much better than the ones nearer home.

'She's not quite black you know,' her husband said peaceably. 'Quite a pleasant sort of brown.'

Harriet Collingwood sniffed. 'People might think he had some sort of connection with her.'

'She's married, my dear, and the man's a hero. The hero of the fire. The Mayor's already said he's to be given a special medal.'

'You don't think Stephen was up to anything?'

'Of course not, Harriet. Stephen was devoted to the memory of that poor little creature his late wife. We must try to think generously about this thing. After all, it is not as if we were on our own home ground.'

The vicar from the neighbouring parish conducted a short service of thanksgiving in the Chapel of St Catherine on Haul Down, thanksgiving for the deliverance of the people from the fire and for the sacrifice made on their behalf by their curate. It was poorly attended, partly because it was held on a weekday afternoon at three o'clock, when most of the inhabitants of Haul Down were either at work or if they had no work were past caring and possibly drunk, and partly because thanks had already been rendered most warmly to Wilf, and to the fire brigade who had eventually arrived and extinguished the fire, and partly because there was a feeling among those who might have attended and who had indeed been deeply shaken by the events of that night that someone was trying to keep them out of the Abbey. In this they were right. The Bishop had encouraged the vicar in his entirely well-meant endeavour because he did not think it appropriate that people from that part of the City should come to the funeral service in the Abbey. He thought it much more suitable that they should offer prayers for their late curate in their own parish church. He failed to take account of two things, the first being that the people of Haul Down very much enjoyed a good funeral, and the second that Stephen Collingwood had come to be looked on not only in his death but of late in his life as well as a Haul Down man.

It had been decided that the coffin should rest the night before the funeral in the church at the foot of the hill, a not very good example of Commissioners Gothic built about twenty years earlier at the height of the Victorian religious revival; it was deconsecrated in 1969 and is now used as a community hall. It was felt that the journey from there to the Abbey and from the Abbey to the cemetery would be of sufficient length for the undertakers' horses, rather than committing them to the long pull up the hill and the slow slippery descent. The undertakers were of course Messrs. Pearce and Whitcomb, whose high-class drapery and furnishing store took up most of one side of the main shopping-street and whose funeral department dealt in a seemly manner with the last rites of all the City's most distinguished citizens; this service in fact they still perform, though Pearce's, while keeping its own name, has passed into the hands of one of the big chain stores. They had in those days a formidable supply of funeral accoutrements, fine black horses and carriages, mutes, plumes, drapes, everything to meet the most exacting requirements. They were only allowed in this case to use a few of them; Charles Collingwood and the Moores had agreed that Stephen would have disliked anything more, and Harriet Collingwood's feeling that the family honour was being severely let down was subdued by the consideration that after all they hardly knew anyone in the City. She explained to her friends General and Mrs Stapleton that her brother-in-law had been an ascetic.

'I suppose every family has to have a saint,' was her way of putting it. 'Trying though they may be for general purposes.'

The hearse with its four black horses left the church followed on foot by the four black-clad mutes, wearing top hats and melancholy faces, and by a similarly adorned carriage containing Mr and Mrs Charles Collingwood, Wilf and Petchumah, all equally in black. Harriet Collingwood wore a large black bonnet and a thick black veil. Petchumah wore a black sari, whose purple braiding she had been sewing for two days, and kept her eyes fixed on the almost invisible face of Harriet, to whom she looked for guidance as to what demeanour it would be proper to adopt. Wilf sat very straight, eyes forward, as if on parade. Having made their slow way across the bridge – the river moving brightly beneath them, it being a day of soft autumn sunshine – and past the warehouses, where men stopped work and doffed their caps as they always did for a funeral, they came to the crowded street through which Stephen had walked late on his last night when he had thought in his despairing mood that it was like a street in Pandæmonium, the City of Lucifer. Here the front carriage drew briefly to a halt, and the four mutes, moving with surprising agility for men of such impregnable dignity, hoisted themselves up beside the coffin. Both carriages then set off at a rattling pace, the respectful populace scattering to either side of them. As soon as they reached the better part of the City and the quieter streets approaching the Abbey, the carriages slowed down, the mutes descended and resumed their solemn walk behind the hearse, and the little procession proceeded at its former slow pace. It was soon joined by other carriages, containing, all in black, the Moores, their friends the Tranmers, the Corfields, Major Spottiswoode and Lady Dalrymple Smythe, and Edwin Hanbury, immense and alone. As these people took their seats in the Abbey there was time for quiet conversation, agreement as to the shocking sadness of the occasion, an exchange of such information as was available as to what had actually happened, whether it was true that there had been a locked door and where it was supposed Mr Freeling had gone to (Madame Sofia's absence having not yet been noticed), whether that was the man who had been so brave and what a fine-looking fellow he was. Under cover of all this Charlotte was able anxiously to ask Rosalind Tranmer if her husband was quite well and to be told that he was not, and that Rosalind was afraid it might be his heart.

Our Abbey is not one of those monuments to the soaring imagination of the Gothic craftsmen of the Middle Ages in which England abounds. It was built later than most of those masterpieces and was anyway much restored in the early nineteenth century. The result, appropriately enough for the eighteenth-century city which surrounds it, is a building which lacks mystery but achieves a most reasonable harmony. There is very little stained glass, and the huge aisle windows admit an even light which often bathes the pale stone in filtered sunlight, showing up the confident fan-vaulting of the roof and making it easy to read the monuments and memorials from the City's grander past which crowd its walls. This was the light which shone on that October day on the small crowd of respectable citizens who had come to attend Stephen Collingwood's funeral, on the black-draped coffin and the attendant mourners, and on the Bishop, Rector and choir waiting by the vestry door to make their entrance. Into this clear light and waiting space there came the people of Haul Down.

It was the sound of heavy boots on the stone floor which first made heads turn among the group of quiet conversers in the front pews. A sombre crowd seemed to be swelling behind them, pushing in from the doors and encroaching on the nave, black shawls and capes, black crêpe, the occasional shabby black bonnet, black bowlers, armbands, knotted neckties, and still those noisy boots. They came without other sound but with confidence, taking their places without hesitation in pews for privacy in which worthy citizens not that day in attendance had paid their dues, working their way up the nave and into the side-aisles ever closer to the ranks of the respectable. They had been joined on their way from Haul Down by others of the City's poor. They had made a noticeable group coming as they did at a steady pace down their steep hill. There were children with them, and one or two babes in arms, but even these wore something black; not to wear black would have been to brand themselves infidels and outcasts, and though there were those among them whose knowledge of the Christian or any other faith was negligible and whose lives ran their course on the wrong side of most forms of authority, they knew what was required of them in regard to a funeral.

The leaders of the group were anything but outcasts; they would probably have counted as part of that great Victorian body, the respectable poor. They consisted of Mrs Tucker, with her husband, who worked on the railways, and their four sons, two of whom were old enough to have already followed their father in his profession and two of whom were schoolboys (there were two girls as well but they had left home to go into service some way away). There was old Mrs Bennett leaning on the arm of her daughter, who worked in the paper mill. There was Holloway the blacksmith, an important man in the community, with his son, who helped him in the forge. There was Anne Smallwood walking sedately beside her husband the carter, to whom she had recently become reconciled, and the family from the corner shop where Stephen had bought his tobacco. After that the respectability became less noticeable, with Joan Greenway, whose illegitimate child was considered a disgrace to the neighbourhood, some doubtful characters who frequented the Bear and knew Stephen as a passer-by who wished them a good morning but none of whom had ever been inside the church, and one old man with no roof to his mouth who turned up every few weeks at the night refuge where Stephen used to read and who, though he wore an old black hat, had not washed for weeks. They crossed the river soon after the two carriages, though not observed by their occupants, and as they walked through the crowded streets immediately after the bridge they were asked whose funeral it was, and much interest was shown in the answer. Everyone knew about the fire, and the rescue of the children, and the death of the vicar. Apart from the accounts of eye-witnesses, the whole story had been in the *City Herald*, with a portrait photograph of Stephen in his younger days provided by his brother and a posed group in front of the destroyed dispensary consisting of Wilf and the four children standing in a row staring fiercely at the camera; the children looked pathetic and in varying degrees patched and bandaged as if they ought all to be in bed. The general feeling about the curate was not only that it was a sad end but that he had been a good man, and a friend of the poor. That he had chosen to live on Haul Down rather than in a more salubrious part of the City was of course counted in his favour, but a number of actions and opinions were ascribed to him which would have surprised him. He was said to have been quite against landlords, on the strength of his having once or twice pleaded with the rent-collector on behalf of Joan Greenway, and to have stood no nonsense from the School Board man when he tried to take children away from useful work and set them to book-learning, and to have been in all sorts of ways against the Government and no enthusiast for the police.

At the same time there were those who were quite sure that many a poor child had learnt to read at his knee and that he had been a lifelong member of the Temperance Society.

For all these reasons, and doubtless others, such as there not being much else going on that day, the mourners from Haul Down gathered followers on their progress. Here and there someone ran to one of the nearby basements — those basements which had been painted up on the outside for the Queen's visit — and fetched a black shawl, or a cape of funeral crêpe; men put on their black bowlers.

To the Bishop this sombre and swelling influx into his handsome Abbey seemed a portent of the future, confirming his worst fears. He nodded to the Rector to indicate that the service should begin, the crucifer raised his silver cross, the organist, observant in his distant loft, began a solemn introit. The Bishop, walking slowly after the raised cross, wore an expression of controlled disgust.

Charlotte put her hand on Harry's arm and whispered, 'They've all come!'

Harry turned to look behind him and caught the eye of one of the quarrymen whom he knew. He slightly raised his hand; the man nodded in reply. As the service began Charlotte knelt and opened her heart to God the Father, as she had done ever since she had been a very small child, without having any clear idea of what the nature of such a being might be and indeed with a feeling, which had grown stronger rather than weaker since those childhood days, that it was beyond her capacity even to speculate on such a matter; this uncertainty did not seem to make it any harder for her to pray. She exposed her sorrow, and her hope that Stephen somehow might know that the people he had felt he was failing had come to pray for him at his funeral, and her ardent wish that he might not now be altogether separated from those things he had truly loved. She concentrated so hard that she remained on her knees not only during the solemn words of the funeral service but while the rest of the congregation rose to its feet and sang the psalm; Harry lightly touched her shoulder but as she did not move he left her kneeling, and after the next prayer when they rose from their knees together, she turned on him a clear untroubled gaze, as of one who had done all she could.

The Bishop meanwhile was mounting into the pulpit. He had prepared a short address, expressing first of all his personal sorrow at the loss of so valuable a minister in the diocese, then briefly eulogizing Stephen's qualities and devotion to duty, and ending with a recommendation that those assembled should remember to support and be grateful to the Church which had provided them with such an example of the truly Christian life. As he read from his notes, in his measured and mellow tones, he looked over them from time to time down the long light nave of the Abbey, and as he looked his indignation grew. It was not the sight alone, it was the smell. There was no incense to cover it, for he was a Broad Church man and did not countenance its use. It seemed to him that from that sombre mass of drab humanity at the back of the Abbey a smell of sweat and dirt and unwashed clothes came rolling up the aisle towards him, overwhelming on its way the faint messages of gentility from the front pews, the drop of eau-de-Cologne on fine white handkerchiefs, the echo of lavender bags on ladies' gloves. The faces back there seemed as far as he could tell to be turned towards him with the same attention as those nearer to him; the incidence of sleep seemed not much different in either group. In fact he thought he saw something more earnest in the faces at the back, something almost desperate, a kind of hunger. It was hunger, he felt, not for bread but for the bread of life; they wanted spiritual sustenance and it was his duty to give it to them.

'Oh, ye of little faith,' he suddenly apostrophized them, departing from his text. 'Why come ye not more often to the house of the Lord?' He paused dramatically. A slight stir passed along some of the furthermost pews, a kind of settling, such as children make when listening to a story. 'If the future is in your hands,' continued the Bishop, 'if it is that to which you lay claim, regardless of the advice, of the example, of the generations of service given to you by those in a position to know what is best, then this is what we have all to ask ourselves – what will you do with it? You proliferate, you breed, without a thought of how you are to be fed, you reach out your hands in greed for everything the world has to give, with not a moment's consideration of what may be left when you have taken what you want, or of what you will be destroying when you sweep away the barriers which you believe have kept you from wealth and power. Power! What would you do with power? Have you prepared yourselves for it by years of education and training and self-discipline? What do you know of the arts of administration? Or of art of any kind? How under your sway can our cities fail to spread and deteriorate and become ever uglier and more vulgar, our culture be lost to barbarism, our morals be undermined by atheism, our politics be poisoned by demagoguery? Where is deference, where the due order of hierarchy? Are we all to be drawn down into a vortex of moral chaos and mere animalism, sucked into that spiritual void which calls itself democracy? We have to ask ourselves these questions, in the name of humanity.'

Mrs Tucker looked along the pew and caught the eye of Anne Smallwood; Mr Tucker, following the direction of her glance, met the gaze of his friend the tobacconist. All four nodded sententiously. Nearer to the pulpit, Charlotte put her hand on Harry's arm again and whispered, 'I don't like this sermon.'

'Pompous ass,' said Harry in a peaceable tone but rather loud.

Rosalind Tranmer poked him two or three times rather hard in the shoulder to show her agreement. Edwin Hanbury gave her a look of lofty reproach. Lady Dalrymple Smythe, unwilling to be excluded, sneezed.

'We have to ask ourselves these questions,' the Bishop continued, as sonorously as before, 'whether we have been born in exalted positions or whether we count ourselves among the lowest. We have to ask ourselves for what purpose we have been made.'

Charlotte whispered to Harry, 'Don't move, I'll be back so quickly. I need a little air.'

Before he could answer she had slipped out of the pew and rustled down the side aisle.

'And when you come to play cricket,' the Bishop was saying, a tremor of emotion in his deep voice, 'will you play for the honour of the game, or will you play to do the other fellow down? The friend we are here to commemorate played for the honour of the game. He did not win it. Is he not the English gentleman at his best?'

But he had lost his audience, particularly that part of it which was sitting in the front pews. Perhaps they were not yet ready to receive his message. Referring with outward calm to his notes the Bishop could not for the moment recall what his message was. Edwin Hanbury, twice the size of everyone else even when seated, had stiffened into an attitude of protest, a fearful glare on his face; Lady Dalrymple Smythe, looking pained, had raised to her eyes a pair of miniature opera glasses; Rosalind Tranmer had put her hand over her mouth like a schoolgirl with the giggles; and Harry Moore, the benign, easy-going, pacific Harry Moore, was frowning.

'Let us consider the life of Our Lord,' said the Bishop, tentatively shuffling his notes.

Charlotte had reached the door. A verger jumped to his feet to open it for her and would have followed her solicitously outside had she not assured him that a breath of air was all she needed.

'In those first two days might he not also seem to have lost?' The Bishop could suddenly see his way clear. 'And on the third day,' he said. 'On the third day ... ' It was a straight run now through resurrection and eternity to the peroration in which he would ask death where was its sting and the grave where was its victory. As the door quietly closed behind Charlotte the Bishop's voice once more reverberated confidently through the Abbey.

Outside in the sun one of the shining black horses was asleep. It had taken the weight off one of its back legs and had shut its eyes. The others stood motionless except for the occasional swish of a tail to ward off the last of the summer's flies. Skirting the waiting carriages and ignoring the few curious bystanders who were waiting to see the funeral cortège leave, Charlotte walked a little way along the pavement and thought of her father, who had been vicar of a country parish and with whom she had never talked of religious matters since it would have seemed to both of them unnecessary. She supposed that after a sermon such as the one which had just driven her out of the Abbey the most he would have said would have been, 'Oh, Bishops . . . ' in a tone she knew well and would have found quite sufficiently reassuring.

When she reached the side-entrance to the Pump Room, the one through which she had walked with Edwin Hanbury when he had taken her to see the warm-water springs, she paused and breathed deeply two or three times. Then she walked resolutely back towards the Abbey, attracting an attention of which she was quite unaware among the bystanders, who were disposed to be moved by her beauty and her black silk. The attentive verger would have walked her back to her pew, but shaking her head at him with a grateful smile she slipped into one of the pews at the back of the church beside Mrs Tucker. The sermon was over and the congregation was on its feet for the final hymn. As Charlotte sang heads turned in the pews in front of her; she sang on smiling and some who knew her smiled back. After the blessing came the slow descent of the coffin down the nave towards the great west door, now opened to admit the sunlight. Mr and Mrs Collingwood walked after it at a solemn pace, followed by Wilf with his military bearing and Petchumah close to his side, her eyes lowered. Charlotte was aware of sighs, even sobs, here and there from the people who surrounded her, and as they heard the sound of the carriages leaving for the cemetery and waited for the congregation from the front pews to make their way out of the Abbey before them she turned to Mrs Tucker and said to her, 'He would have wanted . . . I think he would have wanted . . . '

But Mr Tucker from beyond his wife interrupted her to say it had been a fine sermon; other voices immediately agreed. Finding Anne Smallwood on the other side of her as they began to walk out towards the sunlight, Charlotte said 'I think he would have wanted the Bishop to say . . . ', but there was young Holloway, the blacksmith's son, whom really she had to admit she had never liked, looking at her in that way he had which it was no use pretending was anything other than dreadfully familiar. How could she possibly say in front of him that she thought Stephen would have wanted the Bishop to say something about how they ought all to love each other? She almost laughed at herself.

'Look,' said Anne Smallwood, with the customary emotional charge to her voice. 'There he is.' She nodded towards Harry, who was waiting by the great door with his usual look of being quite at ease. As Charlotte walked gratefully towards him, old Mrs Bennett put out a trembling hand saying, 'Would that be Mrs Moore?' and asked her to come and read to her again. 'There's no one reads like you,' she said.

'So that's my little crumb,' Charlotte said to Harry. 'Mrs Bennett wants me to read to her.'

'Of course she does,' said Harry. 'You read very well.'

It seems that Caspar Freeling never risked a return to the City. He had one meeting with Arthur Corfield in London, at which he told him that pressure of business left him no time to pursue Corfield's political interests any further. He implied that he was busy with a special mission, and claimed to be answerable directly to the Prime Minister. If that meant he had become some sort of Government informer, or spy, perhaps he had found his proper métier at last.

I can find no evidence of Marianne Hanbury's return either, although there is one slightly puzzling photograph of the City Surveyor at the official opening of the hotel accompanied by a woman referred to in the caption as 'his lady'. She bears no resemblance to Marianne. The hotel took years to complete and its design had to be considerably modified, mainly for financial reasons; it remains a mockery of Peter Tilsley's exalted vision. The arguments and delays were said to have darkened Edwin Hanbury's life for ten years, and indeed he exudes slightly less than his former massive self-confidence in the *Herald* photograph. If Marianne never came back, it is to be supposed that she gave birth to Freeling's child in Ireland, but whether or not the two of them stayed there I have not been able to discover. I have odd notions sometimes, reading the subsequent history of that nation.

My mother was the third child of Charlotte and Harry Moore; there were two more after her. Some of them went up in the world, some down. My mother went down, marrying a shell-shocked soldier who was never much good at earning a living. She always seemed to me mysteriously contented, and when I was a child she was a great story-teller; her mother in a variety of different disguises seemed often to be part of the story. Along with their myth I may have inherited the desire to tell stories. I had to fight it down in order to try to be a historian, but as time went on I found I could be a better historian if I allowed myself, just for myself, to tell stories.

If I could tell you why, when I walk on the City's periphery and look down on it, held in all its promise between the surrounding hills, when I seem to pass the striding figure with the questioning grey eyes or pause on the hillside from which he watched Charlotte and her children in their garden, or when I walk in front of the Abbey and feel myself brushed by the elusive form of Caspar Freeling returning to his lodgings, or walk between the Circus and the Great Crescent and remember Madame Sofia in the warm evening meeting her own shadow walking on the pavement, if I could tell you why all this fills me with such intense happiness — well, then I suppose I should be telling you something about imagination, or if you like about the soul, and what it is which makes it, as Yeats said, clap its hands and sing. But I have never liked to spend much time on theory, preferring rather to hold on to any good feeling while it lasts. On bad days, you see, I feel much like the Bishop.

The beeches suffered in last winter's gale. Stephen still walks there and the leaves fall round him. My friend Arthur Morrison is taking me to see a dig they have started not far away on the site of what some people say was once Camelot. Another City, another dream.

The Abbey cemetery was laid out in the 1840s by one of the masters of Victorian cemetery design. The gravestones line the grassy paths thickly now, here and there almost submerged beneath the willow herb and bramble which have taken over from the original shrubs. The trees are still handsome and the steep slope on which the cemetery is laid out gives a good view of the City below; on one side are thick woods and on the other a little valley where a square church tower is half concealed by trees, beyond which the land rises again towards the houses which march up towards Capo di Monte, where the Corfield girls grew up, and Tivoli, where they died. Higher up and a little further to the south-east the Moores' house sits squarely on the hillside, looking down the valley.

If you wander up one of the grassy paths towards the plain chapel in the Norman style with its tall west tower, between the stones commemorating devoted husbands and wives and gallant officers, those whose lives were spent in strenuous and fruitful labour among the Zulus in Natal, those who fell at Balaklava, those who dispensed justice in the Straits Settlements, you pass two charming angels and a number of draped urns and broken columns and come to a simple headstone in memory of the Reverend Stephen Collingwood, placed there by his loving brother and sister-in-law. The wording briefly commemorates the circumstances of his death and underneath it is written the text from Hebrews XIII, verse 14, which Stephen had used as an epitaph to the small volume of Peter Tilsley's prose which he was in the course of editing when he died and which Harry Moore later saw through the press: 'For here we have no continuing city; but we seek one to come.'

Early one November morning Charlotte walked down the hill on the grassy path which had been cropped low by sheep but was wet from the morning mist. The tower of the chapel rose from the surrounding trees, now mostly bare of leaves, and was touched by sunlight, since even now the summer seemed not quite to have given up its hold on the year. She was bareheaded and had only thrown a shawl over her light morning-dress; she carried a bunch of Michaelmas daisies. She crossed the road and opened the cemetery gates. As she made her way up the path towards the chapel she suddenly paused, then went on more slowly. A figure was sitting on one of the graves, knees bent, head hanging forward, back against the headstone, evidently asleep. She hoped it was not Stephen's grave but as she came nearer she saw that it was. She forced herself to walk. Not until she was very close did the figure suddenly raise its head and stare at her.

'You thought it was him,' said the boy, distressed.

'For a moment. But I wouldn't have wanted it, not really. At least I don't think so. What are you doing?'

'I was looking to sleep in the chapel but it was locked. I'm on my way home to Devon.'

'That's a long way.'

'I've been working in London but I don't like it there. I'd rather be back on the farm.'

He stood up and shook out the coat he had been using as a cushion. He was a big healthy boy of sixteen or so. He looked abashed.

'I meant no harm, sleeping here. It was late and I'd no money, except for the train fare today.'

'There's a night refuge up on Haul Down, where you might have gone. His was the church next to it.'

'He was a reverend then?' The boy flushed, looking at the headstone.

'His name was Stephen Collingwood,' said Charlotte, realizing that he could not read. 'He would have forgiven you for sleeping on his headstone.'

'A good man, was he?'

'Yes.'

'Earned his rest then, you might say.'

The boy raised a hand half-way towards his forelock and strode away down the hill towards the station and towards, she supposed, his distant Devon village. She put her flowers on the grave. He had earned his rest, but she did not believe he had wanted it, not then, not yet. And it was such a beautiful morning. The horsedrawn traffic on the road below was already busy; it was time to go home. Above the sound of the traffic came suddenly two childish voices, talking both at once. Turning in surprise she saw Ella and Ned hand in hand climbing up the path towards her with every sign of urgency. She waited without anxiety, knowing that if anything really serious had happened – like Harry being ill, for instance – some grown-up person would have come to fetch her.

'It's all right,' they were telling her. 'It's quite all right.'

They ran the last few yards towards her.

'I held his hand all the time,' said Ella breathlessly.

'I didn't move until she said.' Ned was flushed. 'I'm boiling,' he said. 'We looked both ways all the time and we didn't run across, we walked.'

'But why did you come?'

They could not remember. They were so anxious to set her mind at rest as to how extraordinarily carefully they had crossed the road that they had quite forgotten what had made them set out in the first place. Probably they had seen her from the top of the hill, a tiny figure walking up the path in the morning mist, and had run to join her without thinking.

'We haven't had breakfast,' said Ned, quite shocked by his own rashness. 'We came without having breakfast.'

She took them by the hand and led them home.

A NOTE ABOUT THE AUTHOR

Isabel Colegate's previous novels include those in the Orlando
Trilogy, and *The Blackmailer, A Man of Power,* and *The Great
Occasion. The Shooting Party* (1981) was made into a film starring
James Mason and John Gielgud. She lives in Bath, England.

A NOTE ON THE TYPE

The text of this book was set in Palatino, a type face designed
by the noted German typographer Hermann Zapf. Named
after Giovanbattista Palatino, a writing master of Renaissance
Italy, Palatino was the first of Zapf's type faces to be introduced
in America. The first designs for the face were made in 1948, and
the fonts for the complete face were issued between 1950 and
1952. Like all Zapf-designed type faces, Palatino is beautifully
balanced and exceedingly readable.

Printed and bound by
Fairfield Graphics, Fairfield, Pennsylvania

Title page and binding design by
George J. McKeon